The Cosmati Prophecy

A HISTORICAL FANTASY ADVENTURE

THE COSMATI CHRONICLES

JANE THORNLEY

RIVERFLOW PRESS

Preface

Though historical personages are referenced in this book, it is entirely a work of fiction and any resemblance to real individuals, living or dead, is probably a figment of your imagination.

No part of the book was generated by AI. All intelligence witnessed herein is my own, which is worrisome enough.

Chapter One

To Geri, a good day was one where inanimate objects remained where they were put, at least long enough for her to find them again. So far, this had been one of the better days, and a Friday at that. Had she but known what was coming, she would have thought differently but that probably wouldn't have changed anything.

That afternoon, she had just led her last session of the day, the graduate study group on British Cathedral Design in the Middle Ages. The students had fired intelligent questions at her to which she had responded with a volley of thought-provoking comments. How she loved those moments when the interaction with her students seemed to ensure that a passion for history, archaeology, art, and discovery would live on.

Someday she would have to retire but it was heartening to think that the next generation of "underground operatives" (her term for archaeologists)— would live on at least partly due to her inspiration.

Geri trundled back towards her office brimming with a sense of a job well done. Now, she had only to mark a few essays for an hour or so before walking two streets over to her flat, which would welcome her with the promise of tea and books accompanied by the best takeout curried lamb and chips in London. Add a glass of red vino—all right, so maybe a bottle—to the mix and the launch of the perfect weekend would begin.

No husband, no partner—never had one, never would. Hers had always been a solitary existence for a very good reason, if not entirely of her choosing. She even avoided the staff parties and afterwork pub meets. Most of her colleagues didn't like her much, anyway, and she didn't try to alter their opinions.

For one thing, she couldn't bear how they labeled her. She could literally read the thoughts behind their eyes: *has-been, clutching a tenured spot that should go to a younger professor like me, me, me.* The *me* part was always screaming in her ears. Why was it that those accusing her of being selfish were motivated by such self-interest? Ah, the irony.

Everybody seemed out for themselves. There were exceptions, of course. Still, it was easier to remain apart from her colleagues and to focus on her students than to try being something she wasn't—safer that way, too.

She was halfway down the hall when her phone began to jingle in her pocket. Blasted thing! With her satchel in one hand and her cane in the other, it was not as if she were bursting with handling options.

Backing herself against the wall, she lowered her leather bag carefully to the floor, told it to stay put, and fished out her phone. Randall's name dominated the screen. Her only sibling refused to use his mobile's text feature based on the notion that shortcuts were somehow a fast-track to hell. Also, he knew that his big sister was hardwired to answer phones immediately. Texts and emails could be conveniently postponed, which made them preferable, in her opinion.

Sighing, she hit *Talk.* "Randall, give me two minutes to get to my office and I'll call you back."

"Be very quick about it, Geraldine. This is an emergency."

Geri returned her phone to her pocket, rolled her eyes—she really had to stop doing that—gave her briefcase a quick pat and continued trudging to her office.

Emergency? What kind of emergency was the Right Reverend Randall Woodworth experiencing that would require summoning his much older and less nimble sister? Was the Abbey on fire, had some wayward parishioner refused to obey the Ten Commandments.

Actually, she would be rubbish at assisting with any of those issues, seeing as she was hardly religious in any traditional sense. However, should Randall require assistance with dredging up the minutiae of the Abbey's history, she would be all over it just as long as she could do so at a distance.

But that sort of thing would hardly constitute an emergency. Tremors coursed down her spine as she considered other possibilities. She was almost at her office door when she heard someone call out her name.

"Geraldine?"

She swung around to see George Bolton dashing up behind her. Around thirty years old with shoulder-length red hair so unkempt that colleagues teased that he was modeling himself after his area of study and would row up the Thames in a longboat if he could.

One look at his stricken face told her that she didn't have time for this.

"Geraldine, sorry to ambush you, but I just wanted you to know that what I surmised has come to pass." He held up a pink paper. "I received notice today that I'm being axed."

"Terminated, George, not 'axed'. The college has yet to behead its junior staff."

"Soon to be ex junior staff," George said.

She stared at him, feeling the distress that pushed off him in waves. "Nevertheless, I am most sorry to hear that news, though it is not totally unexpected. The college isn't creating new positions this year, as you know, and Dr. MacDonald is returning from sabbatical, as anticipated. I had hoped that they'd make an exception for you, however."

She knew that they wouldn't, of course. She had certainly spoken stridently on the need for the University to keep fresh blood such as George with his full-emersion approach to Viking Studies, but there were only so many teaching positions and limited funds. Tenured staff like herself commanded the biggest slice of the economic pie, of course, as was only fitting. "It's a financial decision, you know."

Of course he knew. He also knew that if those of retirement age were to bow out, the field would be open for bright up-and-coming teaching lights like himself. "Surely you don't expect me to simply retire so you can have a position? I've been here for almost twenty years. Don't you think I have a right to leave the profession I love when I'm good and ready?" Maybe a bit harsh, but still.

He looked ready to cry. "I'm not asking that of you—well, perhaps I am, but Susan and I just bought that house in Camden and I just can't lose my job now, Geraldine."

So why did you buy a house when you knew your position wasn't permanent? "Nonsense," she said turning back to fiddle with her keys. "You'll find another position, George. Excuse me, I must make a call."

With her back turned, she waited until he retreated down the corridor, his footsteps thudding on the tiles. He wanted her to retire, of course—they all did, except the students. She owed it to them to stay as long as possible.

And then, as if she conjured one such student from plain air, another voice demanded her attention: "Here, Doc, let me help," a female voice said.

Geri swung around again. It was Lynette/Lin Balay—"Lynette" being the girl's "dead name," Lin being the handle the girl had assumed for her new sexu-

3

ally ambivalent identity. "Lin" held gravitas, apparently, and was a handle sufficiency androgynous enough not declare one's gender in any obvious manner.

Lynette/Lin had declared that she was *they* and not he or she, despite all evidence to the contrary. It caused Geri no end of confusion when fishing for the acceptable non-binary pronoun, but she supported the young person for being brave enough to declare her true self. That was more than she could say.

"Where did you come from?" Geri asked.

Lin only grinned, holding her hand out for the keys which Geri dropped into her palm.

"Thank you. Much appreciated. Never could figure out these technical things." Geri leaned heavily on her cane while the girl (at least in Geri's eyes which were influenced by habit) hefted Geri's bag over one shoulder with ease and expertly unlocked the door with a flick of the wrist. Lin had an appointment booked with her that afternoon—the third this week. Geri had almost forgotten.

Geri opened her office door and watched as Lin set her bag carefully in the visitor's chair before turning back to her professor with an expectant expression. Delicate heart-shaped face, wiry black hair hacked into a shocked and startled cut with what may as well have been garden shears, the kid was petite, almost waif-like. Elfin features, a Goth-goes-to-the-the-rubbish-heap fashion sense packaged with a brilliant mind, Lynette/Lin had become her favorite student, if more than a little needy and extremely annoying at times. She arrived at London University on a scholarship and worked twice as hard as everyone else.

"Have you read my essay yet?" the girl demanded, flashing a charming grin. Piercing in the left cheek, a ring in the nose, tats—sometimes it was painful to look at her. Her parents had been Ethiopian—both gone—but now she lived with her maternal aunt.

That was another reason why Geri liked her—a sense of loneliness clung to the girl like stale cooking vapors. She no more belonged to the dominant tribe than did Geri. No entitlement there, either, just plenty of irritating insistence that her voice was worth hearing—and it was.

But the girl could be such a pain sometimes. "I have read it, and I do want to discuss the points with you in depth—excellent insights into iron-age Britain," Geri told her. Though not Geri's specialty, archaeologists required a broad knowledge level.

"The Iron Age? But I'm still working on that one, it's my revaluation of the excavation at Sutton Hoo that I wanted to discuss. Time we tore up all those old theories and took a new look at the evidence."

"Oh, was it?" Geri paused. Yes, it was. "My mistake."

4

"Wait—how'd you even know I was writing about the iron age? I never mentioned it."

"Lin, I really can't talk right now. I must attend to an important call first. Wait outside, please."

"Sure thing." Lin cheerfully breezed from the room, closing the door behind her. Already, the bag the girl had placed on the chair had moved itself to the window ledge—better view, presumably.

"Are you happy now?" she asked her backpack. "Just stay put."

That settled, Geri took a quick glance around her office—book cases, posters of her favorite excavations, the mounted miniature of Salisbury Cathedral she'd purchased years ago—before lowering herself into her chair and speed-dialing her brother.

He picked up immediately. "Geraldine," he said in that imperious, no-nonsense tone he assumed sometimes, "come to the Abbey immediately. Something alarming is occurring." He always had been a bit high-strung and becoming one of the top clergy in the church hierarchy did nothing to lessen the tendency. She hardly saw him these days.

"Can you be more specific, Randall? If I leave now, I shall be caught in the peak traffic, and you know how I despise being jostled by crowds."

"I cannot disclose the events over the phone, obviously, but let it suffice to say that I believe that our biggest fears may have been realized, do you understand? If am unable to contain the activities soon, I fear I will lose control completely."

Geri heard the tremor in her brother's voice, a slight wavering as though the wind were vibrating a sheet of steel. He was a strong man and a good one, if a bit uptight. "Very well," she said. "I am on my way."

"Head to the Abbey's west gate and then to the Queen's Jubilee Museum at the Weston Tower. I am now occupying an office on the top floor. Ring when you arrive and I'll have security let you in." The call ended.

She sat for a moment staring into space. They had always handled "the matter" differently—Randall by believing that somehow a higher power would curb what plagued him while assuring that nothing mutated into outright evil along the way.

Geri, on the other hand, took a different approach. To her, their shared problem must be dealt with in the same manner in which adults generally managed any affliction—arthritis in the knees, for instance. This involved finding a workaround, avoiding flareups by taking the necessary precautions, and, above all, by outright ignoring the issue where possible. So far, these steps had permitted her to live an almost normal life. There were exceptions, however, and she had a sense that the exceptions were about to become more exceptional.

"What do you think's going on this time?" she said aloud before getting wearily to her feet. Her bag remained silent, as usual.

Randall had devoted his life to Westminster Abbey and had risen through the ranks of the hallowed institution with a profound and unwavering dedication. Though briefly filling other posts for the Anglican church worldwide, he always longed to return home to the UNESCO World Heritage site that had once been their parish church; that was back in the days when she attended church. Finally he had arrived at the epicenter of his dreams, and perhaps simultaneously at the ground zero of his undoing—of everyone's undoing, for that matter. Damn.

It would take thirty minutes to get from the Goodge Street Station via the Northern Line to the Embankment Station and on to Dean's Yard, the site of Westminster Abbey, all of it bound to be damnably unpleasant and feverishly frustrating. What was worse, she would need to take her laptop home to mark essays that evening, eating into her precious weekend. Cabs were out of the question in London at this time of day. Besides being outrageously expensive, they became gridlocked in traffic and ended up going nowhere fast.

Shrugging into her long black coat, she ordered her bag into backpack mode and waited until it had settled over her shoulders. "Behave yourself," she warned it as she trudged to the door.

The non-binary girl was still waiting in the hall.

"Regrettably, Lin, we must make another appointment as I must dash"—as if her corporal self could dash anywhere these days. She shuffled down the corridor.

"Dash where?" the girl asked, scrambling after.

"On a family matter."

"Family matter?" Lin fell into step beside her. "I didn't realize you had a family—oh, wait, do you mean your one and only brother who works at Westminster Abbey?" Lin was an only child.

"He doesn't just work at Westminster Abbey, he holds the esteemed title of a right reverend, a fairly lofty position." Now why did she feel the need to add that bit of fluff? Totally unnecessary.

"Is a Right Reverend better than a wrong reverend?"

Geri laughed out loud. That's another reason why she liked Lin—the same irreverent humor. "Absolutely. Right is always better than wrong, apparently, though I would argue that it depends upon the circumstances. Anyway, in my brother's case, he attempts to be much righter than most."

Lin snickered. "I have no idea what a right reverend even is. My mum was Jewish but I'm just not into it—any of it," the girl said. "Sounds important, though. Did you get him the job when you were working as the Abbey's archaeologist?"

That almost made Geri guffaw. It amazed her how one so bright could simultaneously be so clueless. But, she reminded herself, the girl at twenty years old had yet to put enough living under her belt to know better, whereas Geri had accumulated more than enough for both of them.

"The Abbey archaeologist does not have the authority to appoint clergy, Lin. Besides, I left that post nearly two decades ago. Please make an appointment online for Monday. Have a good weekend."

Outside on the sidewalk, huffing her way down Torrington Place past the nondescript buildings of London University, Geri wondered if she would lose a bit of weight from this jaunt. Sometimes it took everything she had just to get from A to B, which mostly explained why she rarely wandered too far from the university enclaves these days. Her flat lay two blocks down on a tree-lined street and required just enough exertion to convince her that a return trip fulfilled her daily exercise quota.

With her bag on her back and her cane in hand, her long wool skirt billowing around her legs, she made good time heading for the Goodge Street Station despite her excess baggage on and around her person.

It helped that her satchel was attempting to play it light, something it would do whenever Geri was on the move. It was a good bag, overall, and she had grown fond of it. Meanwhile, there was just enough tartness in the autumn air to feel as though her senses were biting into a crisp apple. Lovely.

The closer she came to the tube entry, the more congested the foot traffic became. Everyone dashed past, diving for the subterranean trains that pulsed in the veins of the great city of London, the same city that she had devout her life to study, or at least its past life.

She allowed her bulk, enrobed as it was in her usual black-on-black ensemble, to serve as her protection. *Push me and you push a wall.* Besides, she carried a big stick and an equally big bag and would use both, if necessary.

As anticipated, the trains were packed. She managed to squeeze in only by hefting herself against the kid who was too fixed to his phone to notice the gaping space behind him. Of course, all the seats were taken, which left no alternative but to grasp the center pole and glower down at the much younger people sitting heads down over their books and devices—not that they noticed. Oblivious, the lot of them.

"Hey, you, get your lazy butt off that seat and let this lady sit down. Are you blind?"

The kid with the yellow earbuds sitting below Geri gave a startled look when the fierce-looking girl nudged his knee and indicated for him to move with a jerk of her thumb. He promptly vacated the space, muttering apologies. Geri shrugged off her backpack and lowered herself down into the still-warm spot.

"Are you following me?" she asked Lin as the girl maneuvered herself between her and the crowd like some kind of elfin bodyguard.

"It's on my way," the girl said with a shrug.

"Doesn't your aunt live in Kensington?"

"Yeah, but who said I was heading home?"

Geri nodded and soon fell into her own thoughts. She avoided the Abbey at all costs these days, even when it meant requesting that other professors and archaeologists manage the periodic student tours and fieldwork. She always blamed her health and nobody prodded. Most of the faculty believed she should have completely retired long ago, anyway. Being semi-retired left too much skin in the game, apparently. She'd stay on for the students, and maybe just to annoy some of the staff. There certainly were a few who deserved it.

Meanwhile, something very bad had to be happening for Randall to summon her like this. Was it erupting all over again, even after they had worked so hard to keep these energies in check? It was bound to happen someday, especially after the coronation. A prophecy can't be ignored forever.

She had been in the abbey choir as a girl, blessed with the voice of an angel and spirit of a little devil, the choirmaster had said. To be so cruel to one so young can leave lasting scars. While her presence provoked occurrences that she couldn't control, that hardly made her evil. She was just a kid with supernormal abilities and even when she was trying to keep them in check, they oozed out in all directions. Of course, nobody knew what was really going on. If they had, matters would have been far worse.

Everything had gone terribly wrong terribly fast, in any case, at least for her. Luckily, decades later, the clergy and staff had either retired or passed on, so nobody recognized the head archaeologist as the same little girl who had caused so much chaos all those years ago. In the end, she had to resign her post—either that or have the whole mess start up again. She hadn't meant to cause harm, of course. Her presence had simply stirred things up.

She would have missed her stop had Lin not tapped her shoulder.

"Right." Geri rose to her feet while the girl reached down to snatch up her bag and, once again, it went willingly. That left Geri to nudge her way to the doors and then onto the platform unencumbered, "Mind the Gap" booming in her ears.

They climbed the stairs to the exit, Geri anchoring herself step-by-step with her cane, the surge of homeward bound bodies swarming around her in a rushing stream.

After a short walk, the Abbey rose into view.

"You cannot enter with me, Lin. The Abbey is closed to visitors after 3:30, at least in the public areas, and the Queen's Diamond Jubilee Galleries where I am heading will be locked, too. Unless you want a quiet moment of prayer in the church proper, you best go off home."

"Prayer—are you kidding me? Can't you get me in as a guest or something?" the girl asked.

"No, I cannot. The Abbey doesn't come with a backstage pass like in the theatre. I have a personal matter to attend to, I said. Do scuttle home and many thanks for the assistance."

Westminster Abbey loomed before them, a veritable monument of towering time-washed stone rising behind what seemed like acres of wrought iron fencing. A shiver hit Geri's spine. She could sense the whole structure vibrating.

She dialed her brother. "I'm here."

"Good. I'll send security."

She turned to Lin standing nearby and held out her hand. "My bag, please."

The girl hesitated and in that second of possible obstinance, the bag tugged out of the girl's fingers and transferred into Geri's. Just a flash and it was done. Lin gaped as Geri quickly turned her back.

The security guard had arrived. "Doctor Woodworth?", he asked.

"Yes, t'is I," Geri said.

"Wait, what just happened?" she heard the girl call from behind her.

Geri did not reply as she sailed through the gates.

Chapter Two

The security guard, a youngish (most people seemed youngish to her) man with a noticeable combover, led her through the hallowed halls of the Gothic masterpiece that was Westminster Abbey. The graceful tree-like columns soaring overhead in a symphony of tracery and stained glass always left Geri a little breathless—more than breathless, today, actually—almost gasping.

Being in that lofty space again hit her on an almost cellular level. Everything tingled and a haze of light surrounded certain objects. The whole Abbey, as in the building itself, felt as if it were alive with unleashed energies and it was all Geri could do to remain upright as she followed her escort. And then there was all the whispering.

There were other people about, of course, as this was a monument to both the holy and the secular and accommodated many activities after visiting hours, including special prayer groups, meetings, choir practice, restoration efforts, and on it went. It was akin to an ancient undercover hamlet humming with mysterious activity, much of it hidden behind walls, wings, and screens, or simply invisible to the human senses.

When the energies were particularly active as they were now, people would find themselves feeling unaccountably weary, irritated, or experiencing sudden headaches, depending on their sensitivities. She was prone to irritability at the best of times.

Her escort did not know that she had spent three years as the top archaeologist at the Abbey which meant that he felt obliged to give her a tour en route, pointing out this sarcophagus, that plaque. Twice she caught an error in his facts but let it ride. This was not the time to reveal that she knew more secrets about this ancient site than perhaps nearly any other person in Britain, living or dead, and, no, Lord Salisbury was not buried inside that recumbent effigy, you bonehead.

She kept her eyes averted from the statuary, avoiding gazing at certain features on the floors and walls while clutching her bag to her chest as though it were a frightened puppy. Actually, the poor thing trembled—or was that vibration? Either way, she considered herself lucky that the guard hadn't insisted on putting her backpack-cum-briefcase through the X-ray scanner. That would not have ended well.

Finally, she was taken into a light-filled space completely at odds with the shadowy, forest-like realms behind them—the star-shaped Weston Tower which had opened in 2018 in what had once been the Abbey's triforium. *The Guardian* had described the then-dean's tower as being "tucked into an armpit of Westminster Abbey" and that fit since it had been almost invisibly inserted between the thirteenth century Chapter House and the sixteenth century Lady Chapel. It was much quieter here.

Wood, bronze, and leaded glass created faceted views like a tall lantern designed to catch and reflect the exterior abbey in marvelous vignettes. The stairs alone were worth the price of admission. Back in the days when she could manage them, each landing framed some incredible view—a sweep of flying buttresses or some magical aspect of the abbey structure. At points, it felt like one was soaring far above the roofs like an inquisitive angel.

The guard unlocked the elevator and explained where to find Reverend Randall Woolworth's office—behind a hidden door on the top floor. With that, he bid her good afternoon and left her to ride solo.

How odd that Randall would choose a modern space when his previous nest had been behind one of the abbey's venerable old walls below. They both preferred traditional to modern. But then, this was only part modern since the museum environs were tucked high up into the ancient rafters and displayed many ancient objects.

The doors opened onto a landing filled with the rays of the setting sun beaming through the glass beyond. Directly ahead, one of the Abbey's stained glass oriels had been framed in leaded panes, almost close enough to touch, while to the right, another section revealed the Houses of Parliament stark against the golden sky. Around the corner from that, the pinnacles of the

Abbey itself rose like some kind of gilded fairytale confection. Behind that, the Gallery Museum sat hushed and shadowy.

The museum was open in a grid of protective railings that formed a kind of balcony in a square that followed the inside of the tower far above the Abbey floor. This display of artifacts was further enhanced by a safety barricade that both protected visitors from falling down to the Abbey floor and provided a safe viewing point for the glories of the stunning architecture. No other place in Westminster Abbey could offer visitors a view like this.

Geri hugged her bag, gazing at it all. "Oh, I had forgotten how wonderful this area is."

"Geraldine."

She turned. There stood her lean brother in his long black robes with his fine-boned features and grey-streaked dark close-cropped hair. His face was strained but no less handsome. He took after their dashing dad, she after their golden-haired mum, only in her case she had also inherited her mother's love of pub food. "Why did you take an office up here?" she asked.

"It's far more peaceful. No vagrant spirit finds its way up here. Come in, please, Geraldine. I have been waiting," he said.

"Yes, of course."

She followed him through the door into a small office where a side window framed a leering gargoyle. Other than a desk with a computer, bookshelves, and two chairs, the office was devoid of furniture and decoration but for a photograph of Randall shaking hands with King Charles following the coronation. Of course, there was also a cross on the wall—Randall would have to have that. This space was completely different from the old oak paneling that had graced his previous office.

He bade her to sit in the padded visitor chair before sweeping his elegant self behind the desk and taking his own seat. No sooner had he sat when her bag leapt from her arms, onto the desk, and into his lap. Startled, Randall threw up his hands. "Geraldine!"

"It's all right, Randall—take a deep breath. He only wants to get acquainted. I've told him so much about you."

Randall's eyes widened before giving the bag a tentative pat.

"There, come back here, you." She snapped her fingers and the bag hopped from Randall's lap onto the floor to where she pointed and settled.

Randall brows arched in an expression of askance.

"I know, I know. One day my satchel suddenly became animated and proved so useful and such good company, that I couldn't bear to banish it, all right? It's perfectly harmless—at least, to me—and rather handy, if you must know."

"We agreed not to take companions."

"First of all, I didn't take it, it took me and, secondly, we agreed not to marry or to live with anyone of the human variety, a rule to which I've abided. May I remind you that while you have your brotherhood, I've lived alone my entire adult life and having a cat has never been an option due to my allergies and general distaste for animals. Now that I'm an old lady—well, maybe not the lady part—I've decided to allow myself a bit of company."

"You are not old unless you choose to think of yourself as such, something which I've said many times to no avail. At 55, you are still a vibrant woman," he protested.

"Thank you, dear brother, but wait until you hit the next decade before you make such proclamations and then we'll see how you feel."

Randall lifted his hand and sighed. "Your unfortunate attitude towards aging is not why I asked you here and, yes, I know of the sacrifices you have made—that we've both have made—but what choice did we have? To encourage intimacy with..." he paused to find a fitting word "anything so extraordinary that someone may notice our uniqueness would only invite trouble."

Geri sniffed. "Actually, I put my bag into more of the pet category."

"The *familiar* category, would be more apt. What is it exactly?" he asked, his tone softening.

"I believe it holds the spirit of a dog, though it occasionally exhibits cat-like tendencies and seems highly intelligent. Either way, he's good protection and very loyal and, unlike animals, doesn't smell or require regular walks in inclement weather."

"Perish the thought."

"I call him Eddy, by the way."

Her brother appeared to be praying silently. "Eddy?"

"After Edward the Confessor. I tell him everything, you see, and no matter how audacious my confessions, he never talks back or judges. Actually, he doesn't speak—a blessing, I'd say."

"I could arrange one of my brethren to hear your confession, Geraldine, if that is your desire." That had to be a joke.

"Wouldn't that be fun? Which one of us would run out screaming first, do you think?"

Her brother sat back and folded his hands on the desk, his face stern. "All jesting aside, Geraldine, you know the risks."

She did know the risks. Had they lived in an earlier century, she would have been burned at the stake as a witch and her brother most likely roasted alive as a heretic, though there could be no more devote man in Christendom. "I do, and yet I have chosen to accept the risks in this instance, much as you have done by returning to the Abbey." Unfair, but on point. "Now, tell me about this emergency."

Something bleak appeared in Randall's eyes. "The portal is opening, Geraldine. At first, I had hoped that by increasing my prayers, I could seal the leak but it is proving exceedingly strong, much worse than ever before. The whispers grow more insistent by the day; the statutes and recumbent effigies actually move at times—so far, visible to my eyes alone, thank God—and then early this morning, I saw a dead ghost."

A moment of silence followed. "Most ghosts are dead, I believe," Geri said after a moment. "I'm not being facetious but requesting clarification."

"You were being facetious, as usual." He cast her a wry, indulgent look before returning to his usual tense expression. "Let me be more clear: I glimpsed the manifestation of the body of what I believe to be a deceased person."

"Why do you believe it was deceased?"

"I cannot state positively that it was deceased as I could hardly feel for a pulse, but seeing as it was facedown on the floor, I believe that to be a reasonable assumption."

Geraldine pondered that for a moment. "Possibly, though we don't know for certain without thorough investigation, do we? If it was deceased, this is a first—a spectral presence of a corpse, I mean. An animated dead person—a ghost, in other words—is more the norm, at least for us. It must be a sign. Where did you see this...'dead ghost'? Describe the circumstances."

"I was walking down the nave under the crossing tower, keeping my eyes averted from the sacrarium, when the whispering grew so intense, that even my prayers could not control it. I cast a quick glance toward the altar and spied a body splayed on the Pavement. It shimmered briefly and then disappeared."

"The Cosmati Pavement?"

He closed his eyes. "Where else?"

"Damn. Then the recent Coronation has activated it, as we feared."

"So I believe."

The Cosmati Pavement, named after a style of inlaid stone perfected by Italian artisans centuries earlier, was commissioned by Henry III in 1268 and had been the powerful heart of the Abbey ever since.

A magnificent composition of cut stones and glass, some reportedly taken from ancient Roman and Egyptian monuments, and laid with incredible artistry, described the world in a complex pattern of medieval symbolism accompanied by a brass inscription that prophesied the world's end. Nearly every British monarch since its creation had been crowned over that floor, most of them having no concept of what lay beneath their feet.

"We knew that this would happen someday," Geri slumped into her seat. "And I suspect that years of conservation has been stirring things up topped off by the jolt of a fresh coronation."

"Indeed. I came here with that in mind, Geraldine. Who better to be a guardian than one who recognizes the true danger? I believed that God would keep the energies in check with me as His agent, and that my presence would act as a guarantee."

"A bit ambitious, little brother, given that we're talking about the end of the world here." She said it without rancor. Randall had always been so certain of his importance and becoming a right reverend hadn't helped.

He was gazing at her intently, his expression fierce in that sword-of-God way. "I was misguided only by thinking I could perform this act alone. I came here as a protector, Geraldine. When the late queen passed—may God rest her soul—and the coronation of our new king loomed on the horizon, I strengthened my efforts to claim a post here, and succeeded thanks to our dean, the Very Reverend Dr. Henry Morris and our Lord, Himself. Now, I pray that you will be at my side and help me do what must be done."

Geraldine scowled. "As in the abbey, the priest, and the witch? Now there's a good one."

"Geraldine, you are not a witch in the truest sense of the term but a woman of immense power—"

"Which is the original definition of a witch, may I remind you."

"Permit me to finish—who has yet to tap into her full potential. We always wondered why God created us the way we are and now we know our true purpose."

"She has a brilliant sense of irony, that's why She gave us our 'gifts'." Geri only used the feminine pronoun to annoy him. In fact, she believed the Universe to be genderless much like Lin claimed to be. "So, the coronation has activated the pavement's energies, despite your efforts to contain them, and now our worst fears are being realized. Had you remained away, the portal may have stayed sealed. Now you want us both to risk life and limb to tackle the Cosmati Prophesy?"

"Do we have any choice? If we do not heed the call, the world will end, regardless, and take all humanity with it. Already, the storms increase, the seas are rising, and disaster looms on every horizon. You more than anyone understand the meaning of that prophecy."

Geraldine stared. The mosaic, designed as it was by a medieval artist, had been encoded by its maker according to the conviction that symbolic patterns could impose order upon the universe and thus channel God. Only in this case, the Cosmati floor had the power to either enforce or destroy. The designer mason had fashioned a kind of door between the dimensions, an opening between life and death, a rent through time itself. Whether its creator had been a wizard or a "person of God"—Geri did not believe them to be mutually exclusive—he had to have possessed immense ability.

"If we do not intervene, you know what will happen. Geraldine, only we can stop the Cosmati Prophecy from coming into fruition."

Geri was back on her feet, her cane thudding against the floor. "I know no such thing. It is more likely that we will be swallowed alive—or dead—long before we can learn how to repair that thing."

Randall rose. "You are a brave woman—my hero, if you must know—the one who taught me how to survive when our 'gifts' appeared and threatened to drive me mad. With your help, I was able to turn my life around, and now I believe that He has placed me here for this great purpose but I need you by my side. We must reseal the pavement! I cannot do this alone."

"Oh, stop. Flattery never works on me, you know that. What do you expect me to do, anyway?" she asked. "I have deliberately stifled my magic all these years for a reason and so have you, despite your most Right Reverend this and holy that. Do you expect us to now conjure enough capacity to stop the End of Days?"

"Yes! We must find a way. The world is in our hands." Now he was intoning in his sermon voice, the decibels intense enough to wake the dead, if they weren't up and about already. "If we do not attempt this mighty task, all will be lost! We will—"

At that moment, Eddy leapt from the floor to the desk and reared onto its bottom with its two handles waving like a pair of ears. It was almost comical had the topic not been so serious.

Randall stared.

Geri flopped back into her seat. "I guess that settles it; Eddy has weighed in: indeed, we must save the world. And here I'd been hoping for a quiet weekend. Do sit down, Randall. You are not on the pulpit now. And, you, Eddy," she snapped her fingers, "get down from the desk immediately. How many times must I tell you to stay off the furniture?"

As Randall sat back down, Eddy hopped back onto the floor. For a moment the office was silent.

"Tell me more about this ghostly corpse you spied," Geraldine began. "Was it male or female and what was it wearing?"

Randall pinched the bridge of his nose. Judging by the dark circles under his eyes, the poor man hadn't slept for days. "I could not really tell since it was sprawled on the floor and the Cosmati mosaic was giving off a glowing mist that shrouded the image. However, I do believe I saw what appeared to be two legs in hose and a loose tunic—a man, in other words."

"Thirteenth century?"

"Very likely."

"Lord or a tradesman?"

"Impossible to tell."

"We must consider the body as a kind of clue that may lead us back to the floor's beginnings, and thus to its maker. If a murder took place while the floor was being laid, it could be significant."

"I did think of that."

"In what way did he look dead?'

"Suggest to me what a dead body looks like when it's face down in a mist, if you will."

Geri waved away the remark. "Yes, well, regardless, this could be the most important clue in our investigation. There is nothing for us to do but begin interviewing."

Randall removed his hand from his nose and stared. "Interviewing whom?"

"Anyone buried in the Abbey who may have lived while the pavement was being laid, one who might know of a murder or an altercation, of course. That includes the Bishop of Ware and King Henry III himself, though I am not looking forward to that. Through them we need to locate the Cosmati designer —probably the master stonemason—in order to discover how to reseal the portal as soon as possible. How's your Italian?"

"Passable, but my Latin is far better."

"Only, I doubt that Petrus spoke Latin fluently, though clearly he knew it well enough to craft the inscription, if he even crafted the inscription himself. French might be a better option since that's what the mucky-mucks spoke at the time."

"Petrus?"

"Petrus Odoricus, the master artisan who laid and designed the Cosmati floor. His name is on the inscription. Surely you remember that?'

"I had momentarily forgotten," Randall said.

"In any case, we must approach this initially as detectives might a murder investigation and do the gumshoe work by seeking possible witnesses to ferret out useful information.."

"Only, in this case, the possible witnesses have all been dead for centuries, Geraldine." A note of panic there. "As you are fully aware, many spirits retain the trauma of their last moments, or are caught in some kind of cognitive loop, and therefore rarely coherent."

"Nonetheless, we must begin somewhere. What did you expect us to do?"

Her brother sighed. "I had hoped that perhaps I could pray fervently while you muttered incantations or something of that ilk." Catching her eye, he managed a thin smile.

"And I would say that praying and muttering incantations could be one and the same if the intent is aligned but we won't get into that debate at the moment. In any case, neither type is bound to work until we know what we are doing. I, for one, have never learned how to do the incantation thing. I've used Mum's book for odd jobs but that's it."

"I understand."

"Meanwhile, we have a great deal of groundwork to do if we are to succeed before the earthquakes and climatic catastrophes intensify to the point that the end of the world draws nigh. We will proceed by employing a certain investigative rigor, which is my domain." Geri heaved herself to her feet. "Let us head to the scene of the possible crime."

"Now?"

"Of course now."

"But the Abbey is very busy at the moment and will remain so until at least nine o'clock."

"Which reminds me, what about security footage—have any aberrations been caught on film?"

"It's not film anymore, Geraldine, it's digitized."

He always did this under stress—fix on some piddly detail. "I know that, Randall. Don't do that sort of thing or I will become even crankier."

"I apologize, but nothing observable has appeared thus far. I replayed the security data early this morning but saw nothing unusual. Blessedly, these manifestations are not being detected by modern surveillance devices any more than they are by the ordinary naked eye."

"Yet. Until they do, we have a bit of time. How do you intend to explain my increased presence in the Abbey as we proceed?"

"Perhaps I could bring you on as a part-time consulting archaeologist. Our present head, Dr. Leadbetter, has not been well lately, a malaise I believe may be related to the Cosmati fissure. I continue to pray for him."

"What he probably needs more is a stiff drink."

"Be careful when we reach the main floor," her brother warned as they made for the door. "Though I doubt that security personnel will attempt to listen into a private conversation where I am involved, it's best not to do anything unusual." He lowered his voice. "At some point, you will need to deactivate the surveillance system."

"And how do you propose I do that?" she asked, turning towards him.

"I don't know—a spell, perhaps?"

"Yes, I'll just consult my book on *Spells for Deactivating Modern Day Conveniences, the Security Edition*, shall I? And while I'm at it, you can see if there's a prayer for that. Really, Randall, the most expedient way is for you to access the security depot and fiddle with the system."

"Me, fiddle?" He couldn't have looked more shocked had she suggested that he go skinny-dipping in the baptismal font. "That would be illegal and completely unacceptable given my position as a right reverend of this Abbey!"

Geri rolled her eyes and called Eddy onto her back. "Let us proceed to the Cosmati Pavement. What exactly is going on at the Abbey at the moment?"

"A choir practice is in session, there is a prayer meeting in the The Lady Chapel, and a private Blue Badge tour is in progress for visiting dignitaries. The Abbey will return to peace at approximately 9:00 p.m., as I previously stated."

"That late?"

It was already nearly half-past seven and Geri's stomach was rumbling noisily as they made their way down the elevator towards the sanctuary pavement. So much for curried lamb and chips.

The Cosmati mosaics extended in three levels from the chapel tomb of Saint Edward the Confessor—currently not open to the public—beneath the high altar screen, a later creation, and down to what is known as the sanctuary altar pavement where most of the significant church events were held.

Though recently exposed to the public, the mosaic was still not available for the visiting hordes to walk upon. A chain barricaded the way. Nevertheless, it was there on that recently restored surface where the coronation of King Charles III had taken place.

That evening, the surface glowed so intensely that it was almost painful to look at. Geri fished out her sunglasses and popped them onto the bridge of her nose. That was better. Now at least she could distinguish the swirling energies rising like a mist several centimeters above the patterns of cut glass and stone. The central rondel in the main *quincunx* appeared to be rotating.

"That can't be good," Geri whispered.

"No, indeed," her brother agreed.

"And this is where you saw the twice-dead person?"

"Exactly over the center," he replied.

They heard a cry. "Holy shit!"

Geri and Randall spun around. Lin stood behind them, her mouth agape, her face alive with shocked excitement.

Chapter Three

"Lin! How did you get in?" Geri exclaimed.

"I entered with a bunch of do-gooders off to a meeting some-where. What's that?" She was pointing at the hyper-active floor. "Is it, like, lit from beneath or something?—a hologram, maybe?" She stepped closer to peer at the mosaic. "Super cool! It moves and everything. I didn't know these places did special effects." She looked toward the ceiling far above. "Is it projected from somewhere up there like some kind of holygram? Haha—get it? *Holygram?*"

Randall caught Geri's eye.

"She's my student," Geri explained with a shrug.

"*They*, as in '*they* are my student'," Lin corrected without removing her gaze from the rafters. "I'm non-binary with exceptional hearing."

"She—*they*—can see?" Randall whispered.

"Apparently so." That shocked Geri, too, though it did explain a few things.

"See what?" Lin asked, wrenching her gaze away.

"Why don't the three of us go for a bite to eat? There has to be a cafe around here," Geri asked as a guide delivered a small group to view the mosaic.

"Of course," Randall replied. "There is an excellent one nearby. I shall just fetch my coat and will meet you by the west door."

As her brother hurried off, Geri linked arms with Lin and drew the girl away. "Hush!" she whispered fiercely. "Most people cannot see what you are witnessing."

"What, like the moving Cosmati mosaic? I loved the lecture you gave on that a couple of months ago but you never mentioned that the floor was animated," the girl said, keeping pace beside Geri.

"It isn't. You have witnessed something extraordinary that most cannot see, something supernatural, which means that you have a special gift, or perhaps a curse, depending on to whom you speak. We'll go for supper and discuss the matter. Do you need to call anybody to say you'll be late going home?"

"Aunt Soo is home watching *Masterpiece Theater*. I'm supposed to join her for leftovers but eating at a restaurant sounds brilliant to me. I'll text her. She'll be thrilled to think that I might actually have a social life on a Friday night. I won't mention that I'll be dining with a witch and a priest, though. You are a witch, too, aren't you?"

"You don't believe in gentle transitions, do you? And why do you think I'm a witch?"

"Oh, come on, Doc. I've always known—all the super odd things that happen around you and then there's that bag of yours."

"His name is Edward—Eddy for short."

"How do you know it's a he? Does he have balls or something? It could be a they, like me. Also, it's all the black you wear—true super witchy stuff."

"I wear black out of convenience and because it's slimming."

"Slimming, seriously? You should talk to my aunt about that. She believes that the older you get and the wider your girth, the brighter your clothes should be so nobody can pretend that you don't exist."

"Keep your voice down. Better still, stop talking entirely until we're outside."

Once standing on the front steps, the breeze blowing across the Thames nipping at her cheeks and swirling her coat, Geri turned to Lin. "Now, listen carefully: your presence here is clearly not solely due to your general tendency to be persistent and annoying. I don't believe in coincidences. You are obviously here for a reason and are meant to be useful, possibly to assist my brother and me on a special task."

"Brilliant! I'm in! I don't have to pray or anything, do I?"

"We'll leave the praying to my brother."

Who arrived at that very moment. "How do you do? I am the Right Reverend Woodworth. You may call me Father Woodworth."

"Not happening," Lin smiled up at him.

"I beg your pardon?"

"Sorry if I seem rude but I'm not going to indulge in that patriarchal church stuff by calling you 'Father' anything. I'll do 'Rev', though."

"'Rev' will do, won't it?" Geri asked her brother quickly.

His face smoothed into a look of patience as he held out his hand. "Yes, of course, though I do prefer *Reverend*, and you are?"

"Lin Balay." She shook Randall's hand vigorously. "I'm Ethiopian which explains my coloring, in case you were wondering, though it's not politically correct to wonder anything these days let alone say it, right? So, you might be a right reverend but I'm a right witch, like your sister—pretty certain I'm a witch, anyway."

"A witch?" He shot a startled dance to Geri.

"It seems that way," Geri. "That explains why Eddy took to her as well as her ability to see the mosaics fully."

"I can do other things, too, but I'm very much a newbie and really am just trying to sort this stuff out by myself. My mom had the gift and my grand mom, too, but I didn't know them long enough to learn anything useful. Maybe you can teach me, Doc?" She turned to Geri.

"Probably not," Geri remarked. "Not really my field of study."

"Anyway, I'll do anything I can to help you two to do whatever it is you're doing. What *are* you doing?"

Randall shot his sister a worried glance. "Do pardon me, Lin. I must speak to my sister privately for a moment."

Randall steered Geri off across the pavers. "Surely you did not suggest to this girl—this *person*—that she—*they*—join our mission? Need I remind you of the extreme danger this involves and that we cannot risk the life of a youth while we are about it?"

"Calm down, Randall. Take a deep breath, pray, whatever, and remember that if the world is about to end, that young person is in a precarious position, regardless. This world we're saving belongs to them as much if not more as to us elders. Besides, she can get into tight spaces in ways that we can't."

"What tight places?" he demanded.

"It's just a figure of speech. Plan ahead, little brother, plan ahead. Now, let's get out of this wind and have supper. Does this cafe serve liquor?"

It did, for which Geri was very grateful. Over a plate of chicken pie and chips served with a mug of lager, she filled Lin in on the hyperactive Cosmati mosaic while Randall listened in with obvious unease. She recited the floor's inscription from memory. "It reads—and it has been the subject of much debate as there are missing letters:

In the four years before this Year of Our Lord 1272,

23

King Henry III, the Court of Rome, Odoricus and the Abbot set in place these porphyry stones.
If the reader wittingly reflects upon all that is laid down,
he will discover here the measure of premium mobile;
the hedge stands for three years,
add in turn dogs, and horses and men,
stags and ravens, eagles, huge sea monsters, the world:
each that follows triples the years before.
Here is the perfectly rounded sphere which reveals the eternal pattern of the universe."

"Consider this sentence again," Randall added, "the part that has an alternative translation of: *If the reader prudently considers all that is set down, he will find here the end of premium mobile*—in other words, the end of the world."

"But what does that mean?" Lin asked. "I know what it means literally but what does it really mean?"

"In the Middle Ages, they believed that it made sense to measure the end of the world by compounding numerically the lifespan of all living creatures within it," Geri said. "I touched briefly on that in my lecture. To modern ears, it makes no sense but in a society that fused the concepts of classical philosophers like Plato and Aristotle with the Bible, it had a kind of logic and they loved their riddles. If we use the medieval calculation, the world ends after 19,683 years."

"Of course," Randall continued, "how many years a creature lives is not a fixed number and over the centuries we have lost entire species, so even that foundation of belief is shaken. Added to that is the fact that the medieval philosophers do not define when the world began—is it before or after the birth of Christ, for instance? And, if they did know the true beginning of the world, which is highly unlikely, how could they calculate its end? Nevertheless, to the medieval mind, this floor lays down the end of the world."

"Do you mean like the end of the world for real? I thought that climate change and all these warring bastards were going to do us in," Lin said while digging into her fish and chips.

"Those are just the probable means, not the prime agent," Geri remarked. "The pavement designer or designers constructed a work of art built on the spiritual principles of sacred geometry intending that the pavement would protect the world through a kind of power grid. The sanctuary pavement above which British monarchs have been crowned since William the Conquerer, is the main area of concern. Though an older Cosmati floor exists in the Chapel of St. Edward the Confessor, the sanctuary area is by far the most powerful."

"Now, it's crumbling from the inside out and the wards are leaking as a result," Randall added. "It appears that we must be the ones to fix it. If we are not successful and the protective spells fail completely, chaos will reign across the world."

"Do you mean that if we seal the Cosmati leak, it will all be reversed?" the girl asked, looking up with a chip speared in her fork.

"Not reversed exactly, but if the energies are resealed, the earth may have at least a chance to heal and thus we can back away from the precipice. God will once again reign supreme," Randall continued, his voice deepening to his pulpit tone, "and He will once again regain the power of good—"

"My brother calls God a Him while I prefer to call Her the Universe," Geri interrupted. "Actually, I only add the female pronoun to annoy him rather than because I believe that a universal spirit can ever be a single gender. That makes no sense. Otherwise, it's all semantics."

Lin nodded. "But language matters. It can shape our thinking. That's why I insist on not being genderized."

Geri nodded. "I don't believe that's a word but it certainly works."

"My sister does much to annoy me," Randall said, clearly trying to be a good sport about it.

"Though we disagree fundamentally on matters of religion, we still are in sync on the principles of good and evil. I say to him that, while I understand the language of religion well enough, I choose to use different words to impart the same meaning. Dogma tends to get stuck in my throat. Still, I believe absolutely that the power of good is under siege at the moment. The evidence is everywhere."

"But you think that all this chaos is because a medieval floor is breaking up internally?" Lin asked.

"It clearly is no ordinary floor," Randall remarked. "It is one of many laid at approximately the same time though the others are in Rome. Besides each being in ancient churches and at the sites of countless rituals, it was laid at a time when an intense belief in magic and miracles existed. Belief is a powerful element."

Geri picked up the narrative. "And the powers were very focused and intense in the past. Miracles did happen and those with extraordinary abilities did exist. In the case of this Cosmati floor, the combination of intent and artistry created a unique and powerful portal which could be anywhere in the world but happens to be in England. However, to create something this powerful, there needed to be two opposing forces of equal strength who retain a perfect balance by working together—one good, one evil."

Lin looked from one to the other. "Seriously?"

"Seriously."

"But which is which—who is the good element and who is the evil one?" Lin asked.

Randall cleared his throat. "Seeing as we have only three individuals named in the floor's creation and one is the king, we must assume that our two prime players are Petrus Odoricus and the Abbot of Ware."

"Both of whom must have had great magic to have created such a portal, yet one had to be a bad guy and one a good guy," Geri added.

"But since the Abbot is a man of the cloth, it follows that Petrus is likely to be the negative force," her brother posed.

Geri rolled her eyes. "It means no such thing. In any case, if we do not find a way to repair the tear, the catastrophes will continue to become more frequent until the ultimate big one arrives to whack the world into oblivion." She nabbed another roll. "We probably need both players to fix it."

"Well, damn!" Lin said, chewing her French fry. Pending doom did nothing to dampen her appetite, either. "What exactly are we trying to fix again?"

"The floor is broken, period, and since we can't see the damage with our naked eye, we're only surmising that the problem is a rent or a tear in the magic power field. Equally, it could be a crack or a hole," Geri said. "Otherwise, we have no idea how to work a repair since it is not of the actual mortar variety."

"Will sealing or healing the Cosmati mosaic really restore the balance of good and evil and smarten humanity up enough to prevent us from annihilation?" Lin asked.

"That is the hope," Geri replied, chewing thoughtfully.

"But why would these Cosmati dudes even create such a thing? I mean, I get that they want to create a beautiful mosaic but why the magic part?" she pressed.

Geri sipped her beer. "As a means by which to protect the world, is our belief. The world must have a balance of good and evil to survive. Without one, the other cannot exist. As to why it was created, we need to speak with the designers to find the answer, provided that we can locate them. I have long believed that the stone mason who was probably a great wizard named Petrus Odoricus, created the actual design but he was certainly not buried in the Abbey—probably somewhere in Italy. The other has be the Abbot Ware who is named as enabling the floor's creation by bringing the materials back from

Rome. He, at least, is certainly buried in the Abbey, right below the altar in fact —cheeky bugger."

"Only my sister would refer to an Abbot of Westminster Abbey as 'a cheeky bugger.'" Randall sighed. "Nevertheless, the said abbot's tomb inscription reads: *Abbot Richard of Ware, who rests here, now bears those stones which he himself bore hither from the City.*"

"The city being?" Lin asked.

"Rome. In the Middle Ages, Rome was the heart of the holy universe, so to speak, and the pope the right hand of God," Randall replied.

"The inscription doesn't sound really complimentary, does it? I mean, it doesn't spew hyped-up things about the abbot being noble, a great guy, or any of the stuff you usually see on tombs," Lin pointed out.

"It's true that the abbot was not well-liked," Geri explained. "I suspect he had an eye on his own self-aggrandizement. The fact that he had designed a tomb cover for himself right under the altar is telling in itself."

Geri took another bite of her pie. It wasn't curried lamb but was tasty, though she'd pay for it later because of all that fatty pastry. "Did we mention that my brother spied what may have been a body—as in ghostly corpse—lying on the Cosmati floor this morning? I'm hoping that was not Odoricus but I believe that the body is somehow related to the floor's creation. This is part of the mystery that we must unravel."

"Did King Henry know about the pavement's true power?" Lin inquired.

"Doubtful," Geri said between chews. "I would venture to say that King Henry didn't know half of what was going on in his kingdom at this point. The Plantagenets weren't too swift in the leadership department with the exception of Henry II. In this case, Henry III was more about one-upping the French king who had a number of glorious cathedrals going for him, and appeasing his French wife by making Britain just as impressive. Our Henry probably commissioned the floor—in fact, his new addition to Edward the Confessor's Abbey—as a way of keeping up with Le Joneses."

Geri chuckled at her own joke. "Also, he hoped it would be his ticket to heaven. He probably considered the Pavement to be no more than a magnificent ornamental mosaic—which it is and was—that honored his Abbey and the Shrine of Edward the Confessor, his saintly hero. Abbot de Ware, however, was another matter."

"So what was Abbot de Ware up to?" Lin prodded.

"That is the question. He was only elected by the Benedictine brethren because the man they really wanted for the role died on his way to Rome. Rome required a tithe as well as a personal appearance from all would-be abbots.

Anyway, I believe that Ware had seen similar mosaics in the churches in Rome and brought Petrus Odoricus and his artisan team back to England to fashion the Pavement in both the Confessor's shrine and the high altar. He also managed to have his own resting place created with a tomb cover of exquisite Cosmati mosaics directly below the sacred pavement. Odoricus and Ware were definitely working together at some point."

"Both men were central to the Cosmati Pavement's creation and together they must have forged a powerful seal to protect the world against global disruptive forces. Now we must engage them to heal the rift," Randall added.

"You really are talking magic," Lin pointed out.

"Magic was most certainly involved," Randall told her. "Nothing of that nature can be created without binding two opposing forces in perfect harmony, which takes immense skill in both the light and the dark arts. If the two forces are out of sync, calamity occurs, such is what we are seeing now. It's a question of balance."

"As in the Moody Blues song." Geri cocked an eye at her brother and Randall smiled. There was a time when Randall fancied himself a guitarist but that was long before he entered the church.

"Who or what are the Moody Blues?" Lin asked.

"A music band back in the 70's." Geri stabbed another chip.

"Okay, so like, *old*."

"Don't say 'old' with such contempt," Geri admonished. "You are in the business of studying old, remember."

"Right—sorry. Back to the balance thing: is it like yin and yang?" Lin asked.

"Yes. Good and evil, positive and negative, in other words," Randall remarked between spoonfuls of leek soup. He never slurped, of course. Her brother was as precise in his eating habits as he was in everything else. "That, however, is a great simplification of the true meaning behind the mosaics."

"Doc, in your lecture on sacred geometry, I remember you going on and on about the mosaic. Here." Lin set down her fork and picked up her phone where she swiped through her photos before laying her device in the middle of the table open on a picture of the Cosmati pavement as seen from above. "I thought it was pretty amazing and detailed like one of those posh antique carpets you see sometimes."

"Those are no ordinary floor mosaics, even by the standards of the day. Cosmati-style mosaics were then known to only a handful of skilled artisans and only found previously in churches, primarily in Rome that we know of."

"Fashioned from green serpentine, porphyry, onyx, jasper, glass tesserae, each color and stone is significant in some manner," Randall recounted, peering at the photo. "The original colors are now much subdued since the sealant used by recent conservation efforts has dimmed their luster. Observe how the design features a *quincunx* of double-bordered circles within an angled square framed by another border in which four loops were centered by intricate roundels. Note how the outer guilloche border contains four intricate rectangles flanked by five medallions each—twenty in total—that encompass the central matrix, all of it worked in a complex inlay of glass and stone. This truly is an artistic masterpiece as well as a sacred object."

"There," Lin placed a finger on the large central medallion fashioned from pink-toned onyx that appeared almost like the earth as viewed from space. "That central medallion is what we saw spinning, right?"

Geri nodded. "The monad, the Great Unity. In sacred geometry, the number one remains unique and represents the One."

"And those four circles on the inner and outer edges of the great matrix represent the four elements, right?—earth, fire, water, air?" Lin asked.

"Excellent—you remembered." Geri grinned at her student.

The girl grinned back. "My aunt is also big on that stuff but takes a different angle. Hey, do I get special mention for working on this project?"

"If we all survive the task ahead, that should be reward enough," Geri said mildly.

Randall cleared his throat. "Yes, well: '*The heavens declare the glory of God; and the firmament sheweth his handiwork*'—Psalm 19. No doubt the Abbot and Odoricus believed that the mosaic, being secured in a church, would assure that negative forces would never tip the scales. However, they did not take into consideration—nor could they—that the very force of the population explosion in the centuries to come would increase the surge of violence, pollution, corruption, and negativity to the point that even the Cosmati pavement could not withstand the pressure. Everything wears down over time and the mosaic is showing its age."

"But it's been restored extensively, right?" the girl asked.

"Structurally, yes, but every conservation effort has contributed to its decline," Geri said. "They can replace slices of stone and Purbeck marble, even repair grout here and there, but those efforts can't fix the weakened power grid which holds it—and our world—together, especially when they replace the original matrix with other materials. Thus, over time the wards have disintegrated."

"And then the coronation of King Charles III acted as a kind of shock to the Cosmati system," Randall added as he buttered a roll.

"Think of it as a faulty car battery getting a boost—either nothing happens or the charge will blow out all the electronics in your car—in this case the mosaic's energy core," Geri said.

"We believe that occurred during our dear King Charles's coronation," Randall continued. "Normally coronations act as a kind of positive charge to the Cosmati's energy field but here the opposite occurred—due to no fault of our king, you understand. Had the mosaics remained unsullied, each coronation would have continued to energize the power in the floor through ritual and communion, as was the original intent." Randall placed his roll on his plate uneaten. "However, that did not occur. Petrus Odorous probably had no concept of the effects eight centuries of wear and tear could have on his creation."

"So we're fucked." Lin slapped a hand over her mouth. "Sorry, sorry! What can we do?"

"We must interview the key players to repair the wards," Geri said, draining her glass. It all sounded so simple when in reality it was a bit like fumbling blind in a hurricane.

Lin stared. "But they're all dead."

"Good point," Geri said. "So, we wake them up—in particular, King Henry and the Abbot Ware. If they can tell us more about Petrus, that's a start. Actually, I'll be the one to rouse them as my brother has no stomach for that kind of thing. He's good at putting them back to sleep with prayer, so to speak."

"Ha!" Lin cast Randall a mischievous glance.

"Have you ever seen a ghost?" Geri asked Lin while Randall continued to gaze at his sister with pained patience.

"Well, sure," Lin replied, "but the ones I've seen were all wispy-like and just kind of drifted around before disappearing."

"These might not disappear easily once aroused and most of them are not particularly wispy." Geri caught the waiter's attention and pointed to her empty glass.

"Surely you are not going to have another, Geraldine, in light of tonight's work?" Randall whispered.

"I most certainly am." She shot him a fierce look. "If I'm going to interview a ghost or two, I require fortification." Catching Lin's look of surprise, she added: "Monarchs in particular have hefty egos which can anchor them to the living, leaving them hanging around longer than ordinary spirits. They are a royal pain in the neck, if you want to know. Henry in particular is very attached to his tomb."

"Have you interviewed a royal ghost before?" the girl asked.

Geri gave the waiter a thumbs up when he returned with another foaming glass of ale. "Unfortunately, yes, long ago when I was the Abbey's head archaeologist. In those days, I'd just see them by accident and occasionally attempt to prod them for information. That's probably unethical in archeological terms but if it works," she shrugged. "Anyway, it turned out to be a great deal more effort than I anticipated and not worth the bother in the end."

"Something that I was obliged to remind her of frequently," Randall remarked.

Geri pretended not to hear. "Once one stirs, he or she can begin remembering how important they were in life and demand more of the same—tiresome, I can tell you. At least they were all very religious sorts back then so they usually take well to being subdued by prayer, which Reverend Randall here is very skilled at."

"And tonight?" Lin whispered, her eyes wide.

"Tonight, I will attempt to have a little chat with King Henry and possibly rouse the Abbot while I'm at it, if there's time. Hopefully, Henry will be more receptive than the first time around." She downed her beer in several deep gulps, wiped her mouth on her sleeve which provoked a wince from her brother.

"What's he like? I mean, what *was* he like—King Henry, I'm referring to?" Lin pressed.

"Vague," Geri replied. "He was a bit dithery when he died and before that, more than a little inept, plus a thieving crook, if you consider that he bankrupted the Jews and plundered the lands of his barons. No doubt he'd chalk that up to the Divine Right of Kings. Never mind, I shall persist. Meanwhile, do call your aunt and tell her that you are working on a special assignment with your professor this the weekend—just in case."

"Okay. I've already texted her that I was going out to supper with friends. I am of legal age now but she's so used to protecting me..." Lin let her words hang as she dashed off a quick text on her phone. She glanced at Geri. "Should I say that I may be staying overnight?"

"Yes. I have guest accommodations, if needed." Silly how delighted she was at the thought of having company. "Tell her that she can text me if more information is required." She provided her cell number. "Now, it's nearly 9 p.m.. Best to get at it then, shall we?"

Randall folded his hands on the table. "One moment, please. There is still the matter of security. The cameras may not yet be able to detect ghostly presences in the Abbey but the sound of a voice addressing the late King Henry III will certainly register."

Geri leaned forward. "Then I advise you to ask for holy forgiveness and fiddle with the machines, dear brother."

"I do not have the knowledge to fiddle with the machines, even if I were to agree to infiltrate the control system."

"I do."

They looked at Lin. "It's just technology—cameras and recording devices, right? Is it connected to New Scotland Yard or the Metropoltian Police?"

Randall gazed at the girl. "Both, certainly."

"I'll start with the camera feed, then. You just have to get me in."

Randall opened his mouth to protest.

"Good, it's settled." Geri heaved herself to her feet. "I'll get the check." While her brother went to the loo, Geri unzipped Eddy and dropped in a roll.

"Do you actually feed them?" Lin asked.

"Not feed him, exactly. I just toss bits of food sometimes and it all disappears. Not sure what that's about. This is a relatively new development. Are you ready?"

"Ready."

Chapter Four

The Abbey had finally emptied by the time Randall had keyed them into the western gate. He nodded at the guard and drew his guests over to the control booth to explain that his sister Dr. Geraldine Woodworth and her graduate student would be doing a walkabout in the Abbey under his direction. He'd like to give the student a tour of the inner workings of the Abbey's systems while he was at it. Could the guard team arrange that?

Apparently, the opportunity to do something other than stare at the monitors all night held enough appeal for the guard captain to readily agree to the reverend's request. Geri whispered to her brother to meet her at King Henry's tomb and left them to work out the details as she made her way through the warren of monuments and tombs.

The Abbey's lighting system had switched to night mode which created a considerably gloomier mood to the nave than regular daytime spotlights. Added to that, the Cosmati mosaic now appeared to be glowing with an almost neon-like intensity—or was that just an illusion?

Geri stared past the steps towards the spinning central medallion which seemed to have increased in velocity and now included the other companion roundels in its incessant twirling. Not an illusion, then—real, or at least, one version of real. The Cosmati mosaic was coming undone.

Geri stifled a jolt of panic and shuffled past the sanctuary towards the tomb of Edward the Confessor, her cane echoing against the stone. She could only hope that Lin and Randall soon fixed the security system and joined her before things became too interesting.

The long hall stretched far ahead, the Abbey feeling even more huge when emptied of its influx of visitors. Of course, places this old were never truly empty and the occasional spectral presence was to be expected. Ghostly monks were all the rage, apparently. Geri had seen plenty in her day and they had never bothered her.

As she rounded the corner of the north ambulatory, the shadows seemed to thicken, deep and impenetrable. Geri hesitated. It felt so much like wading through murk here that she almost expected to step on something slimy. This was not typical Abbey behavior. In the past, the shadows were just that—if occasionally deepened with hints of ghostly presences—but not like this. Here, the shadows felt, well, *busy*.

Geri had always used her instincts to feel her way around and through anything supernatural. There were always more dimensions than what the human eye could detect, and one of her many gifts was the ability to see fully in ways that most could not. In her profession, that could be very useful.

Cautiously, she took another step and then another while tapping her cane before her as a blind person might. The stone walls with their inset tombs, statues, and carvings rose all around her, everything seeming watchful and not all of it friendly. Three thousand bodies had been buried in the Abbey over the centuries, most of them remaining peaceful despite occasional ghostly activity, but this felt different, very different. It was as though everything had been activated—the good, the bad, the ugly.

Could evil already be leaking through the Cosmati cracks? It was something Geri had not considered but now found it impossible not to. These shadows were deeper than she'd ever seen them, and Geri knew her shadows.

Supposing demonic entities were coming through? Usually a church with its frequent prayers and hymns, could keep these energetic free radicals at bay. But if they were *that* strong, and the Cosmati wards *that* broken...

Ghosts never frightened Geri but demons were something else. Clutching Eddy to her chest with one hand, her cane in the other, she turned to look behind her.

There, where the corridor turned a corner, and opposite the chapels of St Edmund's and Saint Nicholas, something scrambled across the floor—not scrambled exactly, more like loped, as if the arms were too long for its body. Maybe a large rat, only darker and thicker, and with what looked to be arms? Not a rat, then, but something far nastier.

"Get away!" she hissed.

The shadow thing paused the way a dog might, one paw half-raised and head cocked as if to say *You talking to me?* And then took a step towards her.

Any medievalist could name these entities. In the Middle Ages, the craftsmen were forever carving imps, gargoyles and demons into the cathedral stone and woodwork as a kind of talisman against more of the same. Apparently that trick was no longer working here. Had the enemy breached the gates?

"Stay back!" she cried.

Geri suppressed a shiver, wishing desperately that she could call up some kind of incantation to send this creature back to where it belonged. She knew nothing so useful. All her life, she had saved discipline for the applied science of her profession, not for the weird things that tugged on the edges of her perception. Now she wished she'd done her homework. Girding her loins, she turned her back on the thing and carried on, her neck hairs prickling.

"I don't like this," she whispered to Eddy, "I don't like this at all."

Adding to the infiltration of evil entities and maybe partially because of it, the Abbey's dead occupants were agitated. Occasionally Geri could make out a word or a phrase amid the whispering, most of them coming from the surrounding tomb chests and occasionally from beneath her feet.

Most of it was confused stream-of-consciousness stuff but at least one voice had the high-pitched imperiousness of a queen demanding the presence of her lady-in-waiting. Queen Elizabeth I? No, she was buried in another wing...unless that Queen Elizabeth had become a floater.

Geri kept her eyes averted and refused to engage. It was bad enough that she would soon have an audience with King Henry III's ghost much less become ensnared in some random royal decree.

Without looking left or right and attempting as best as possible to block her ears, she approached the wooden stairs leading up to the Chapel of St. Edward the Confessor, the Anglo-Saxon king who had reportedly been a pious and goodly man as well as an able ruler.

One of the main reasons that he had been canonized was because they had opened up his tomb long ago and discovered that his body remained "uncorrupted". At that point, reportedly miracles began occurring—always a good thing for an up-and-coming saint. Apparently, these were grounds enough to nab a sainthood back then. A petition was sent to Rome and it was done.

Henry III idolized Saint Edward, building this chapel in his fabulous new addition to Edward's original monastery as a means to honor his early predecessor. The king may have hoped that this might pave the way for his own beatification but that never transpired. At least, Henry had ensured that he would rest for all eternity as close to his hero as possible by arranging for his own tomb nearby.

By commissioning the shrine's pavement and sarcophagus ornamentation in the Cosmati style, it also set the stage to receive a regular troop of alms-paying pilgrims. Pilgrims were critical to the medieval church economy. In the thirteenth century, hundreds of years before King Henry VIII's anti-pope temper tantrum which turned Britain officially into the Church of England and thus, Anglican, Westminster Abbey had been Catholic, and saintly relics were key to keeping the medieval coffers suitably plumped.

The raised chapel was almost completely dark but for the faint illumination of the night lighting in the main Abbey when Geri reached the top stair. Ornate coffins resting between arched pillars lined the space with the majestic shrine to Edward the Confessor crowning the central area. One last look over her shoulder assured her that the demon thing had not followed her in ,but it also revealed that neither had Randall and Lin. She briefly considered texting her brother but knew he wouldn't likely respond.

All right, then. Best get at it. Carefully, she shuffled around to the other side of the shrine. If she was to rouse King Henry, she needed to remain out of sight. He wouldn't take well to an unknown woman appearing at his bedchamber— that is, if he remained fixed on the last moments of his life, which had been the case the last time.

Meanwhile, it was difficult to tell whether any other spirits were active nearby. There were fourteen tombs surrounding Edward's shrine alone, including a few that remained unidentified. Henry's, of course, was the most magnificent after St. Edward's and Henry's tomb lay to her left. At least, the surrounding spirits seemed at peace at the moment. If her brother had been here, he'd pray to keep them that way but she had to do this on her own.

The Shrine of Edward the Confessor was a work of art in itself and was positioned over another sweep of Cosmati mosaic work. In fact, as she had discovered in her previous investigations, this floor predated the sanctuary pavement by at least a year. Whatever the case, the looming tomb structure made the perfect place behind which to hide while addressing the king.

She doubted that King Edward would rouse while she was at it. Of all the times she'd worked in this area, including the days when she had been using ground-penetrating radar to scope out the floor burials, the ghost of St. Edward had never made an appearance. Since his body had been moved around so much while the shrine was being constructed, maybe his spirit was understandably confused—or disgusted. If she had been him, she'd haunt the daylights out of all those who shoved him about, stripped him of his burial robes, and stole his ring.

On the other hand, many spirits truly are at peace or, at least, find something better to do in death than hang around their graves for all eternity. *Get a life.* Geri smiled at her noir humor before suddenly sobering. She knew that Henry III was another matter: he was obsessed with his cathedral, the mosaics, and with this tomb, in particular.

But it was still so dark. She badly wanted to use her phone light but there was no telling what an intense digital beam might do to aggravate the spirits. She made her way as stealthily as possible behind the tomb of St. Edward where she could fix on King Henry's tomb without being seen. At least, he would stay put. King Henry wasn't a "floater" as she called spirits that liked to move around.

Meanwhile, Eddy was twitching. Slowly, she lowered her bag to the floor and clutched her cane with both hands. "Stay!" she warned. The bag quivered briefly and then stilled.

Now, all she needed to do was wake the king. She peered out from behind the monument, her eyes scanning the tombs before fixing on King Henry's recumbent effigy. Once, it had been covered in gorgeous Cosmati work but over the centuries, most of it had been picked off by vandals calling themselves pilgrims. Souvenirs were big then, too.

"Thy majesty King Henry, pray grant me audience," she began, heart pounding in her ears. Instead of speaking French, the tongue commonly used by nobility since William the Conqueror, she used early English. Henry would know a smattering of it enough to address the occasional serf that made his way into his presence and since she was pretending to be lowly born, it was more fitting.

Surprisingly quickly, a spectral bearded image materialized on the top of Henry's tomb. The figure of a man wearing what looked to be some kind of nightgown with a cap upon his head was not exactly transparent but not quite solid-looking, either. He appeared to be sitting on the edge of his effigy, his ghostly bottom resting below the gilded image of his sleeping self. The floor had been raised since the tomb was first installed.

Well, that was easier than she expected.

"What ho! Who goest there?" His majesty was peering into the darkness trying to catch sight of her but his eyesight was notoriously poor, something she'd work to her advantage.

"Tis I, Your Majesty, your humble servant, cometh to apprise thee of the matter of Abbot de Ware." Geri well knew that the king had emptied his coffers —and everyone else's—bringing this surrounding magnificence into fruition. His passion to rebuild Westminster had never wavered but his interest in governance had. His abbot, on the other hand, had been fixed on the Cosmati mosaics and on his own self-aggrandizement, in particular. He had not been a popular man.

"What art thee about? Speaketh!"

Geri closed her eyes and scanned her memory desperately for her Middle English equivalents. She was rusty and had to remember that a boggling mix of French, Anglo-Saxon, and Latin words had infiltrated the yet-to-be-born modern English lexicon. It was practically undecipherable to the modern ear. It would have been easier had she spoken French but now that she had begun, she needed to excuse her poor diction somehow.

"Ich have a sore tooth," she ventured. "Pray forgive that Ich mumblae." She held her breath and waited. It was a long shot but worth a try.

"Art thee ain woman?"

She stared out into the dark with the faintly luminous figure of the seated king not more than ten feet away. Best get him off the topic of her gender.

"Thy majesty, Ich cometh don behalf ope Abbot de Ware." She went on to explain that the abbot was ill and that she was his nurse. It was all nonsense. However, since this king had been ill himself and had probably had many nurses visiting in the last few months, a supposed nurse addressing him on behalf of his ailing abbot might not seem so far a stretch. They lived more or less next door to each other: the king in his palace across the road and de Ware in his abbey next door.

But it worked. Actually, it worked too well. Henry, used to having an audience, clearly missed it. Once he began speaking, it was impossible to make him stop, let alone pin him down to one topic.

His majesty was a babbler. He asked for his dear wife, Queen Eleanor of Provence; he mumbled on about his late father, King John of the Magna Carta and Runnymede fame; he condemned his lazy courtiers who were nowhere to be found when he needed them most; and, where was the Abbot de Ware? Should he not be here at his side? Sick, you say? What right had he to be in ill-health when his sovereign lay dying?

The topic of the abbot was a sore point, obviously, but she soon had him waxing on about the Cosmati floor, at least in terms of its beauteousness. There was no sign of him knowing about the floor's cosmic powers but he did fervently believe that it depicted the universe of God and that he was thus connected to its mysterious wonder.

As for magic and miracles, the king believed in them both absolutely, not that he permitted Geri much opportunity to steer the discussion. When she interrupted his monologue to prod him on the whereabouts of one Petrus Odoricus, master stone-layer, it provoked a fit of righteous indignation. A stone-layer? Why would he, the most rightful king, knoweth of a mere stone-layer? Is this a jest? For if so, he was not amused by such foolery.

Then she asked about possible violence over the sanctuary floor. Did His Majesty know of such a thing, a man killed, perhaps?

"Ask the Abbot!" he cried for he knew nothing so mundane.

By that point, his majesty had left his perch and was sailing towards her. She noted with alarm that his form was growing more opaque by the minute and that she could now make out every hair on his long flowing beard. He had become a floater!

Instinctively, she took a step back and then another. Eddy had begun to glow on the floor in front of her. She needed to send the king back to sleep and quickly. Where was Randall? She couldn't do this on her own.

"Oh, thy majesty! Ich beseech thee!" And then she tripped over something and fell backwards in a heap on the mosaic pavement. For a moment, all she could do was stare up at the swirl of shadows overhead. It had grown so dark, not even the night lighting seemed to penetrate the gloom and, what was worse, the air around her had thickened to the point where she could hardly breathe.

She could make out figures of people and things above her—nasty things, demonic things with green eyes and long limbs and at least one gargoyle. Spirits floated past wringing their hands in various states of distress—one was headless. Many she could not recognize because they pre-dated formal portraiture but she guessed them to be kings, queens, and related royal family members, each one frightened and crying for help. Her heart broke at their pain and suffering. How she longed to comfort them but her mouth wouldn't open.

Something snarled in the dark.

"Eddy!" Geri tried to cry but her throat clogged with sludge. And then, as if from a faraway place, she heard her brother's voice reciting the Last Rites, followed by prayers of wholeness and healing.

Geri heaved herself onto her elbows.

"May the light of God surround you,
May the love of God enfold you..."

. . .

39

She spied Eddy glowing intensely on the other side of the chapel. He seemed to be perched on top of King Henry's tomb right between the effigy's hands. Her brother was standing nearby, praying fervently, and beside him, Lin was yelling at a black demon thing, ordering it back to hell using good Anglo-Saxon expletives—a bit rough but effective.

Geri grasped onto the edge of St. Edward's tomb and hefted herself to her feet. With her cane in her other hand, she swiped at the demon, pushing it back until it fell against King Henry's tomb and appeared to fizzle in Eddy's glow. Seconds later, the thing had completely incinerated, leaving behind nothing but sulfurous smoke and a now ruined leather satchel.

Finally, after several minutes of swiping and praying and yelling, the chapel subsided back into its usual gloomy peace.

Geri, Randall, and Lin stood temporarily stunned.

"Please tell me that the security cameras didn't catch all this," Geri whispered after she caught her breath.

"I shut it down," Lin replied, "but like we had a hard time even getting here. There are black slippery things everywhere and Rev had to pray them to death before we could even walk down the hall. What's going on? Is this the end of the world?"

"The first few cracks, yes," Geri told her, "And it's going to get much worse." No use coddling the young. Let them see the true scope of problems so they could join the fight, especially since the older generations caused most of it.

"Indeed, the Abbey is in complete spiritual and physical disarray," Randall said, turning to his sister. "It is falling apart! Quickly, we must leave and form a strategy!"

Geri called a smoldering Eddy onto her back, seeing that parts of her bag were hanging in charred strips. There'd be time enough to figure out the reason for his demon-singeing capacity later.

"Eddy's a demon-toaster!" Lin whispered.

Leaving the chapel was easy enough, but once they reached the ambulatory, the floor appeared to be coated in foot-deep sludge. Randall prayed fervently which cleared enough of a path for them to proceed, while Geri kept muttering the first thing that came into her head.

"Are you casting spells or something?" Lin asked of her teacher. "I don't know how to handle all this stuff!"

"I don't know, either," Geri said, "but you're doing a good job by using your instinct. Just keep doing what you're doing until we can figure things out. Randall," she called ahead to where her brother was busy clearing their path. "I must speak to Abbot Ware before we exit tonight!"

"That is highly unadvisable, Geraldine, given the state of the Abbey and, indeed, of the Cosmati floor! Look."

They had arrived at the sanctuary and the Cosmati Pavement. Geri stopped dead and stared. Now the mosaic had lifted nearly a meter into the air and the roundels were spinning so furiously, they appeared to be achieving lift-off.

"Where's Ware again?" Lin asked.

"He's buried under there," Geri said, pointing to the pavement.

"So, does that mean we have to stand on that thing to get him up?" Lin asked. "That sounds pretty damned risky!"

And there appeared to be a vortex forming over the neon mosaic, a mini tornado that tugged on their clothing and attempted to drag them closer.

"Abbot Ware!" Geri called. "Come forth, I beseech ye—"

But Lin, by far the slightest of the three, suddenly flipped forward and began to slide towards the mosaic.

Chapter Five

I f it hadn't been for the steps blocking Lin's slide into the vortex, they might have lost her. It took Geri and Randall everything they had to drag her back by the ankles before they could all scramble away to safety across the south transept and out into the Cloisters, Randall praying every step of the way.

There, the three of them collapsed onto one of the ancient stone benches and huddled shivering into the night, Randall on one side, Geri on the other, and Lin in the middle. The siblings held the girl's hands in each of theirs, everyone too shocked to speak, at first.

"That was close. Are you all right, Lin?" Geri asked after a moment.

"Yeah, sure. I almost got sucked into a super-colored whirling hole, but what of it? I didn't have anything better to do on a Friday night, did I?"

Geri smiled and squeezed her hand before quickly releasing it. "I am very sorry that you had to experience that but fair warning—this will only get worse."

Randall was leaning against the back wall with his eyes closed, praying. "God preserve us," he muttered. After a moment he opened his eyes. "Did you have any success with King Henry, Geraldine?" he asked.

"None whatsoever. Henry remains as confused as I recall from last time, perhaps more so, and now there is so much activity in the Abbey that it is working him up even more. All the spirits are restless and some are in distress. You did a fine job soothing them tonight, Randall, but I'm afraid it won't be enough. Hopefully things will calm down, at least until dawn."

"The Lord has provided succor through my prayers, for which we should all say a prayer of thanks. Let us pray."

"How are we going to fix this?" Lin asked quickly. "I mean, there are ghosts and horrible things everywhere. Seriously, it's freaking me out! What did King Henry say exactly?"

Geri responded. "Nothing important exactly, as I feared. He knows—sorry, *knew*—about the floor's powers only in a general sense and didn't appear to grasp any deeper significance. He believed in miracles, period, but appears to have no knowledge concerning a murder and didn't acknowledge the existence of a stone-layer named Petrus."

"And what about those creepy things hanging all around?" the girl asked, leaning forward.

"Demons coming in through the Cosmati cracks. If we don't soon find a way to stop them, their numbers will increase. Unfortunately, I cannot access the Abbot Ware, let alone track down Petrus and whatever murder—if it was a murder—that the Reverend here witnessed. I sense that they are all somehow related—the body on the Pavement, the floor's wards, Petrus Odoricus, and Bishop Ware."

"What do we do now?' Lin asked.

"Have a good think," Geri replied but, admittedly, she was out of ideas for the moment and too exhausted, anyway.

Meanwhile, Randall continued praying. At their back, the cold wall of the Abbey, while ahead stretched the cloister's manicured lawns surrounded by the other three arms of the cloister, everything dark but for occasional nightlight.

Once, long ago, this space would have been busy with monks working by candlelight, the open arches half-closed against the autumn winds, the braziers burning for warmth.

If she peered too long into the dark, Geri could see tonsured heads bent over their tasks and feel the communion and comfort of a close-knit community. It was akin to a family, she realized, and she envied Randall's sense of belonging unified by common beliefs.

But she was tired of ghosts, for the moment. A little human companionship was in order.

"Come, Randall. Let us all take a cab to my place. I have two spare bedrooms, as you recall, and we could all do with a rest before we study this matter further. Admittedly, we don't have much time. We will need to find the solution and heal the broken floor by the end of the weekend, if the current activity is any indication."

43

Randall straightened. "I cannot leave, Geraldine. The Abbey is on my watch. I cannot simply walk away."

"And you can't keep going without sleep, either. You know that your very presence in the Abbey increases activity as does mine. It's best that we stay away for a few hours until we get this thing sorted—do our research."

And then Randall's phone rang. He pulled it from his robe's pocket. "It's from the Dean. Pardon me." He strode away talking quickly into his phone.

"I have a spare toothbrush, by the way,"

Geri said, getting to her feet. So far, it seemed as though Eddy had returned to his version of normal, which was a relief. Somehow her bag held together despite its scorched parts. "Every time I go to the dentist, they give me a new toothbrush and I've collected quite a few."

"I could always use another toothbrush," Lin said absently.

Randall returned quickly. "The Dean has instructed me to retire for the night. Security has requested that all non-guard personnel leave the premises while they perform a thorough sweep. He says that there appears to be some malfunction in the surveillance systems—God forgive me."

"What he doesn't know, won't hurt him, right?" Lin remarked. She was unusually subdued.

"If only that were true," the Reverend replied. "Nevertheless, I will return with you to your apartment, Geraldine, and attempt to sort this out. I keep an overnight bag in my office. Excuse me while I fetch it and I shall meet you by the Poet's Corner."

They headed out the door to the south transept where Randall paused long enough to issue a prayer of peace towards the Cosmati floor. It appeared to be successful, at least to the point of dialing down the vortex and calming the fractious energies. Lin and Geri waited, keeping a nervous watch.

Meanwhile, all around them, the whispering continued, though much fainter than before. Various security personnel were on the move, dashing around the Abbey in a sense of alarm.

"Pardon me, would you mind terribly if I ask you to wait outside?" one guard addressed them. Though maintaining the outward appearance of unflappable professionalism, Geri could sense that the man flapped like a wind-blown flag inside. Something was going on; he just didn't have a reasonable explanation for what exactly that something was, poor man.

"Everything okay?" Lin asked the guard.

"Oh, yes, everything is good but for a few technical difficulties but, until we get them repaired, it is best that all visitors wait outside."

"You look like you've seen a ghost," Geri said, adding a laugh for good effect. She was testing him, of course.

Though the man cast her a tense smile, he made no comment before ushering them down towards the north entrance at such a pace that Geri could hardly keep up. He left them on the steps outside, seeming unaware of the glowing Cosmati floor or the restless spirits that they had passed along the way.

"It's like he doesn't see a thing," Lin whispered when they were alone.

"He doesn't—not yet, anyways, but he knows that something is very wrong. If the security systems are off-line on top of everything, no wonder he's in a spin. How hard will it be for them to get the systems back online?" Geri pulled her coat close around her shoulders.

"I didn't do much to harm anything, really, but I tried a bit of magic. By clouding the cameras and then creating white noise on all the audio equipment, I think I messed things up pretty badly but not in a permanent way. All smoke and mirrors stuff, really."

"Did you use a spell or something of that ilk?" Geri pressed.

"Not a spell, no, just my imagination." She tapped her skull with one finger. "I imagine something really intensely—like put my whole self into it, you know?—and then make it manifest. It doesn't always work but if my intentions are good, a lot of the time it will. Like tonight. I could see the mist blurring the monitors in the control booth. You've tried stuff like that, too, right?"

"Right." Geri looked away. She had done something similar but unconsciously. It was too difficult to explain her approach—or lack of it—regarding her latent powers. Anyway, she needed to focus on larger matters for the moment. "Oh, good, here comes the Right Reverend now."

Randall strode from the Abbey carrying a leather doctor's bag that had been their late father's. "I spoke again with the Dean. He appears to be satisfied that matters are all under control." With that, he led them to the curb and hailed a cab.

Almost half an hour later, they finally arrived at Geri's flat. While Randall paid the driver, Geri led Lin up the walkway to the three-story mansion that had been converted into flats back in the nineties and greeted the doorman, John, a sturdy little man who always reminded Geri of a bulldog.

She had been lucky to have purchased her third-floor unit all those years ago when spacious accommodations were still available in London for a semi-reasonable price. It had everything she needed; a wall of windows looking out onto a leafy street, room for her books, her passions, her ideas, and a kitchen suitable for reheating takeaways and making toast and tea. Unfortunately, the pipes also moaned at night, the hot water took ages to arrive, and electrical appliances were prone to go on the blink without a moment's notice. In other words, the building was old and therefore required a great deal of appeasement to keep things running smoothly. Geri mostly despised new buildings. They were so soulless with their gaping lack of history and previous occupants.

As the three of them rode up on the lift, they were still too weary to speak, each of them lost in their own thoughts. It was already just past 11 o'clock.

Lin's phone beeped from her pocket. "It's from Aunt Soo," she said, pulling out her device and peering down at her screen. "She wants to know the address of where I'm staying. Says she wants the particulars."

"That means she cares for you and wants to ensure that you are not being kidnapped or stolen away by some wayward person," said Randall. "I do admired the support of such a vigilant guardian. Here, I shall type in my sister's address."

"I'll do it, Randall. You'll inevitably type something incorrectly, activate autocorrect and become cross. I'm cross starting out so it makes things easier." She took Lin's phone and typed in her location herself, adding that Lin was in the company of her professor, Dr. Geraldine Woodworth, and her brother, the Right Reverend Randall Woodworth of Westminster Abbey. Seriously, could one get any better credentials than that?

"My aunt is super-protective. I keep reminding her that I'm twenty now but she doesn't get it," the girl told them. "It has something to do with when she escaped Ethiopia during the revolution and lost my mom. I was still a baby. She's never really gotten over it."

"Your aunt sounds like an amazing person and, yes, I would think traumas that deep would leave a scar," Geri said as she unlocked the door of her flat and switched on the lights.

Her beloved threadbare Persian carpets and wall-to-wall books, the plants, the deep red tones against cream walls with her somewhat shabby antique furniture all embraced her with heartfelt hugs of color. She felt sorry for those without the Sight because they never realized how inanimate objects hold love in their very fibers.

After ushering her guests into the comfy lounge with its gas fireplace and flea market finds, she dropped Eddy onto the ottoman and announced: "Make yourselves comfortable while I put on the kettle and check that the spare rooms are up to snuff."

Scurrying out of the room, she hung her coat onto the hall hook and dropped into the kitchen long enough to plug in the kettle.

Things were just as she left them—the teapot sitting ready beside the single mug, the digestive biscuit on the plate. Those little touches provided the illusion that somebody loving waited at home. In a way, that was true. Nobody was ever truly alone, at least, not if they looked beyond just human companionship. Besides, she did have Eddy and her plants.

She took out two additional mugs from the cupboard and added more biscuits before slipping down the hall to the guest rooms. One was actually an office and the other an extension of her library. Both were kitted out with single beds which she kept made up in case visitors arrived, which seldom occurred.

Otherwise, she decorated each room with forest green paint, a mix of colorful textiles collected on her travels, and far too many bookcases to leave wall space for paintings. She did have the occasional oil painting propped on the shelves here and there, most of them having belonged to her parents.

"Yes," she whispered to the house spirits as she plumped up a pillow. "You'll like this, won't you—people to keep you company in the dark? Just don't bother them with any nonsense, understand? They'll be onto you, anyway."

They were good spirits, overall, as she had trained them well over the years. They just became testy if abandoned for too long a time or if she failed to talk to them upon occasion. Once she had altered their behavior away from the infernal wall-knocking and the moving things around bit, they got along just fine. Any time one got out of hand, she lit the candles and muttered a line or two from the book her mother had given her.

Once long ago, she had considered acquiring a cat or a dog but decided against it because pets were too demanding—kitty litter, regular walks. Who had time for that sort of thing? Besides, they smelled and often mewed or slobbered and, in the case of cats, assumed they were queen of the estate when there could only be one of those. No pets, in other words.

It was enough just keeping the invisible companions in line. She paused, thinking so hard that her head pounded. Would any of those poems—she refused to call them *spells*—work to reseal the Abbey spirits? Not strong enough, she reminded herself quickly. Those little ditties were designed for managing household spirits like random energies that set up shop in houses because they prefer human company—not for the entities and ghosts such as those oozing out of the Cosmati cracks. It was the floor itself that needed fixing there.

Taking one last look at the room, she returned to the kitchen where she found Randall pouring boiling water into the teapot.

"Do you still have the tea cozy I gave you?" he asked without removing his eyes from the kettle.

"I do." She fetched the Gothic church-shaped knitted cozy from the cupboard and tugged it snugly over the pot.

"And the crucifix?"

"It's in one of the spare rooms beside the Star of David, the statue of Shiva, my Buddha, and my Hand of Fatima. Why are you asking me this, Randall? We are in dire straits here and you want to know if I treasure your gifts? I treasure every one. Now, let us focus on the crisis at hand."

"I apologize. It's just that I am once again faced with the fact that I have asked for your help with a holy site when you are not indoctrinated into the religion that created such. Geraldine, it is not too late for you to return to the fold. God will always welcome you."

Geri glared at her brother. "I respect all religions, Randall, though I have never approved of the sins against humanity that have been inflicted in the name of religion—all of them. At the same time, it is the gathering of people with the intent to support one another and to do good in this world of which I do approve, even though I choose not to join any of the congregations for one reason or another. You know all this because I've told you many times before but allow me to restate it one more time: I will not 'return to the fold,' as you say. I am far more goat than sheep and will never swallow carte blanche any doctrine, understood?"

Randall swallowed, his Adam's apple working like a frenzied elevator. "Geraldine, I mean only to remind you that this is an abbey we're working in, a hallowed site, a—"

Geri held up her hand. "Enough. We will never agree on this. Drop it."

Randall frowned. "Very well. However, because this is an abbey and because of the enormity of the task we face, I am considering alerting my colleagues—perhaps even the Archbishop of Canterbury himself—in order to authorize prayer warriors to gather both beyond and within the Abbey," he told her. "The Dean would certainly give my concerns credence, at least to the point of hearing me out."

"But you can prove nothing," she told him. "Without having visible manifestations to show the Church of England mucky-mucks, you are in danger of sounding a bit of a crackpot. What would you tell them—that the Cosmati floor is fractured to the point of emitting real gargoyles and setting the Abbey's ghosts into restless prowling?"

"That is the truth."

"Which sounds bonkers and will not help us in this instance." She paused, staring glumly down at the crafty cozy—some lady of the church bazaar's rather amazing offering. It even had beaded stained glass windows. There are so many different kinds of magic. "Besides, we don't have time to organize grand gatherings. We need to repair the floor within in the next day or two, at the absolute latest."

"But how?" be asked, one hand wiping his face as if to clear his thinking.

"How about an exorcism?" They turned to see Lin standing behind them in her stocking feet. "I mean, isn't that what priests do to return demons back to hell?"

"In point of fact, yes and no," Randall replied. "Exorcisms are performed to evict demons, in particular, from an inflicted person or place, but this is an entirely different situation, and more of a global danger. It is as if time itself is cracking at the seams. Demons aren't the only horror escaping that void. No exorcism alone can repair this."

"What, then? I mean who do we ask how to fix this if we can't get to the Abbot of Ware?" Lin paused for a moment, shifting her weight from foot to foot with one hand holding her phone. "Wait," she said suddenly. "What if we come at this from a different angle?"

"What do you mean?" Geri asked. The girl was a divergent thinker—who knew what tangents she could open for inquiry?

"What if we come at this scientifically?" the girl continued. "Aunt Soo always tells me that magic is just science that we have yet to understand."

"As in science is magic and magic is science?" Randall asked.

"Something like that. But look," she held her phone up to the picture of the Cosmati pavement, "if the medieval designer, this Petrus dude, saw this as symbolic of the universe and all the circles are currently spinning the way the planets spin, maybe it really is meant to represent the cosmos?"

"The *sacred* cosmos," Randall clarified.

"Is there a difference? They wouldn't have thought so back in the Middle Ages, would they, Rev?"

She had a point. Geri turned and leaned against the counter. "Go on, flesh out your theory, Lin."

"So, like in physics, space/time is a mathematical model, right? And the Cosmati floor is designed around the principles of sacred geometry. So what if we look at this in terms of physics—which is a bit like magic better understood by our rational brain?" Eyes flashing, the girl literally percolated with ideas.

Something tingled in Geri's belly. The girl was onto something.

And then the buzzer rang. Startled, Geri stared at the jingling wall unit. "Who could that be at this time of night?"

"Probably my aunt." Lin shrugged. "I didn't invite her, honestly, but she has a habit of inviting herself, probably because I brain-pinged her."

Brain-pinged? Geri reached for the phone. "So does Aunt Soo have powers, too?"

"Not in the way you mean. She's a retired scientist but she just doesn't get such a big difference between patterns of thought the way most people do. My mum was witchy so she's used to it. Let her in, Doc, please. You'll like her."

Geri caught Randall's eye as she picked up the phone.

"Hello, Dr. Woodworth?" said the voice on the other end. It was the security bloke downstairs. She had always imagined him as an English bulldog—same jowly snout. "I have a lady here that says you have her niece in your care. Probably related to the guest you brought in earlier, you know, an immigrant."

She could almost picture the man slobbering over the phone, maybe emitting a growl on the side. She knew he was referring to the woman's skin color, which annoyed Geri so much that she buzzed the door release without comment. She'd reprimand the small-minded ass privately later.

"Right, then. Randall, please take down another mug and I'll grab the tray."

Moments later, Geri opened the door on an amazing woman dressed in a bright green coat over a long orange cotton dress with a towering fabric-wrapped headpiece. Eyes warm behind spectacles, smile bright and wide as was the woman herself, she held a carryall in one hand. "Dr. Woodworth, I presume?" she said in a precisely modulated English with just a touch of an accent.

Geri beamed. "It is indeed but please call me Geri. You must be Lin's aunt."

"Call me Soo, Soo Belay, and contrary to my niece's insistence, she will always be Lynette to me."

"Soo, then. Please come in." She stepped aside to open the door.

At that exact moment, Eddy dropped onto the carpet behind them and a glowing orb slipped from his innards to roll across the floor.

"He is male—look at that ball!" Lin exclaimed, clapping her hands.

Chapter Six

"How extraordinary," Soo remarked, stepping forward to gaze down at the orb.

Approximately the size of a large snow globe, the sphere glowed from within as if lit by swirling pinkish-gold gas. Actually, it appeared to be too hot to handle.

"Is it meant to be a nightlight? If so, it truly is a novel work of technology. Only," Soo crouched down, "this example appears to contain actual gaseous matter as opposed to the illusions of light and pattern that I have seen in similar examples. How is that possible? Quite amazing. I wish I had such a thing when I was teaching astronomy all those years ago."

"Best not to touch it," Geri warned.

Too late. Soo had already cupped the orb into the palm of her hand, twisting it this way and that as she studied the sphere intensely, the colors reflecting in her eyes.

"Hi, Auntie," Lin said, giving her a sideways hug. She pointed to the orb. "Meet Eddy, or I think that's Eddy."

Geri swallowed and cast a glance at her bag's seemingly empty cavity. "I suspect it is, indeed, Eddy."

Soo, standing now, caught Geri's gaze over the top of the sphere—eyes sparkling with intelligence enhanced by the orb's glow. "Eddy?"

"Eddy is the name my sister has given to her pet bag which became unexpectedly animated one day and..." Randall stared at the globe. "I'm at a loss for words concerning this, however." He held out his hand. "Nevertheless, how do you do? I am the Right Reverend Randall Woodworth of Westminster Abbey, Geraldine's brother. And you are?"

Soo offered her free hand. "I am Sofuchi Adeeze Belay, aunt of Lynette here. As a kindness, you may call me Soo as most people cannot pronounce my name. Very pleased to meet you, Reverend. I apologize for the sudden appearance, but I wanted to assure myself that Lynette was safe while also bringing her a change of clothes, toiletries, and my special ginger snaps that always settle her stomach before exams. Am I to understand that there are anomalies at work here?"

"A reasonable assumption," Randall said with a nod. "Anomalies are a common occurrence around my sibling and me." A strained smile tightened his face. "At the moment, they are totally out of control."

Geri remained uncharacteristically silent—a bit stunned, more like it. Eddy had just emitted an extraordinary ball of light—either that or Eddy *was* an extraordinary ball of light—and it left her gobsmacked either way. "Anyone want tea?" she said quickly.

"Tea would be lovely. Many thanks," Soo said, still fixed on the sphere. "I prefer herbal with honey and no milk, if it's not too much bother."

"Not too much bother," Geri assured her.

"Eddy looks just like the Cosmati floor's central roundel—look!" Lin exclaimed, pointing. "That can't be a coincidence."

And the sphere did—the same coloring, the same twisting pattern in animated form. This was all getting too much. Geri lifted the orb from Soo's hand and lowered Eddy carefully onto the table where he appeared to rotate slowly on his axis.

"Eddy, is that you?" she whispered. The sphere briefly flashed before subsiding into a soft glow. "Do you mind terribly staying still?" she asked. Another flash and it stilled. Geri sighed. "This is Eddy, all right."

"Eddy's a demon-slayer, Auntie," Lin said.

"A demon-slayer? And here I thought it was a nightlight." Soo said, her eyes wide as Lin filled her in on the night's activities.

Turning away, Geri busied herself with handing everyone mugs while Lin poured the tea and Randall delivered the biscuits—chocolate-covered digestives, another of Geri's little sins. She needed to keep her mind occupied with trivialities to allow her thoughts to settle.

Lin was speaking. "Auntie, I've just been telling the two docs here about how you always say that science and magic are flip sides of the same coin. I'm thinking that taking that approach may help us figure out how to heal the Cosmati rent. Obviously, Eddy is here to help. That part's no accident, either."

Soo's brows arched as she stirred in a bit of honey into her chamomile tea.

The poor woman seemed like a person who found herself suddenly dropped headfirst onto an alien planet and must now decipher the language. "The Cosmati rent?"

"The Cosmati floor—you know the medieval mosaic in Westminster Abbey where King Charles' coronation took place? It's damaged," Lin explained.

Geri studied her guest. Close to her age but perhaps slightly older, Soo was magnificent. She held herself with a regal bearing as if daring anyone to deny her right to wear the clothing of her heritage—the riotous color and pattern—while remaining open to everyone else's unique persona.

"Soo," she began, "am I correct in saying that you are accustomed to anomalies such as what some might consider witchcraft and magic, for instance?"

"You are correct," the woman acknowledged with a brief smile. "My late sister had the gift, as did my mother and many others in my maternal line. It has skipped me but manifested rather strongly in my niece here. As a result, I have learned to stretch my mind beyond that which the establishment believes to be true in order to better understand the universe as a whole."

"That is such a healthy way to look at things," Geri remarked.

"It is important to constantly adjust one's thinking when new information enters the mix. Nevertheless, I admit that extraordinary glowing demon-slaying orbs that appear to heed one's call are a bit beyond my experience. May I ask for further details regarding the Cosmati pavement?"

They all began to speak at once, Randall winning by slipping into his pulpit voice. Calmly, he went on to recount the odd occurrences, explained his and Geri's relationship with the Abbey, and ended by describing that evening's events.

If Soo Belay was shocked, she smoothed it down under an exterior so serene she could be in a meditative state. "And you believe the world will end should this crack not be repaired?" she asked mildly.

"Most definitely," Geri acknowledged.

"And would this be just the earth we are speaking of or the entire cosmos?" she posed.

Good question. "Actually, we don't know but since the medieval designers centered their efforts on their conceptualized world, I'd venture to say the earth." Geri visualized the whirling roundels. They could represent the birth of the universe. "And possibly the solar system."

"And am I to understand that this is an extremely dangerous enterprise given that the floor literally tried to suck my niece down the vortex?" Soo asked, suddenly taking a different tact.

"Yeah, Auntie, it's super dangerous but world annihilation is even worse."

She held up her phone to a news clip from the BBC. "Remember that comet you told me about that is predicted to swing too close to earth in the next few days? Well, now the news channels have picked up the story and are talking about margins of probability. You get that, don't you? Anyway, you came here to help us, whether you know it for not, so let's get started."

Soo's full lips twitched. "And how exactly am I to do that, Lynette?"

"By studying the Cosmati floor and seeing how the principles of physics may apply, of course," Lin pointed out. "I get where you're coming from but let's get on with it, Auntie. Here's a photograph of the floor. Give it a think and give us your opinion." Lin swiped her phone away from the news and back to her photos before passing over the phone.

Clearing her throat, Geri began to fill the woman in on additional details concerning Petrus, the Abbot Ware, and King Henry while Randall and Lin added tangential details.

Soo Belay sipped her tea and listened without interrupting, gaze fixed on the picture. "And you say that this mosaic formed a moving vortex that appeared to drag Lynette towards its center?" she asked at the first moment of silence.

"Totally," the girl said. "I felt like I was being sucked towards a giant vacuum cleaner."

"A vacuum—curious," her aunt mused, setting the phone down on the side table. "Gravitational, then. Perhaps the floor does, indeed, symbolically represent the solar system or more likely the birth of the cosmos with possibly more accuracy than was general knowledge at the time. I am no theologian or historian, but as a scientist if I view those roundels as revolving planets and consider that the central sphere appears to be revolving to such an extent as to create a vacuum, then I will hypothesize that it may be approximating the birth of the universe or, in scientific terms, is either a star being born or one ending."

Eddy began to spin with luminous intensity.

"Ah," Soo said, catching sight of the orb. "With that note of encouragement from Eddy, I will add that, if I extrapolate further and think in terms of world's end, then that central roundel could represent the end of the world as much as its beginning. It appears to be behaving like an anti-gravitational black hole that is absorbing all the matter around it in which case, it may widen to an even greater extent and swallow us whole."

Lin stepped forward. "So, if it's behaving like a black hole, could it suck us right back into time itself?"

Lin gazed at her steadily. "As is an Einsteinian concept? Well, why not? If the dead are up and walking, couldn't this be a time tunnel, really?"

Geri's eyes widened. "As in it could suck us back into the thirteenth century when the floor was being laid?"

"Quite possibly," Lin acknowledged, "if we align with the Theory of Relativity."

"Indeed, that would explain why the ghosts are prowling and why the Cosmati Cosmic leak is emitting so much negative energy," Randall said. "It is a black hole."

"As in a rent in the space time continuum?" Geri didn't really understand that sort of thing but it sounded reasonable.

"However," her brother interjected, "to believe that the principles of physics may in some way be aligned with the sacred beliefs that laid the foundation of the Cosmati floor is simply astounding."

Soo stood and picked up Eddy in her palm. "Perhaps not. As astounding as everything may seem to our limited understanding, the universe has always been in divine chaos and endless contradiction. We can never understand it all."

"God does, indeed, work in mysterious ways," said Randall.

"So," Lin began slowly, "if I had been swept down into the Cosmati vortex, I might have ended somewhere back in time?"

"Maybe, but that's not going to be allowed to happen, Lin," Geri stated as if her word were law.

"Why not? If anyone has to go back in time, it should be me. I'm small enough to fit down that hole and, besides, I'd love, love, love to go back in time."

"Absolutely not!" Randall asserted.

"I agree—absolutely not," her aunt agreed. "I vowed to protect you, Lynette. You are all the family I have left."

"Oh, Auntie, you're the best, but this isn't about just you and me. You know that."

Geri glanced at Soo's stricken face. "Nobody is going to be sucked anywhere, indeed, if that could even happen," she concurred, taking a deep breath. "It's mere speculation at this point. Besides, should it be true and this is a time chute, we have no idea how to return, not to mention that medieval England—if, indeed, that's where one would end up—was an exceedingly dangerous place." Though she figured that everywhere was a dangerous place at the moment, just in different ways.

"Then how do we find out how to fix the floor?" Lin demanded.

Geri took a deep breath. "I shall anchor myself to the here and now and demand an audience with Bishop Ware— at a safe distance from the Cosmati floor, of course. I will call him up and request the answers we need. *And then what?* A voice cried in her head. "We will proceed with this tomorrow night." She said that as if it were the most logical plan in the world and it was settled but at that point, it was the only one they had.

Considering her size, she really wasn't too worried about being sucked down a chute, providing the aperture remained the same circumference. Randall would pray fervently to keep everything as calm as possible, just in case. Lin and her aunt (Soo refused to leave her niece from that point forth) were to remain at a safe distance away up in the Queen's Jubilee Museum which overlooked the transept and afforded the best view of the Cosmati floor.

Altogether, it seemed the safest way to proceed, if the only one they had at the moment. Though Geri knew that it was woefully inadequate, the alternatives were too fraught with unknowns to even consider.

That night—or actually morning, as in the wee hours before they went to bed—Soo and Randall each took one of the spare bedrooms and Lin camped out on the couch while Geri took the orb with her into her room.

She had always slept with her bag on a chair beside her bed, comfortable in the odd companionship to which she had become accustomed. Now everything had changed. She wasn't sure who or what her companion was.

She lay on her back in bed, Eddy—what *was* Eddy?—balanced on her night table, still glowing beside her. Geri used to talk to it, and though Eddy had never responded, she believed that he listened the way a dog might listen, not understanding every word but knowing its master's voice. Now Geri wondered who really was the master in this situation—certainly not her.

Clearly, Eddy had appeared in her bag for a reason. Now, it was she who must listen. She turned on her side and gazed at it/him/her/them—for, of course, it was genderless—sensing that the orb was closely in tune with her thoughts.

"Are you an angel?" she whispered. Not that she believed in angels of the winged variety any more than she did of God sitting on a throne way up high. All those were symbolic concepts to help the multitude better comprehend the incomprehensible, but she believed absolutely in powerful entities of both good and evil, regardless of what name they went by.

Eddy's glow intensified before subsiding. Okay then, communicating with this orb was like playing a game of warm, warmer, warmest—the brighter Eddy shone, the righter Geri was.

"A guide?" she asked.

Eddy flared red, sustained that glow for at least ten seconds and then subsided again.

"Alright, then," she whispered. "You're my guide and I will begin listening to you. If you agree, we'll use colors to communicate, alright?"

Eddy turned green and Geri laughed. "Green for go. Goodnight, Eddy," and she flipped over to her other side and fell into a deep, restful sleep without any of the nightmares that usually plagued her—the burning, drowning nightmares.

* * *

The next morning arrived bright and chill, passing clouds threatening rain one minute and delivering sun the next, typical London-style. Geri bolted up in bed and shot a quick glance out the window which she always left open a crack—daytime already! She had actually slept that late? Her alarm clock said half-past eleven. Now she must scramble. Into her ensuite bathroom she went to shower and dress, shocked that she had been allowed to sleep for so long.

She could smell coffee brewing and Eddy still sat by her bedside colorless, but revolving slowly.

"Morning!" she greeted the orb as she rushed by. How does one say good morning to a mysterious a ball, anyway?

Once inside the shower, she wondered what in her closet she had to wear that wasn't black. Black had never been her best color but she wore it because it was so practical, didn't show dirt since she was always spilling food on herself, and maybe (hopefully) slimming. As long as she looked respectable and some- what dignified, it had always been enough. Now for some unaccountable reason, enough wasn't good enough. She wanted to, well, look *better*—her best, in fact. Soo had inspired her to get her color on.

She even fixed her hair, smoothing her blondish grey-streaked bob into the coiffure her hairdresser had intended. Then she donned a lovely wool dress in a peacock blue Liberty print and added a coordinating silky scarf. The former colleague who had gifted it to her had her claimed that it matched her eyes. That was during a hot summer dig at Sutton Hoo when she briefly considered romance as a possibility. Such a long time ago...

Gazing in the mirror, she declared herself almost unrecognizable. It was tempting to add a lick of lipgloss but that would be over the top. What was she doing? The world was ending and here she was thinking of lipgloss? But then the newsstands were full of articles on the world falling apart while pushing beauty products. Even she had been influenced.

Taking a deep breath, she gently lowered a now blue-green Eddy into her bag (the leather now back to its pre demon-singeing condition) opened the door, and headed for the kitchen.

The only person there was Lin.

"Wow!" the girl gasped as if seeing her professor for the first time. "You clean up brilliantly, Doc."

"I didn't realize I was that dirty. Anyway, thank you—I think. Do I really look as bad as that most of the time? No need to answer. Where is everyone?" She found herself unaccountably disappointed.

"Auntie's gone to our place to change but will be back soon and the Rev took off to the Abbey first thing this morning. Says he'll call later. We're all to convene at Westminster at nine o'clock tonight."

Geri stiffened. "We shall have to go to the Abbey long before that." What was Randall thinking? She sipped the coffee Lin handed her, pondering. "I must attempt to rouse Robert de Ware as soon as possible."

"So, like, is the Abbot down deep or something?" Lin asked. Today she had turned herself out in a pair of black leggings and a bright green hoodie, the latter no doubt her aunt taking advantage of the situation to impart a little color onto her niece.

"Not physically," Geri mused.

"Obviously not physically. I meant is there some reason why he doesn't rouse as easily as the others—King Henry, for instance?"

Catching the attitude, Geri turned to her student. "Speak precisely, then, Lin. Say what you mean. I have made the same comment multiple times on your essays, explaining how important it is to be clear, especially among academics in the field that you wish to enter."

Perhaps she came on a bit too strong but Geri believed there was a danger when becoming familiar with one's students, especially if they bordered on being disrespectful even for a nanosecond.

Lin opened her mouth to counter that statement but closed it again. For a moment it appeared that she might fall into a sulk but suddenly pulled herself together. "You're right and I'm sorry. I do need to catch myself, hone my thoughts, and communicate more clearly. I will improve, just watch. In the meantime, would you like some of Auntie's frittata? She's a mean cook. Please try it. I've been keeping it warm in the oven but it should still be good."

Geri never refused a peace offering. "Sounds wonderful, thank you."

"Want toast with that?"

"Absolutely." She beamed.

It was a strange sensation being served by somebody else in one's own kitchen, to sit down to a delicious home-cooked breakfast while being fussed over. Most of the time, she'd pick up a sticky bun and a coffee from a cafe on the way to work. On Saturdays like today she might treat herself to a boiled egg and a few store-bought croissants, that is if she remembered to go to the bakery.

"How's Eddy today?" Lin asked as they sat across from one other.

Geri glanced towards her bag propped on the counter. "You can take him out and ask him if you want."

Lin slipped Eddy out of the bag. He was shining like the sun. "He feels warm to the touch."

"He's telling you that he likes you and is here to help us on our mission. We reached a kind of understanding last night, but it's no use asking me who or what he/she/it/they are because I have no idea. It's probably best that we don't understand absolutely everything. For now, let's just accept all the help we can get."

"Sounds good to me." Lin carefully set the orb on the table. "Auntie just texted. She's on her way up."

"Buzz her in, please. The guard isn't on duty in the mornings."

"K."

In minutes, Soo had entered the flat, today wearing a red and orange block print gown that hung beneath her red coat like a banner of honor. In both hands she had carryalls filled with what looked to be food and clothes. "Good morning, Lynette and Geri. I come bringing good things to eat in case we are forced to camp out to fight the ghosts and demons." She caught sight of Geri's outfit. "Are we celebrating?"

"In a manner of speaking," Geri replied.

"Ah, yes," Soo nodded. "Because color is a celebration of life and, at the heart of it, that is what healing the Cosmati rift concerns, true?"

Geri stared. That was exactly true—fight the darkness with vivid color. Could it be that this woman actually got her? She grinned. "I believe I quite like you, Soo."

Soo grinned back. "Then you will like my cooking, too. I brought snacks."

"If your frittata is any indication, I believe I will. That was the best breakfast I've had in ages. Now, excuse me while I call Randall." She pulled out her phone. "We must get into the Abbey as soon as possible."

"Indeed. Lynette and I will stand at the ready as soldiers of peace." She shot a quick glance at her niece. "Or something of that ilk."

Geri speed-dialed her brother and Randall picked up right away. "Good morning, Randall. We are preparing to join you at the Abbey. Has the situation at all improved?"

"No, not improved at all." His voice came across so crisp, it was as if he were hissing into a tin can. "Things are not back to normal here, do you understand? Not back to normal at all. Security is still reporting anomalies and the Dean and the brethren are running about trying to put out fires, including one of the literal variety!"

"Calm down. Are the security systems still off-line?" She turned and caught Lin and Soo's eye.

"Most certainly. A security firm has been brought in for backup and all events and tours have been postponed—a totally unheard of situation for Westminster Abbey, with the exception of during the pandemic."

"Is the misting of the monitors and the white noise Lin created last night still the issue?"

"Security anomalies continue unabated but there are other unexplainable events that are occurring that maintenance has not been able to rectify or identify—the lights continually flash on and off; a loudspeaker suddenly broadcasts odd sounds; the visitors toilets are overflowing—total chaos! We have police dispersing the visitors' queues outside as we speak and the Abbey will remain closed until the matter is resolved."

"That's good—less danger of anyone getting hurt or experiencing visible phenomena."

"Nothing is good, Geraldine."

"No, of course not. What about the Cosmati floor?"

"Simmering, for lack of a better word. However, the whispering in the Abbey is now so intense, I must suppress the urge to cover my ears as I walk the transept. I fear that it may be only hours before the phenomena becomes visible to all, God help us. Pardon me." He briefly spoke to someone before returning. "I must go. We are convening another emergency meeting."

"Wait—we need to access the Abbey, Randall, as in ASAP! Get Lin, Soo, and me in."

"Absolutely not—tonight at the very earliest. No one is permitted access, Geraldine, not even the conservationists and archaeologists. We're in lockdown."

"But we must speak to Abbot Ware!"

But he had clicked off.

Soo was watching her. "Things are bad, aren't they?"

"Worse than bad. It sounds as though the Abbey has been beset by poltergeists now. The Reverend assures me that we can't gain access to the Abbey until tonight and yet we must."

And Randall knew they must. Why was he being so obstructionist? Because he was following the rule of the Abbey, of course. Try as she may to nudge him off the straight and narrow, he was prone to slip right back into the groove the moment her back was turned.

"Oh, my," Soo murmured, eyes wide.

"There is nothing to do but go to the Abbey and figure out how to get inside once there," Geri said, after a moment. What choice did they have? They must get in somehow.

No sooner had she uttered the words, than Eddy rolled into her backpack and the whole kit settled in over her shoulders.

Soo only gazed on in amazement. "Extraordinary."

"I told you," Lin nodded. "Powerful magic. This woman's a witch and a half."

Minutes later, they were in a cab weaving through the Saturday morning traffic. As the car drew closer to the Abbey, the Metro Police could be seen dispersing the lines of visitors that trailed out through the monument gates onto the sidewalk.

It seemed as though no sooner had a line been scattered when the people began gathering again, this time in angry clusters, everyone demanding entrance to the Abbey. This was the nation of queues, not mobs. Some people were shouting at the police, accusing them of abuse. For England, this was alarming.

"Holy shit!" Lin exclaimed. "Do you see what I see?"

"Yes, a mob of people behaving badly," said her aunt tersely.

"I don't mean the throng, I mean what's among the throng," the girl clarified.

Geri saw what she was referring to at once. For a moment she forgot to breathe.

Queen Elizabeth I was sailing down the sidewalk, crying out and wringing her hands.

Chapter Seven

Her Majesty veered off the sidewalk onto the road, heading to what once had been the Palace of Westminster, as oblivious to the traffic as it was of her.

Geri bounded out of the car, about to call out to the queen but stopped herself.

"Should I go after her?" Lin asked, arriving at her side.

"There's no point," her professor replied. "Look across the road."

Lin stared.

Hundreds of spirits dressed in a veritable timeline of costumes were floating around apparently squabbling with one another.

"They are unaware that they're in the modern world and only see Westminster Abbey and the Houses of Parliament which existed as a palace during their lifetimes. Everything modern remains invisible to them except, perhaps, us. Besides, we'd never be able to round them all up."

"Who are they?"

Geri peered intently, trying to see past the whizzing cars, the honking cabs. "I can't see clearly but I'm guessing the chap with the long curly hair could be King Charles II but why he's arguing with Queen Elizabeth 1 is quite beyond me. Oh, and I believe that small headless lady could be Mary Queen of Scots. And," Geri took a deep breath, "The others I suspect are various and sundry personages—kings, queens, notables, poets, explorers. Is that Sir David Livingstone in the pith helmet? I believe it is. And many of the others I don't recognize but they could be anyone from Chaucer to Dickens."

"But they're all fighting with one another!" Lin whispered.

And they were. In fact it was a scene of extraordinary spirit violence. Lin and Geri watched astounded as a figure dressed in full armor floated across the sidewalk and began attacking a couple of ghostly monks.

"So much for chivalry," Geri muttered.

"Why are they acting like that?" Lin asked.

"Because they're being stirred up by whatever evil is oozing from the Cosmati leak. Likewise for the living people over there." They stared at the raucous crowds. "Take note of your own emotions, Lin, and if you experience intense anger, ask yourself where those feelings stem from, truly. Spiritual assaults manifest themselves in bad temper, sudden acts of violence, and uncharacteristic outbursts."

"Got it," she whispered.

Soo arrived. "What is happening? What are you staring at?" She was gazing across the street but appeared to see nothing amiss. "Have we not better things to do?"

Lin and Geri exchanged glances.

"There are ghosts fighting with one another across the street, Auntie, and all those people behind us that are behaving badly are unconsciously responding to the spiritual assault. We are all vulnerable."

"Oh, my." Aunt Soo stared as if trying to pick out shapes in the wind.

"And they keep on coming," her niece added. As she spoke, more ghosts sailed across the road to join the squabble. There had to be hundreds of them streaming out through the abbey walls.

Lin and Geri watched as a ghostly child caught sight of what must have been her mother among the spirit throng and began to float towards her, arms outstretched. Suddenly, a tall male shape—darker and more shadowy than the others— stepped forward and began to beat the child until she screamed.

"No, I can't bear to watch this spiritual carnage a moment longer. We must race to heal the Cosmati tear before all is lost!" Geri's emotions were roiling, too. Though influenced by the overwhelming sense of anxiety, fear, and sadness suffusing the atmosphere, knowing from whence it came helped her wrestle it into control. "Come, we must get into the Abbey immediately."

"But Doc, shouldn't we be stopping that shit show across the street?" Lin cried.

"There's nothing we can do from here. We must heal the wound, not apply a poultice!" Brilliant analogy, Geri, she thought as she scrambled across the pavement towards the Abbey gates.

They needed to find a way through those doors unchallenged and since the guards were rushing along the outside of the fence attempting to calm the crowd, that meant waiting for an opportunity. It didn't take long.

"Look, there's the Rev," Lin whispered.

Geri's gaze shot over to the main doors where Randall accompanied by two other clergymen, was marching down the steps, past the gift shop towards the crowd, robes flapping in the wind.

"They must be planning to talk reason into everyone," Soo remarked.

As if that would work, but Geri understood why the priests believed that calming words might do the trick. The three men strode along the inside of the gate, her brother among them, nodding and smiling. They were saying things like: "Please stay calm. The Abbey is having mechanical difficulties and we cannot permit the public to enter."

One figure whom she knew to be the dean, addressed those pressing against the wrought iron fence with authority. "My dear fellows, I ask that you understand the situation," he began.

It was as if a film was rolling away behind her eyes. She saw scene after scene before it happened: the dean would begin his reasonable calming address and the horde would briefly quieten. Encouraged, the dean would proceed to order the guards to unlock the gates so that he and his brethren could walk among the people, dispensing smiles and calming words as if they bestowing grace upon the masses.

And then all hell would let loose.

Randall, as if also sensing pending events, turned and caught Geri's eye mere seconds before the throng erupted into howls of outrage.

"What about our bloody tickets!"

"We paid good money to see that pile of stone! Now move yer butt out of the way an' let us in!" or variations of that theme.

The crowd surged through the gates, nearly running down the priests in their path, carrying Soo, Lin, and Geri along in the surge.

Geri clutched Lin and Soo by the hand and lunged for the Abbey doors along with the rest of the storming hordes. Vaguely, she realized that she had lost her cane but for whatever reason, that didn't matter.

Everyone was shouting, demanding to see this and that while the police ran after them, blowing on whistles and ordering everyone to stop. No one stopped. The dean was knocked off his feet while calling for everyone to remember that this was a house of God. Sirens could be heard shrilling in the distance.

Geri pulled Soo and Lin across the nave towards the Weston Tower. Somehow Lin ended up clutching Eddy in his backpack. "This way," Geri called.

As she expected, the doors to the stairwell had been left unlocked and so, too, was the lift. Randall must have received her mind message and listened for once.

"In here." She ordered everyone into the elevator. Geri pushed the button, relieved once the doors hushed closed. No one followed them. The throng were too busy pouring across the Abbey's tombs crying for vengeance. They'd be safe up there.

"What are we doing?" Soo whispered, leaning against the elevator wall. The woman was trembling.

"Escaping the mob," Lin told her. "It's okay, Auntie."

"Are you all right, Soo?" Geri asked, laying a hand on her arm.

"I am very sorry. I am beset by terrible memories from long ago," she whispered, closing her eyes. "Mobs, violence, bring it all to the surface again—all the pain and fear. Oh, my, oh, my." She dabbed her forehead with a bright blue kerchief pulled from her pocket.

The trauma of the Ethiopian uprising, of course. Lin and Soo had lost everything all those years ago.

"Here," Lin retrieved a cookie from her pocket. "Eat this. You always tell me that your ginger crunchies are the ticket to comfort and health."

"Yes, I do say that, don't I?" Her aunt carefully unfolded a ginger snap from its wrapping and munched.

"Everything will be fine," Geri assured her. "The Metro Police will soon round this lot up and send them packing. That should happen in, um, about thirty seconds. Those poor sods below have been possessed by violence not of their making and crowds always intensify such energies. We will be safe in the Jubilee Museum up in the triforium."

And they were. As soon as the doors opened, peace descended like a hush. Up there in the rafters and trusses of the mighty Westminster Abbey, for whatever reason, the dark entities didn't linger. That didn't mean that they were alone. Other spirits hovered about in this refuge.

"Do you see them?" Lin whispered.

"I do," Geri replied. Though there may have once been royalty among the spirits, their energy was as soft as butterfly wings.

"I do appreciate how this place feels," Soo whispered, brushing crumbs from her coat. "Hard to explain, really, but I feel my heart rate decelerating. I'm certain that's not only because of my ginger crisps."

"What are those...entities?" Lin whispered, staring into the shadows ahead.

"You might call them angels," Geri said softly.

"I don't believe in angels," the girl remarked.

"As I have often said, Lynette, if there are demons, there must be angels," her aunt replied. "I cannot see them but I truly feel them."

They stood for a few minutes as the spirits floated among them, offering peace, brushing against their hearts and souls. Geri took a deep breath. "Thank you," she whispered, "but now we must get to work."

As if awaking from a dream, Lin snapped to. "Listen—they're storming the Abbey below," she cried, turning towards the railing.

They ran to the grilled barricade and gazed down. The Cosmati floor glowed far beneath them, its pattern completely visible from this vantage, each of the roundels revolving counter clockwise at a rapid speed. The central one especially was almost a rotational blur.

"It looks like a huge clock mechanism or something," Lin whispered.

"What are you seeing?" Soo asked.

But abruptly attention shifted. A swarm of people had begun attacking the tombs and gilded screens with their bags or fists. Storming through the nave behind them came the Metro Police in riot gear but Geri barely noticed. She was too fixed on the dark-haired woman dressed in a smart jacket and knee-high boots, running towards the Cosmati floor with what looked to be an open bottle of red nail polish in one hand.

"Stop!" Geri cried.

As soon as the words left her lips, the woman flash-froze to the spot, caught mid-flight balanced on one foot.

"How'd you do that?" Lin gasped.

"I have no idea." Geri stared at the frozen figure. How *did* she do that? Were her powers growing stronger without conscious effort on her part?

In moments, the police had surrounded the woman along with the others and the spell—or whatever it was— ended as quickly as it had begun. The bewildered would-be vandal was rounded up and herded from the Abbey with the rest of the mob while Soo, Lin, and Geri watched from overhead.

"There is no way that poor woman would have entered a national monument roiling with such destructive urges had she been in possession of herself," Soo said. "Did you see how shocked she seemed as if she had just awakened from a bout of amnesia?"

At that moment, a slightly battered Randall tumbled into the Abbey accompanied by another reverend. Geri knew that the dean had been rushed to the hospital but wasn't quite sure how she knew that.

When Randall looked up and caught her eye, she saw his panic: *We must fix the Cosmati leak now!* Geri nodded.

As Randall hurried away, a group of other clergy rushed to join them. Soon they had spread off to various points across the Abbey. The nave emptied, slipping into a different kind of peace.

It was at that moment that something could be seen rising from the right side of the Cosmati pavement. For a moment the floor's light was so intense that the object's shape could barely be distinguished. Geri squinted.

"Look, a chest!" Lin cried.

"What are you seeing?" her aunt asked, peering down. "I can't see a thing."

It was, indeed, a chest. Lifting horizontally about two feet above the floor to the right of the central roundel, it slowly began to tip until it was standing upright.

"It's a coffin, I think," Lin whispered.

Geri caught her breath as a shape began to form—the figure of a man growing more distinct by the minute. Short by today'sstandards but wearing a tall conical hat and garbed in what appeared to be richly embroidered robes, he gazed around in confusion before slowly revolving as on an axis.

"Abbot!" Geri cried. "Abbot de Ware, ich beseech ye for an audience!" She tried again in French for good measure.

He couldn't hear her from way up there, of course. Maybe he couldn't hear her at all. She must get down to the floor and address him in person. To that end, she hustled towards the elevator. In fact, she hustled so quickly that Lin and her aunt could hardly keep up.

"Prof, don't forget Eddy!" Lin cried as she dove into the elevator just seconds before the doors closed on Aunt Soo's startled face.

"What's happening?" the girl asked, clutching the backpack. "It's like you're super-charged or something. You don't even need your cane. You're floating!"

But Geri wasn't listening. She must demand an audience from the Abbot; she must beseech him to hear her out and explain the dire situation before all was well and truly lost. The cosmos would not hold together much longer; the fissures were gaping wide with terror and despair.

The moment the elevator doors opened, Geri burst out and dashed across the south transept, Lin right at her heels.

"Doc, take Eddy!" she cried, holding the bag in her outstretched hands.

As they approached the Cosmati floor, the Abbot could be seen spinning more quickly now.

"Abbot!" Geri called. "Abbot de Ware!"

But something else was happening. The Abbot was spinning like a top at the same rate as the central roundel and together, it was as if a tornado was forming. Wind whipped their faces and hair.

Lin suddenly toppled onto her stomach and was being dragged towards the whirling vortex by Eddy—at least Eddy appeared to be the one doing the dragging. "Doc, help!" she cried. Soo began screaming overhead; Randall's voice could be heard crying out in alarm from somewhere.

"Let go of Eddy's handles!" Geri demanded.

"I can't!" the girl cried. "He won't let me go!"

Geri lunged for Lin's ankles, clutching them hard, thinking that she would never let the girl go for anything in the world. What was happening? Both were being hauled head-long towards the vortex.

And then she knew what Eddy was doing, what he planned all along, and wondered why she hadn't realized it sooner.

A blast of air and smoke, a swirl of gases and particles, and then the darkness hit with the force of a million stars.

Chapter Eight

Geri dreamt that she'd eaten something undigestible like lasagna or maybe pie and chips—yes, pie and chips, that was it. Served her right for allowing herself such a stupid indulgence. When would she ever learn? Her gut burned and her head ached. But how did that explain why the whole front of her body felt stabbed and scratched? Best to just to go back to sleep.

Only she couldn't.

Shifting slightly, she felt something heavy weighing her down as if she were on her stomach and someone was sitting on her back. Her eyes flew open. Everything was dark and shadowy yet tinged with a strange green light and she was facedown on a floor—a floor! Something sharp scratched her chin. She tried to move but couldn't—that weight again.

What looked to be an arm drooped down over her shoulder. Her adrenalin spiked as she heaved the thing off in one monster shrug before scrambling to her knees and staring aghast as a body rolled from her back to flop face-down on the floor beside her.

At first she thought it might be Lin, but no—too thickly built. Though the fashion sense wasn't far off, this was definitely a man with long, straggly hair wearing leggings over muscled calves and maybe a leather tunic. She thought immediately of the body Randall had seen.

That strange eerie green glow seemed familiar yet not.

She gazed down at herself and gasped. She was naked; she was in some strange place; a man had been lying on top of her, but was he unconscious or dead? Her body was shivering so badly, her teeth chattered, and she feared she'd upchuck right there on the spot.

Hunching over, she waited until her head stopped spinning and her breathing steadied. Seconds later, she slowly raised her eyes to focus on what appeared to be glass and stone chips everywhere, along with pools of solidifying wax—beeswax, maybe.

She straightened and gazed around. Beneath her, tiles of glass and stone cut in geometric shapes, some neatly stacked; above, a shadowy sky shot with shards of moonlight, scaffolding across the sky—yes scaffolding—and beside her, that guy glowing green in the strange light.

Leaning over, she felt his neck: flesh warm, pulse strong. Okay, then. Had she been attacked by this would-be rapist? That must be it. Bastard had ripped off her clothes...which were where, exactly? She looked around, realizing they were nowhere to be seen.

She heaved herself to her feet and stared, forcing her mind to clear, her brain to think. Nothing about this place seemed familiar and yet it was. If this was an indigestion-induced nightmare, she needed to wake up soon and find her antacid pills. And where was the bloody light switch? The last thing she remembered was being dragged towards the Cosmati floor with Lin.

She paused, grappling with her memories before reality hit like a truck. No light switches here. She would never find such a thing because they had yet to be invented. She was in Westminster Abbey ten centuries before she had even been born, sometime around 1268 when the Cosmati floor was being created. Henry III was on the throne and busily rebuilding Edward the Confessor's Abbey into a Gothic wonder with the amazing mosaic pavement still a work in progress.

Could it be that she had been sucked through the vortex and emerged on the Cosmati floor sometime during its making? Wrapping her arms around herself, she gazed into the green-tinged darkness and trembled.

Where was Lin? She couldn't see her anywhere. And now the man was moaning on the floor behind her while ahead she could see candlelight flickering and hear voices on the way. People coming!

It was at that moment that she glimpsed the glowing object on the floor, the source of that strange green light—Eddy.

"You!" she whispered. "You're to blame for this!" Swooping down, she rolled the glowing orb back into its bag and shrugged the lot onto her shoulders. A quick glance down the corridor and she knew she must hide. A naked woman running around an abbey at night would not bode well, especially if an unconscious man was found sprawled nearby.

But where to hide? Westminster had been an actual abbey in the 1200s, which meant that it would be populated by monks. In fact, she was positive those were monks hurrying towards her now.

With no time to find a better hiding spot, she dove behind a gilded screen, nearly knocking over an enormous candlestick and stumbling over a bag of something hard. There she huddled, shivering, while clutching Eddy to her chest, and cursing silently.

Moments later, three black-cowled men of the Benedictine order hurried up the nave, each holding aloft a flickering candle. Geri was afforded the most perfect view of them through the filigreed screen.

"It is he, as I feared! Did I not tell ye that the man works past the hours of Abbot's decree?" one whispered in a guttural mix of French, Anglo-Saxon, and possibly Latin.

"But what hath befallen him?" asked another, holding his light up to better study the prone man. "His candle lies gutted on the floor, the wax fair melted into the cracks as if a great fire has burned in this very spot."

"I see no singe marks about," said the first.

The third monk, a much smaller person altogether, rolled the prone man onto his back. "It be Petrus, true enough, and he seems fair beaten. Do ye think he was wrestled by the devil? I swear that I saweth with mine own eyes Petrus flailing with a great mass of green light and shadow but two candles ago."

Geri cringed. He'd better not be referring to her as a great mass of anything or there'd be hell to pay. She kept staring through the opening in the screen, suppressing a nervous giggle. The monks were genuflecting now.

"If that be true, then he emerged triumphant, Brother Gregory, for look ye, he breatheth still. Let us carry him to the enfermerie until he regains his mind. He may best the Abbot yet. Brother Stephan take his feet, I will lift his shoulders, and Brother Gregory bring the man's tools. Lauds will soon be upon us."

Lauds already! It was almost daybreak?

A moment later, the smaller monk poked his head around the corner of the screen and held out his taper to scan the floor. There was no way he could fail to see the large shivering naked woman huddled there and yet he did. He picked up the leather bag she had nearly tripped over and backed away without comment or acknowledgment, leaving Geri stunned.

There could be no other explanation: she was invisible.

And being invisible was liberating under the circumstances, though it didn't make her feel any warmer.

Still clutching her Eddy bag, she hauled herself to her feet and padded after the monks as they scuttled off across the transept. She briefly wondered if Eddy and the bag were invisible, too, or whether somebody might see a leather satchel levitating down the hall. No, she reasoned, Eddy would stay out of sight, if he knew what was good for him.

The stone beneath her feet was cold, the air around her colder still, and everywhere signs of a building under construction laced with scaffolding.

The monks ahead of her were making towards the cloisters. Though there were no windows and it was dark, it had to be autumn, possibly October, as it had been when she left her century. She desperately needed warmth but she needed to talk to Petrus, find Lin and track down Ware even more.

The monks entered an arched oak door into the cloisters where candles flickered in wall sconces and lamps suspended on chains from the ceiling. Occasional fires burned in braziers and yet a biting draft blew in from somewhere.

The monks worked here and performed a myriad of tasks in between and all along the four arms of the great square that embraced the garden courtyard. Religious scenes had been painted on the walls and a fresh burial gaped in the floor against one wall. A handful of monks sat on the stone benches, some washing their hands and feet in basins of water, some mending their robes, others talking quietly among themselves.

Even this early, many were hurrying this way and that, everyone greeting one another in hushed whispers. Geri didn't just walk right past them, she walked right through them, a sensation like a mild electrical current. The resulting tingle was strangely invigorating and briefly helped to warm her. Mostly, though, she was relieved to realize that neither her naked body nor the bag she carried was visible to the brethren.

The three monks carried the man down the eastern cloister, panting under the weight they carried, attracting considerable interest from others as they went. Brother Gregory followed behind with the tool bag.

"Who goes there, brethren?" one monk asked while apparently settling down to read a book by candlelight.

"Petrus Odoricus!" called out Brother Stephan, a man with a long narrow face. "T'was spied prone upon the Abbot's floor!"

The Abbot's, not the King's? Odd.

Turning the corner on one arm of the cloisters, they shuffled down another. Geri remained fixed on two things: finding something to wear and interviewing Petrus Odoricus. Add to that, she must find Lin and the Abbot Ware.

She now realized how unlikely it was that Petrus had attacked her and yet it did seem likely that he and her arrival into the twelfth century were somehow interlinked. Obviously, he was the body Randall had seen on the Pavement and therefore it followed that he should have answers. That still didn't explain where the Abbot fit in. It was he who she saw before falling through the vortex. Baffling!

Either way, she needed to discover how to fix the Cosmati tear before returning home, provided she could even return home, all of which seemed monumental tasks. On the other hand, being an archaeologist actually walking through another century in a building she had once studied was rather thrilling once she could stop shivering enough to enjoy it. What would Randall think? This was gobsmacking amazing!

They were heading for the infirmary at the far end of the complex. When King Henry began his Gothic renovations in 1245, the monks' dormitories had been in the great vaulted room that houses the library in modern times. Below that and to the right lay what is known as the Little Cloisters which was the then infirmary. The Benedictine monks were ahead of their time in terms of healing, Geri knew. They believed that the sick and recuperating benefited from gardens, which the Little Cloisters opened onto. Her archaeologist self felt on holiday, if such a holiday wasn't so uncomfortably close to hell on earth.

The moment she stepped into the long whitewashed room that smelled faintly of herbs and who knew what else, the air immediately felt warmer. The walls were lined with beds, some empty, some not. A fireplace crackled at both ends and two monks were moving among the patients distributing drinks and probable tinctures. She stood in awe.

Shaking herself out of her stupor, she followed along behind the trio, peering at the patients, relieved that this period predated the plague—worse than COVID, any way you looked at it. She did not want to witness such suffering. As it was, many ailing monks lay with poultices on their wounds or being bled by leeches—yuk. Some appeared to be suffering from too rich a diet, judging from their florid complexions and portly stomachs. She knew from her research that many monks did not live beyond their thirties despite their relative good fortune and bountiful diet.

She watched as one of the tending brothers pointed to an empty bed near the end of the room. The monks carrying Petrus lowered the patient upon a platform of rushes covered with linen and began to undress him.

Geri watched from a comfortable distance next to the crackling fire while studying the master-stone-mason-probable-wizard. He looked strangely familiar. About forty years old, approximately her height and well-muscled, neither his clean-shaven face nor his lean body was hard to look at. From her vantage about ten feet away, she could see every inch of the man and was not above gawking. After all, if Petrus had been wrestling with her naked self, presumably he'd had an eyeful, too. Tit for tat and all that.

He looked so much like a figure in her nocturnal imaginings that it almost threw her off her stride. Nonsense, she told herself. Stay focused. So what if she had had a dream dude in her youth—didn't everyone?

As the three delivery monks backed away and the tending brothers took over, Geri could observe them cleaning Petrus with a basin of herbed water and a cloth. The man was covered in nicks and scratches plus a gouge or two. Casting a quick glance downward, she realized that she was, also.

"What hast unfolded here?" one rotund monk asked his brother. "See the cuts and scrapes as if a hundred cats doth claw his skin?"

A bit of an exaggeration, Geri thought, but Petrus certainly was a mess. She risked stepping closer to study one of the man's scrapes—surface, she thought, but no less bloody. Certainly his scratches were worse than hers but his bled more profusely. The gouges on those brawny arms of his did, however, look very much like claw marks. Demons? Had they encountered demons on the way through the Cosmati portal and, if that was the case, what role did Petrus play? And then there was Lin—where was she and how had she fared? She was that girl's guardian now. She couldn't let anything happen to her.

The monks worked on bandaging the man where necessary and applied some kind of a pungent muslin herb pack onto his brow. Meanwhile Petrus remained unconscious though the monks declared that they could see no sign of a head wound.

After a few minutes, they covered him with a blanket and went to attend to other patients. Geri hovered nearby, studying the man's features. Damn good-looking, that's what she thought. She'd always had a thing for Italian men, not that she indulged any of her cravings. Still it was just such a lean, sharp-featured man that she had fashioned for her imaginary dream lover years ago. Coincidence, surely? Snapping herself away from the male appreciation fest, she decided that she really needed to find something to wear and fast. And to find Lin. Did the girl come through with her or not?

Slipping from the infirmary, she made her way into the Little Cloister garden, filled as it was by herbs and lovely flowers, many spent in the autumn chill, and sprinted across into the hall leading to the refectory. She must find a spare robe. Westminster was a wealthy abbey and the monks would not be disadvantaged by either a lack of food or clothing. There were enough ample-girthed monks around to assure her that finding something that fit would not be a problem, though her biggest issue might be finding something to fit around her chest rather than her gut.

After transversing what seemed like the full length of the main cloister, she found the cellarium exactly where she expected it to be. A cafe inhabited the windowless space in her own century but back in the 12th, this is where food, casks of ale and wine were stored along with woolen robes hanging on pegs along one wall. There were also linen long-sleeved shifts, most of which were way too short but she found one that fit well enough.

The black robe that she pulled over her head was still scratchy despite the linen she wore beneath but it was still better than being naked. A pair of leather sandals from a selection that lined a bottom shelf solved the problem of footwear. Tying the robe close to her body with the leather rope provided, she was suitably clothed at last, though going braless was not comfortable.

She opened up her bag and stared in. "Look what you've got me into, Eddy —satisfied?"

Eddy glowed a blameless pearly white but remained typically uncommunicative.

"Oh, it's like that, is it?" She tossed the bag over her shoulder and stepped back into the cloisters, relieved to find them empty, too. The robe was beginning to itch like crazy and the voluminous sleeves were just plain annoying.

A bell gonged in the distance: Lauds called the brethren to the first prayer of the day, which briefly left her the full run of the Abbey before the order was called to Prime at 6:00 a.m. Terce, Sext, and None were all said before dinner with the final prayer of the day at 6:00 p.m. The monks would retire to bed at 8:00 p.m. and amid all that to-ing and fro-ing, she must keep focused.

Geri hurried down the cloister, hoisting the hem of her robe to keep from tripping. Several times she had to stop long enough to adjust the tie until she had it right.

She was just turning onto the south cloister arm when she saw a corpulent monk huffing along, obviously late for prayers. She fully expected him to sail right through or past her but, instead, he stopped dead in his tracks and screamed.

Chapter Nine

G eri, taken by surprise, screamed back, which sent the monk scrambling down the hall, crossing himself and muttering Hail Marys all the way.

What the hell? Had he actually seen her? If he'd glimpsed only a floating robe then she would appear for all the world like a headless monk. That must be it. Crud, she thought. So she was a headless monk now. She couldn't remain invisible while wearing the robe unless she played a ghost, which might be fun but hardly on her to-do list at the moment.

Meanwhile, she'd just have to throw the cowl over her head and try not to encounter anyone else until she could figure something out. She estimated maybe an hour of free movement at the most before the monks returned from morning prayer. She'd find someplace to hide while there was still time.

She hurried back past the cellarer's storeroom, down a short corridor to an arched door that led to what in her day was a reception hall and offices. That should be a safe hiding place and she was growing tired. How long had she been awake, anyway?

Luckily, the door was unlocked, allowing her to slip inside without problem. Eddy was vibrating in his bag, and not the good kind of vibrating, either, but she was too awestruck by her surroundings to take note. Where in hell was this? After the monastery's austerity, what she saw was a shock to the senses. She gazed around at the luminous religious art on the walls—the triptychs gleaming with gold paint from the glow of the massive fireplace, the gilded statue of the Virgin Mary in one corner, comfortable chairs all about.

76

A central table lay with gold plate and candlesticks, a bowl of oranges and apples at the ready, plus a lovely dish encrusted with mosaics that glittered in the lamplight at one end beside a single silver spoon. The table was set for breakfast, the scent of frying meat and baking bread wafting from somewhere. Shit. She'd stumbled into the abbot's private quarters and now she had to get as far away from this place as possible.

But then she heard footsteps.

Nabbing an apple from a bowl as she passed, she darted into another room —the Abbot's private bedchambers, as it turned out. His quarters were almost as luxurious as she had imagined. So much for vows of poverty. The big comfy bed looked so inviting, though the thought of sleeping in its unmade linens where the Abbot had just lain gave her the creeps. She slipped into the shadowy room noting the thick draperies closed across the windows and another fire burning in the grate. Voices were coming down the hall.

Then she spied a garderobe—the closet. Dashing in, she noted the man's considerable array of embroidered vestments and robes, hats, shoes all hanging on hooks along the wall or folded on trunks. There, wedged amid curtains of fur-lined velvets, silks, and wools, she trembled, waiting. After several seconds, she realized that by rights, Ware should be leading the prayers so none of those voices she heard could be his. Heartened, she stepped out from the clothes.

The space was unlit and she lacked the means by which to ignite the wall sconces but enough illumination entered the room from the room beyond to see. A floor-sized beveled mirror dominated one end of the space.

What man of God keeps a big silver mirror in which to admire himself? She stepped closer to study her reflection. Yes, indeed, she appeared like a headless monk even to her own eyes. Lifting her arms, she twirled around—a very shabby-looking headless monk, at that.

Quickly she shrugged off her bag and brought out Eddy. "Make yourself useful and glow for me," she whispered. She was used to giving him orders, alternating with bouts of respect—the last bit only recently—but being hauled headfirst into another century tried her temper. Luckily, the orb cooperated by emitting a bright spotlight glow.

"Much obliged." Setting Eddy on the floor, she turned to the mirror, which was hardly clear like the modern variety but certainly revealed enough. Shrugging off the Benedictine garb, she plucked a fur-lined royal blue silk velvet robe from a hook and dropped it over her head, cringing at having the Abbot's personal stuff touch her skin but quickly getting over it. Beggars can't be choosers.

Additionally, it piqued her to find the robe too snug in all the usual places and only mid-calf in length at that, but still it beat the scratchy wool all to bits and so much warmer. Besides, blue was her color. There, she thought, turning this way and that before the looking glass, she looked rather fetching, even if she did say so herself.

Her hair was a mess, though. She froze. She could see herself now? Yes, she could see herself, and what was even stranger, when she moved in a certain direction, her appearance changed to a blond shaggy-haired man. When she turned slightly more to the left, she grew more portly and closer to her own age; another shift to the left and she appeared like a much younger version of herself. What was going on?

Her eyes fell on the orb. *Eddy was what was going on.*

"What's this?" she demanded, leaning over the orb. "Aren't things complicated enough without more of your tricks? Okay," she said after a moment, "make yourself useful and help me find Lin."

Eddy glowed green in agreement.

"Maybe I haven't been using you to your full potential."

In answer, the orb started flashing.

"Okay, okay. You're giving me a headache." She flung her bag over one shoulder and, holding Eddy in her palm, exited the garderobe into the bedchamber where a maid was busily making the bed.

The woman took one look at the figure standing there holding a glowing ball of light and fell prostrate on the floor, praying fervently.

Maybe she looked like a saint or even an angel—a good look in an abbey, either way. That was her cue to exit so she dashed down the steps and across the abbot's hall, holding Eddy aloft as she went. The woman would probably declare that she'd experienced a miracle and in some ways she had.

Geri had to find Lin. Depending on the direction she went, Eddy would change color from cool to warmer. Geri was being led back out into the cloisters heading to the eastern end back towards the infirmary.

Only, the cloisters would soon be filled with monks. Either she hid Eddy's light back in the bag and became headless again, or she took off her robe and assumed invisibility. Walking headless down the corridors would only send the Benedictine order into a tizzy which did not seem a viable option. That left only one choice: get naked again.

But first, she'd check on Petrus. She made her way back down to the infirmary, noting how brightly Eddy was growing as she preceded. Lin was down this way, too but where?

And then the bell rang, signifying the end of prayer. Soon, the halls would fill with monks—about 60, as she remembered from her research. Damn it, she was just getting used to feeling warm and comfortable but now she had to return to being stripped and shivering.

Swearing under her breath, she scrambled back to the infirmary. She'd peel her robe off by the fire. The moment she slipped inside, she blinked in disbelief —Petrus's bed was empty! So where did he go? She looked around for answers but the only attendant was a napping monk.

Standing before the hearth, she pulled off her fancy robe and stuffed it into the bag along with Eddy. She had just resumed her invisibility when two monks entered the infirmary.

"Dost thou believe what Father John says about Abbot?" one whispered.

"Hush, Father Stephan, for it be a sin to speak ill of others," cautioned his companion.

The napping monk cocked an eye at the pair. "Hush, thou should not speaketh so."

"True though that be, should the one so ill-spoken of not bring shame upon this order. He keeps another boy, Father Noah! This be the greater sin! Father John says that he doth keep the boy in the Pyx."

The Pyx! Geri nearly toppled into the grate. Abbot Ware kept a boy locked in the Pyx? The Pyx Chamber was off the East Cloister and was believed to have been used as a treasury during Henry III's reign, making it highly secure with access granted to the Abbot and the king alone. Was Lin the boy they were speaking of? It had to be.

She broke into a cold sweat as she faced the possibility of Ware harming Lin for his own foul purposes. She could not let that happen, absolutely could not! Snatching up her bag, she scuttled from the infirmary and made her way through the passing monks towards the Pyx Chamber.

The low vaulted room was one of the oldest parts of the Abbey. Built around 1070, it had served various uses over the years but had always remained highly secured.

Halfway there, she remembered that the entrance to the chamber was originally just off the vestibule leading to the Chapter House and not off the East Cloister in this century. That meant a long circuitous route back through the main Abbey.

As she made her way there, she suspected that the Abbot Ware had to be the negative force tipping the balance between good and evil all along. Too many things about him didn't add up. That made Petrus the good guy, as odd a thought as that seemed. Had these two warred over the floor when she and Lin came through?

So many questions and not enough answers. Stabbing loneliness hit Geri as she hurried towards the huge oak doors that marked the Pyx Chamber. She missed Randall, she actually missed her colleagues, she missed Lin—she missed her own century!

Ahead, she glimpsed the Chapter House. She had always loved the old meeting chamber with its round arched roof, stained glass windows, and gilded paintings. What would it be like to see the space just after it had been built? Probably amazing to study something so old when it was so new. Yet Geri knew that the Abbot might meet with his monks here that day and maybe with the King, too. It wouldn't do to linger around. Best to just rescue Lin and find somewhere to hide.

Arriving at the mammoth twin iron-studded doors securing the Pyx Chamber moments later, it hit her that wouldn't be easy. What was she thinking? The oak barricade was locked and bolted. Pressing her ear against the wood told her nothing. Either the doors were too thick to hear a cry or Lin was in no condition to make one. She couldn't risk calling out since being invisible didn't mean being inaudible.

Eddy began bumping against her shoulder.

"What are you up to now?" she hissed.

Taking a quick scan of the surroundings, she pulled the orb from the bag to find it a hot, dazzling red.

"Okay, so Lin's in there but how am I going to get her out?"

Now Eddy began flashing like a police car. What was he trying to tell her?

She heard a cry from across the nave: "Hark, Father! What be that light?"

Shit and damn! Two monks were hurrying her way and what they saw besides a ball of light was anyone's guess. She didn't know whether to hold Eddy or hide him but decided to drop the orb back into the bag and resume invisibility at once. No sooner had she done so, then the monks reached the Chamber door.

"Did thou seest what I sawest?" one brother asked the other.

"Aye, twas a ball of red light that gloweth like the sun!" the other said.

Geri squeezed her eyes shut in relief. They couldn't see her—hadn't seen her —but she must find someplace to hide. She was exhausted; the Abbey would be crawling with monks during the daylight hours; and, she was so damn cold, she couldn't think straight.

With that, she spun on her heels and bolted across the nave towards the Cosmati floor, which at this stage was still a work in progress.

Carrying on into Edward the Confessor's tomb—also under construction but much further along than the altar floor—she headed right for an area that she hoped would make the perfect hiding place: an empty tomb.

During Henry III's remodeling of the Abbey and while creating Edward the Confessor's shrine, King Henry had moved his yet-to-be-sainted hero to another location. Empty tombs made perfect hiding places. She climbed up on a block and peered in—deeper than she expected and so dark and dank but, damn it, the last place anyone would look.

In seconds she had wedged herself down into the receptacle, as yet devoid of an actual coffin, and lay there shivering with the bag clutched to her stomach and the cold earth chilling her skin. Daylight washed in from the Abbey windows but it barely penetrated where she lay. This wasn't going to work. She'd never fall asleep in this cold, uncomfortable, damp recess, especially not stark naked.

* * *

She had no idea how long she had slept but clearly she had, if only fitfully. When her eyes opened, it was impenetrably dark where she lay wedged. Maybe she was dead. No, she could wiggle her toes. Then she realized that her bag was emitting an enveloping warmth along with comforting glow.

"Okay, Eddy," she whispered, "I hereby admit that you are a true friend and I'm sorry for all the times I snapped at you. Now, can you help me out of here so we can find Lin and Petrus, please?"

In response, she seemed to levitate horizontally up from the tomb until she was standing upright in the glorious shrine of Edward the Confessor—minus the Confessor. He'd be along in a few years—in 1269, if Geri remembered correctly. They kept moving the poor guy, not to mention opening up his tomb and gawking at him, stealing his rings, and whatnot. If Geri were him, the Ghost of Edward the Confessor would haunt the living daylights out of everyone he encountered. But maybe that was against the rules of sainthood.

Geri shook her head free from her thoughts and pulled out Eddy, who glowed a soft pearly white. "So, I don't suppose you do coffee, too?" she whispered. He flashed red once and subsided back to his pearly thing. "Right. Worth an ask."

Lowering the orb to the floor, she pulled out the monk's habit, thinking that if she was going to float around an abbey, she might as well do so as a headless monk. When she picked Eddy back up, he was emitting a useful flashlight-like glow.

She had no idea what time it was as she transversed the shrine pavement and across the yet-to-be born Cosmati floor towards the Pyx Chamber. All she knew was that it was as dark as death in the Abbey and that the monks had to be tucked into their beds up in the dormitory. She needed them to stay put until she finished her business.

Rescuing Lin was her first priority, and this time she'd implore Eddy to break down the door or do something equally dramatic. Only, when they arrived at the Pyx doors, Eddy was not in the breaking mood.

"Okay, do your worst. Unlock the doors, release Lin," she ordered.

In response, the orb shot forth a beam of light that briefly illuminated the internal mechanism of the huge oak doors in a neon-like purple glow. Bars of something stronger than steel fortified the wood, a jaw-like portcullis hovered in the lintel overhead, and a snarling dog—a dog, seriously?—was showing its fangs as if ready to tear to pieces the first person to enter. Geri knew in a flash that this could only be magic, very, very strong magic. The Abbot Ware was a wizard of incredible power, and an evil one, at that.

She stepped away, her heart beating furiously. "Eddy," she whispered, "how are we going to break this down?"

The orb pulsed yellow.

"Is that your coward color? We have to get in there! What if he's harmed Lin?"

Eddy, hovering before her eyes, returned to his pearly color which this time appeared fog-like, a fog that blew away to reveal the image of Chamber's interior in crystal ball fashion. Geri could see Lin huddled at a table within, shivering, her tear-streaked face resolute and fierce.

"Oh, Lin. Hold on. I'll get you out I promise," Geri whispered.

The girl's gaze met hers through the orb. "Doc?"

"Yes, it's me! Hold tight."

Lin leapt from the table where she had been held, straining against the chains while the dogs snapped their jaws all around. "He's a monster!" she cried. "The Abbot of Ware is a bloody monster!"

Eddy flashed red: Ware had been alerted. *Run!*

"I'll get you out," she called to Lin. "Hold on!"

With that, she dropped Eddy back into his bag and scuttled off across the transept towards the cloisters.

She thought—more like *felt*—Ware being roused from his bed, looking for his slippers and his robe, before heading off to check on his prisoner. He'd know that Geri was there, either specifically or realize that there was an enemy within. Magic left a residue and maybe those monster dogs could tell a tale or two.

Geri rushed down the shadowy cloisters towards the infirmary, desperate to speak to Petrus. If he wasn't there, she'd make one of the monks tell her where he went.

Minutes later, she was inside the infirmary, taking in the scene at a glance: fires burning low in the grates at either end, the patients sleeping soundly, the tending brother dozing in his seat by the hearth nearest the door and Petrus's bed still empty.

Looking at the napping brother, she realized that she must make the monk tell her where Petrus had gone. She'd shake it out of him, if she had to, but first she'd try something else.

Slipping back up the aisle, she stepped back out into the Little Cloisters until she was just outside the infirmary hidden behind the door.

"Brother, rouse yourself!" she said in her best approximation of a male voice.

The monk shifted in his seat and yawned. "What ho, who goest there?"

"Quick now—where be Petrus Odoricus?"

The monk scrambled to his feet. "Who asks such and why doth you speak in such a strange tongue? Step forward."

"I have come on urgent business from thy King. Now tell me quick: where be Petrus Odoricus?" Hell if she knew if monks would talk like that but as long as she got her point across...

The brother stood momentarily confused, rubbing his eyes. "He hath gone to his own rooms, as is his wont."

"And where be those rooms? The King has need of him now!"

The monk stepped towards the door, suspicion darkening his otherwise cherub-like face. "Why doth His Majesty want Petrus Odoricus? This be most strange. Who goest there, I say! Showeth thyself."

"Where be the rooms?" Geri demanded but soon realized that Father What-shisname wasn't having any of it. He was dipping a taper into the embers. He planned to shine his light on her now? Not good, not good at all. And then she caught a glimpse of flickering candles moving towards her from down the hall: the Abbot was on her heels.

Geri backed away and bolted across the cloisters heading for the stairs she knew led to the second-floor dormitories back in the day. She was unfamiliar with those buildings, so much of that structure having been absorbed by the current library and college school, but she hoped that she'd recognize enough to find her way around. Maybe the Abbot wouldn't look for her up there.

Along the way, she had to press herself into shadowy corners not once, but twice, as troops of disgruntled monks roused from their sleep stumbled past. The Abbot must have awoken the Prior who then turfed the monks out of bed to search the monastery for the interloper.

Once they'd passed, she risked stepping out into the dormitory, studying the rows of single beds below the lofty vaulted ceiling. Surprisingly, she saw count-less places to hide—so many doors leading off in many directions with hallways jutting around corners into the dark. Eddy was thudding against her back again. Taking him out, she stared down at the orb.

"What is it?" she asked.

Eddy displayed a clearly-defined green arrow which pointed down a right-hand corridor.

"Upping your game, I see." Without further comment, she headed in the direction indicated, wondering all the while whether Abbot Ware's magic was sufficient to track her down like a rabbit hunted by wolves. Though she doubted the monks were used to being made into a hunting party, an abbot ruled supreme after king and pope. Maybe she didn't have a chance of escaping him let alone rescuing Lin.

She was just moving down a hallway, holding Eddy up for light, when suddenly something wrenched her backwards, hauling her into a dark space, a space so dark she could not see a thing while Eddy left her hands and floated in front of her.

"What, whoah!" she cried. "Eddy, defend me!"

Just as quickly, she was released. Swinging around, she saw her attacker: Petrus Odoricus.

"Geri," he said, spreading his arms. "I have been awaiting thee!"

Chapter Ten

Petrus Odoricus did not look as though he had just been attacked by a demon or anything else, for that matter. There wasn't a mark on the brawny chest that was exposed through the shredded tunic. He stood arms wide, grinning brightly with white teeth, flashing dark eyes, and an expression of absolute joy while Eddy floated in the air beside him throbbing pinkly.

"My love," he said, "how I have dreamed of this moment. My heart, it beats for you. I wait and wait for you across a thousand stars, ten thousand turns of the moon, at every rising of the sun in this world and beyond. You take so long to arrive, but here you are at last, my beloved Geri!" A slight Italian accent but with excellent English mixed with modern diction and a smattering of Medieval English.

Even more shocking: he seemed as though he expected her to fall into his arms. He looked yummy enough to make that appealing, but still.

Geri blinked. "Beloved? You know me?"

Slapping a hand over his heart, he looked playfully wounded. "But of course for we are life mates. You forget but you will come to remember, soon I hope."

"Mates as in good friends?"

Petrus's attention briefly swerved towards the door. Footsteps were thundering down the corridor. He lunged past her to slam the portal shut, snapping his fingers as the great iron bolts slid home at his command.

Turning back, he studied her intensely, the high cheekbones and deep-set eyes radiating a feverish emotion. "We are life mates, as in man and woman, Ariana, Seraphina, Geraldine—all the names by which I've known you across the ages. You forget now, but in time you will recall the many times we have met, the many passionate ways in which we have come to know one another."

She blushed furiously, her face hotter than a baked potato. It suddenly hit her that this was literally the man of her dreams, the same man who did all those knee-weakening things with his tongue that she only half-remembered in the mornings. She thought he was the stuff of a feverishly lonely life but maybe not.

How could it be true? Surely this wasn't true, but neither could anything else she'd been experiencing lately. Anyway, she couldn't get her mind around that at the moment. Lovers? Past lives? Best to just get beyond all this ardent nonsense and focus on the matter at hand. "Yes, well, I can tell that you're Italian through and through. Anyway, you need to fix the Cosmati Pavement and rescue Lin. The Abbot is after me. He knows that I'm here. Oh, and somehow I will have to return to my own century."

He smiled slowly, his expression maybe a bit pained. "Ah, yes, I have missed your to-do lists, my love, and your bossy ways— mostly. I know what needs to be done. I was waiting for you to arrive but now that you have come, we can get to work. As for Lin, no need to worry as yet. The Abbot has a meeting with the King today and several internal problems will keep him occupied, including a possible mutiny. These are matters that he must handle before he can get back to enjoying his latest toy." A flash of vivid anger. "Such a beast! We will put him back where he belongs!"

"We will?" but now she was distracted by the room in which she found herself. Before Petrus had barricaded the doors behind them, she had glimpsed an austere cell with drawings scratched on bare stone walls and a single pallet shoved against one wall that must serve as a bed.

Now she stood in a magnificent apartment-cum-workroom, not rich in decoration so much as layered in fascinating objects—books, drawings, astrological charts (some suspended mid-air), paintings, an entire shelf of odd jars and bottles. A huge stone fireplace held court beside a big double bed and the whole room featured a magnificent stained-glass window on one end, plus a round skylight in the ceiling above that beamed shafts of moonlight into the room.

Eddy was floating around as if he owned the place.

"Where are we and won't Ware know about this room?" She was as overwhelmed and confused as she sounded.

Petrus was smiling at her, his head slightly lowered, his arms crossed as if forcing himself not to touch her—so damn attractive, the whole package. "He knows that I am in the Abbey but not how to get to me. If he were to break down the door—which he cannot do, by the way—he would find a barren cell, while I keep my apartment in an alternative dimension held in place by magic.

He does not even try to find me. We meet by mutual agreement. It is you that he seeks at the moment, but once he realizes that we have reconnected, he will stop his search for he knows that you and I are one."

"I beg your pardon—we are one, wot? Never mind." She held up her hand. "Let's just stick to logistics for a moment, shall we? So, you are a powerful wizard and so is Ware but what am I doing here?"

"You are a powerful witch, though seriously suppressed at the moment. We will work on that. In this age, magic is more intense and easier to create for those so gifted. The willingness to believe in miracles saturates the minds and spirits of all who live now which helps activate the power. You, my love, have spent too long in the 20th and 21st centuries leaving you stunted."

"Stunted?" She'd been called many things in her life but never 'stunted'.

"Fear not, for I will help you and will be gentle—I am always gentle with you as you are with me—and when you are ready, you and I will work together to keep the darkness in place while we rebuild the Pavement."

We rebuild the Pavement—crud. Could she fall any deeper down the rabbit hole? "But in my timeline, the Pavement has been in place for centuries and only needs to be repaired."

"Ah, Geri, Geri, you must not think of time as either finite or linear. It is neither. It is fluid and flows all around us like an ocean, meaning that whatever we do in this century will influence all the others, even if we repair something in the past—which we must do multiple times. You and I will build the Floor again in this century to better secure it for the trials ahead in yours."

She was supposed to help him repair the Cosmati Pavement? "I presume that you mean repair as in the magical sense since I know nothing about mosaic work. Actually, I don't know anything about magic, either."

"Ah, but you do. You just don't yet know what you know." He snapped his fingers and from somewhere overhead, a floating diagram descended, the lines illuminated with inner light, the figures on its surface revolving slowly one minute, madly spinning the next.

It took a moment for her eyes to adjust enough to recognize the Cosmati floor overlayed by a map of the solar system—or, at least, that's what she thought she recognized. Soo was right and the overall effect was very much like the glowing mosaic she'd witnessed in her future version of the Abbey floor. "This is it, then, the Cosmati Pavement?"

"Yes," he said, his gaze now fixed on some far point beyond the hologram thing. "This be my design as commissioned by King Henry through the Abbot Ware. What I attempt to insert to preserve the world—with help from above, of course—Ware attempts to undermine with his insidious undercurrents of deceit, avarice, malice, greed, and a vast litany of other horrors."

"He's the Devil?"

"There are many devils and they take many forms, always striking an underhanded, deceitful bargain in the process. Would that I had known at the time. Balance was our agreed upon goal but already he breaks his end of the bargain. The day I insert the great portal—the round onyx that I sourced from the depths of time—will be the moment that Ware plays his hand by tipping the balance. This will be the most crucial moment when all must be shored up against pending catastrophe. I failed once but will not do so again. This time, you will be there to help me set it to rights, dear Geri."

"Will I?" How was she supposed to unpack that assertion, especially when she felt so weary, she could hardly keep her eyes open? "Why do you speak a mix of modern and old English?" Stupid question but all the good ones came with such damn complicated answers.

"Because I am not of this century but of all centuries, including yours. I go where I am needed and I am needed here. Think of me as the ultimate cosmic handyman, the mason to the stars." He threw back his head and laughed.

Ordinarily Geri would have found that funny but by now, it was all becoming too much. She did something she had not done since her childhood days when she was trying to escape school PE class, only back then, the act was feigned—she fainted.

* * *

When she awoke, the passage of time could have been days or years, yet she suspected that she'd been napping for mere minutes. She awoke clear-headed, exceedingly warm, and comfortably sitting in a reclining chair by a crackling fire.

To the right, Petrus stood chopping vegetables on a long table that she had thought to be a workbench but now seemed to be a kitchen island. Eddy was hovering nearby, apparently acting like an extra lamp. It almost seemed as if the orb and Petrus were great buddies.

Geri stood up. "Don't tell me that you cook, too, Petrus?" she asked. "What, no magic conjuring of dishes?" Humor had always been her way of gaining control, though in this instance she knew that control was unlikely.

"Ha!" he said, turning to her with that flashing smile of his. "A man cooks for the woman he loves. Nothing else will do. I cook to restore you for the work ahead."

The woman he loves. Was she really expected to believe all this? Oh, right: she had been sucked down a chute into the 13th century. What was a sexy Italian wizard cooking her dinner next to that?

It smelled delicious, whatever he was making. Hadn't she always dreamed of having some amazing man cook her exquisite meals? That had been replaced by some amazing pub serving her take-out, of course, but those longings had warmed many a lonely night. It looked as though it might warm another, at least up to a point. Was it even night in this dimension? "What time is it?" she asked.

"Any time you want it to be, my love. I have made it night because you have just spent a semi-wretched vigil wedged into a tomb. Not the best place to rest, no? I will make it up to you with a lovely meal followed by a deep and restorative sleep. Beyond my walls, it is actually daylight but there is much activity in the Abbey, which it is best that we avoid for the moment. Later, I will go forth to manage the laying of the mosaics, to spy, and to check on Lin, but I must do so only while Ware is occupied in the Chapter House. It most important that you remain here where it is safe."

"But what about Lin? We must release her from that monster!"

"And so we shall. Eddy?"

The orb flew from his side to hover at Geri's eye level. In full crystal ball mode, it revealed Lin sleeping with her head cradled in her arms.

"Lin is resting. She has been fed and given ale to drink," Petrus explained. "One of the monks, Brother Eli, is in league with the Abbot and has been tending to her on Ware's instructions. She will be kept safe until Ware has time to—well, we will not discuss such things. It will not be allowed to happen."

"But—" Geri began.

Petrus was before her in an instant, hands gripping her shoulders—not an unpleasant sensation. "Geri, do you trust me?"

She gazed into his deep hazel, chocolatey eyes, thinking that perhaps she could dive deep into those depths and maybe swim around, make a big splash and all that. "Ah, I don't know you," she whispered.

"But you do, my love. I have never let you down and never will. Trust me now."

Trust him now. Hell. Well, why not? "All right," she said. "But when you return into the Abbey, I want to go with you."

The eyebrows arched over those unfathomable eyes. "No, you are not be ready for that."

"Define 'ready'," she said.

"'Ready' means that first you must reach deep into yourself and assume invisibility while fully clothed—or not, as you choose. Certainly, I will be happy whether you are clothed or not—but you must gain control over your own powers enough to cloak yourself in invisibility that will shield you against Ware."

"A cloaking device as in the *SS Enterprise*?"

His lips quirked into a half smile. How strange that he appeared to recognize references to modern popular culture. "Very much like your science fiction shows, yes, only managed by your will alone. You must do this in order to protect yourself against Ware's probing. He knows you are here but thinks you an easy mark, that he will bide his time until he has a moment to spare in which to take his pleasure. He is a despicable being and his monks know it. He has made many enemies and but still has enough followers to make things difficult and he grows more. Each of the swine following him gains from his thieving, evil ways."

"And yet you work with him?"

"Not work with him, exactly—formed a pact, would be a more fitting description. He located me in Rome where I had been forging a floor to further seal the balance between good and evil. He desired that the next and most powerful floor of all be created in this Westminster Abbey at King Henry's bidding and beseeched me to come back to London to create it thus, thinking that I would not know of his foul intent, which was true because I did not discover it until recently."

"And his foul intent is, I mean, *was*?"

"To embed evil influences deep into the floor's mortar thus destabilizing the foundation and tipping the balance until evil ultimately rules the world. Evil must never rule the world but neither can good. Both must exist in harmony. To do otherwise will end the world as we know it. In this moment, we are the great balancers, Ware and I—I bring the light, he the darkness."

"So," Geri said cautiously, "does that mean that he is Satan and you are—"

"Certainly not! I am but a worker for good, he for evil, but I am not the manifestation of ultimate goodness but merely a wizard for the cause. Ware takes his orders from the source of all evil."

"Yes, all right, that's a relief." She could just imagine if she ever had to explain to Randall that she had met God and that He was an Italian making dinner in an alternative universe. He'd never recover. "So, just trying to understand here: you and Ware decided to create this powerful mosaic that would hold the balance of the world together?"

"We didn't decide, exactly. These sacred places exist in different settings worldwide, some natural, some formed by powerful beings like ourselves. My

Cosmati floors are placed in sites of worship—denominations are unimportant —and forged with the intent to protect the balance of the world. Agents of both good and evil must be present when cosmic forces are masoned into a great pavement such as the one I am fashioning. Now I learn that he intends to insert—already has, in truth—instability into my creation, the fruition of which we must prevent at all costs. It is that same flaw that threatens the world in your century and beyond. Your help is critical, my love."

"But why didn't you come to my century and get me if I played such an important role?"

"I cannot leave the Abbey, and will be unable to do so until the floor is repaired. To do so would expose my creation to further tampering. I have bound the floor in a spell that keeps Ware at bay but only if I remain nearby."

"So, you are captive to the Abbey?"

"I am its protector, the steward, you might say."

"And if the Cosmati pavement is repaired, will you then be able to leave then?"

"I will."

"And can you fix it?"

"We can fix it together."

Geri swallowed. "Very well, then..." Another statement she didn't want to poke around in just yet. "So, what happened when I came through the floor yesterday or whenever?"

"I was expecting you but so was Ware. He'd sent a few of his demons to tear you to shreds but I anticipated that move by being there to meet you. I shielded you from the attack, assuring that you would emerge safely into my arms."

"Or onto my back, whichever came first. Was I a damsel in distress, or is that *un*dress?"

He laughed. "Nobody comes through the portal clothed, my dear Geri, any more than we are born in our swaddling robes."

"But you had clothes on," she pointed out.

"I didn't come through the portal but was already here waiting for you. Does it bother you that I saw you naked? I have seen you many times such, and every time is always a delight."

That did it. "Oh, just stop! Look at me: I'm old enough to be your mother, only I haven't even been born yet so I'm not sure how that works. Besides which, I'm overweight, wrinkly, and sagging in all the usual places, whereas you are just—just..." Geri struggled to find the right word. "Bloody magnificent with your biceps and pectorals and everything else placed just as it should be. Who are you kidding?"

Annoyance darkened his mercurial features. He began stabbing the air between them with his index finger, sparks literally flying. "Do you think I see only how you appear? Do you think so little of me to assume that I only see surfaces? No artist sees just the surface. We look below, within. I see who you are, Geri. I see who you are inside—your soul, your spirit. I have seen you across many timelines and have known you as both young and old, and have never measured your worth by your flesh alone, no matter how comely or burdened with age. You have rescued me from the jaws of eternal death multiple times and may do so again once you assume possession of your full self. To me, you will always be the most beautiful woman in the cosmos."

Geri flushed, stunned. For a moment, she thought she might cry. Eddy floated past throbbing pinkly. "Oh, stop." She swatted the orb away.

"There, enough questions for the moment," Petrus said, holding her close. "I am sorry that I was so sharp with you just now. I am an impatient man, you see—patient with my art but not so with matters of the heart. There, you will find me very patient. I so desire you to remember me fully and to see who I am as I see you." He pulled away. "Forgive me." He flashed her that smile that unaccountably caused her knees to weaken. "Now, are you hungry?"

"Famished." Hungry for lots of things she'd always thought beyond her reach, in truth, but she couldn't allow her mind to go there now.

He threw up his hands and grinned. "Then let us eat!"

When Geri settled across the table from this baffling, ardent, devastatingly gorgeous man and took the first bite of his pasta, she knew that she was lost—or maybe found. Whatever the case, she had decided to enjoy the moment, wherever that moment may be, if it existed at all. She would pretend to be a gorgeous damsel tucked away in a lovely castle being wooed by a dreamy knight. Reality hardly mattered under the circumstances.

"Tell me more about yourself, Petrus. After all, you seem to know a great deal about me," she began. It was a strategy she'd used with many people while dining—get them talking about themselves, leaving her to savor her meal in peace, though in this case, she was content to savor him, at least with her eyes. The strategy had been particularly useful at the annual faculty dinners that she'd been obliged to attend. Most of her colleagues would wax on and on about their endless accomplishments, their published papers, their standing at this or that university, their discoveries.

"There will always be depths to explore in every person, especially one such as you, Geraldine," he began, "so never will I say that I know you fully. Instead, I will say only that I know parts of you, facets of the gem that is you. I understand the mortar in which you have designed yourself but not the varied and miraculous design that has settled into place over this particular lifetime. That alone will be endlessly fascinating and I long for the secrets you will reveal."

Geri cast him a penetrating look. "You are off-topic, Petrus—no detours permitted. I have asked about you so do please unfold the details of your extraordinary design, in particular."

"But is it not best to explore a person slowly, element by element?"

"Ordinarily, I would say yes but in this case, it appears that you've had a head start on knowing me of at least a few hundred years, give or take a decade or two, to which you briefly allude. Consider then that we are not on equal footing in the knowledge department and therefore it would behoove you to bring me up to speed. Please tell me a bit about *your* mortar and design in a nutshell, if you must."

He laughed. "Very well. In this lifetime, I am Petrus Cosmati Odoricus, born just outside of Rome in 1222 to a family of stone masons. I have been a scholar, a wizard, and a stonemason for many centuries, but now consider myself to be a wizardly mason. Would you like to hear how we met?"

Geri took a forkful of pasta and winced. "I'm not ready for that, thanks, especially if it comes with some tale of passion, but please keep talking."

"Why not let us just eat and savior being in one another's company once again and leave the talking for later?"

He gazed lovingly across the table at her, his eyes warm in the candlelight, both of them sipping wine between mouthfuls of deliciousness. Somehow, she had ended up wearing a deep velvet burgundy dress trimmed with ermine with long bell sleeves over a creamy-hued undergown. She couldn't help but wonder if the dress would disappear just as easily.

Any time a stray thought entered her head concerning Lin, wizards, broken floors, and any other part of the phantasmagorical world she was experiencing, she shoved it away. She knew that at some point she must grapple with this new reality and prepare herself to wage a war against the forces of evil. But not now. Now was all light, food, warmth, and a handsome man casting her ardent glances.

Meanwhile, Eddy floated around emitting soft music and pulsing pink. It wasn't until he dropped a paper Valentine onto the table that she grew annoyed. "What are you up to?"

Petrus shook his head at the orb and laughed. "Silly girl, but enough. Be off now."

"Eddy's not a girl," Geri commented.

"Not all the time, of course, but certainly now. Do not scowl so, Geri."

"Why is it that you seem so familiar with Eddy?" she demanded. Maybe she was just growing tired or maybe growing too lulled by wine but she actually felt a pang of jealousy.

"I am very familiar with Eddy. I do hope you open your mind soon, my love. Time is running out."

She knew that much for sure and yet she was suddenly so weary, all she craved was a good long sleep. It wasn't as if she were in her thirties and used to being wooed by gorgeous men in alternative universes in between large quantities of wine and carbs.

As if sensing her thoughts, Petrus leapt from his chair and guided her towards the bed, treating her in the most gentlemanly fashion as he tucked her into the deeply comfortable, ultra-cozy, absolutely perfect bed.

He murmured something into her ear that sounded like "Whatever you do, do not try to leave my rooms" but she didn't quite grasp the meaning.

She could have slept for days and awoke so refreshed, it was as if she'd been infused with caffeine-induced vigor only better, much, much better—no wine aftereffects, no indigestion, no headaches or achy bones. Magic sleeps were something else.

Bounding out of bed, she stood in the center of the studio apartment and blinked, baffled: she was alone but for Eddy buzzing around.

"Where did Petrus go?" she demanded, disappointed that the mason to the stars was not in sight—for purely aesthetic reasons, of course.

As usual, Eddy had nothing to say but hovered nearby as if emitting waves of caution.

"I don't know what you're trying to tell me this time." But she did: *patience*. Petrus would return eventually but eventually was never soon enough for Geri. Now was always better than later. Who knew how long she'd been sleeping?

She swept around the room, peering at the astrological and astronomical charts hovering mid-air, those massive full-scale diagrams of the Cosmati mosaics.

Tearing her gaze away, she scanned the wall surfaces looking for a door but saw nothing that resembled the one she had entered. One corner did reveal a fully modern bathroom complete with shower. She stared, imagining warm water pouring over her, maybe Petrus coming in to shampoo her hair. Oh, enough! She shook away the thought. What was she, twenty? She must find Lin.

Eddy floated in front of her. "What?" she demanded. "Are you trying to tell me that I need a shower now? Who appointed you the cleanliness police?" she asked, swinging towards the orb.

In response, Eddy floated across the room to the table where breakfast sat spread. Fresh pancakes, bowls of jeweled-colored fruit, eggs—there was no favorite morning repast that wasn't represented.

"Do you think I can be distracted by food, too? Where is Petrus? Tell me."

But the only thing Eddy was telling her was to either eat or shower, preferably both. In the end, she succumbed, if for no other reason than to burn the edge off her restlessness. Once she had been fed, washed and fluffed—the shower came equipped with a hair dryer, if you could call that gargoyle-shaped wall-mounted thing blowing hot air, a hair dryer—she put on the ermine-lined velvet number she had on the night before, tucked her feet into the matching velvet slippers, and resumed her search for a door.

Petrus had to be working on the Cosmati floor and she wanted to see him at work, and if Abbot Ware was meeting with the King, she wanted to spy indiscriminately there, too—anything but stay locked inside this fabulous cage. If that meant going forth in the nude, she'd do that, too. It didn't matter. All that mattered was that the world was spinning without her and beyond her which, under the circumstances, she found unbearable.

Every time she pressed a wall looking for an opening, Eddy bumped into her. She tried to ignore him until five bumps and five dead ends later, she snapped. "Get me out of here now! That's an order!"

Something happened. The wall exploded. In a flash of moving images and with dizzying speed, Geri crashed out of the magic room, ending up on her back someplace bright with brilliant shards of spinning colored light and the sound of angry men speaking French.

Chapter Eleven

S
he recognized the octagonal vaulted ceiling and the brilliant stained-glass windows unfurling color all around. She had to be lying face up on the floor of the Chapter House and a meeting was in progress, which was alarming enough.

Pushing herself to her elbows, she gazed around at the circle of seated men, each perched on one of the flip-down wooden seats that lined the room. By the looks of the tunics and insignia, many attendees were barons, others wealthy merchants, and, everywhere there stood a sprinkling of bishops, abbots and priests. That bearded guy wearing the crown and a scowl sitting on the biggest seat was definitely King Henry himself, looking a few years younger than the last time she'd seen him, though none happier.

Thankfully, nobody seemed to notice the woman splayed in the middle of the floor, which meant that she was both invisible and—a quick glance assured her—fully clothed. That settled, she began picking up traces of the discussion while checking the timeline in her head: if she had entered the 13th century in 1268, then this was not the Great Council meeting of 1257 that had launched Parliament as it is now known but clearly a council meeting, nonetheless.

That meant that by now the wealthy landowners had wrestled King Henry into an uneasy truce and were not putting up with him bleeding them dry for his wars and projects any longer. Nevertheless, by the sounds of things, the King was after additional funds, his tone sounding more plaintive than demanding, but the barons were resisting the squeeze.

Another man began to address the council, somebody standing behind Geri and partially hidden by the King's throne.

"Gentlemen, preservest thy souls! I sayest unto you, provide for this magnificent Abbey to assure thy place in Heaven. To do otherwise will prove that thou are heathens and will push thee but steps away from the Devil's gate!"

Something about the voice, the tone—everything—hit Geri like a punch in the gut. She risked turning her head. This speaker with his back to her, raised his fist to the sky, sparks flashing around his dark and muddy aura while clutching a Bible close to his chest with his other hand—a Bible that wasn't a Bible, Geri realized, but something camouflaged much like the man himself. Geri stiffened. The Abbot Ware!

The moment she thought his name, he turned, shooting an invisible bolt of ice through her, deeper than it had any right to go and sharp enough to make her gasp aloud. He recognized her!

Scrambling to her feet, she lunged for the door, heart thundering. The Abbot could not follow her while in the midst of the meeting but it seemed he could harm her, regardless. That powerful, that virulent, that he could multitask with the worst of them, he fired a bolt that threw her off her feet. Scrambling back to standing, she raced for the door.

All she needed was to get away, through those oak barriers and out—find Petrus, Lin—but the doors wouldn't open and the two knights standing guard blocking the way were oblivious to her screams. Nobody could see her but Ware.

She fell to her knees as the man warning the barons of God's wrath, hurled invisible fireballs in her direction. Every time one hit, she was flung face-down onto the ground, expelling the breath from her lungs, only to struggle up long enough to be whacked again. Bastard must plan to incapacitate her until the meeting ended when she'd be so weak that he could skewer her into oblivion. No bloody way! She despised nothing more than a wolf in a priest's clothing.

Shoving herself back onto her feet, she pivoted to face her attacker, bursting with so much rage, she thought she'd explode. And she did explode—or it felt that way. Ware was in mid-speech, countering one of the baron's arguments with a spew of righteous indignation, when Geri's fury boomed across the chamber and hit him full in the chest.

She watched, stunned, as the Abbot was propelled backward by the force of a giant fireball, his mouth forming an "o" of shock as the other men rushed to help him regain his feet. The bastard would retaliate as soon as he recovered. Swinging back, she forced the door open with her will—another anger blast—

before the startled guards, who only saw that the doors suddenly crumbled—and ran from the chamber in a headlong rush, oblivious to where she was going.

What had just happened? Had she really blasted Ware?

Halfway down the nave, she spied Petrus rushing past a group of monks who seemed to be tearing after him. He was heading towards her, his face dark, either with fear or fury. For one flash second, Geri didn't know whether he was on his way to rescue her or to reprimand her. She didn't need one and wouldn't put up with the other but she was still glad to see him.

As she dashed towards him, he stopped in his tracks, turned and strode towards the front door.

"I beseech thee for a moment of privacy, brethren." he called over his shoulder to the monks scrambling behind him. The brethren stopped at once, leaving Geri to take the cue and follow Petrus through the doors and beyond the Abbey walls.

"I just blasted Ware," she told him in a rush once he paused long enough for her to catch up. "Knocked him right off his golden slippers while he was attempting to bully the barons into coughing up more funds. He didn't expect my attack and neither did I! I don't even know how I did it. It was like a ball of fire!"

Petrus turned to face her, his hands raised. "You did it because you were furious and you still are. If I were a lesser magician, you would have knocked me over by now, too." "Contain yourself, Geraldine." It was not a request.

Geraldine stared, instantly sobering. Her anger and excitement were still manifesting in negative ways? "Oh." Immediately, she imagined a soft rain shower, a sunny sky over a field of blooming wildflowers. "Better?" she asked.

"Much better."

"Does this mean I'm claiming my power?"

"Yes, Geri, you are claiming your power but not without cost. Now you must learn to control this force within you. Conjuring explosions will be useful at some other time but a far more subtle approach would have had the desired effect without bringing attention to yourself. Now Ware has your signature."

"My signature?"

"Your magic imprint, that which he can detect more easily from hereon in. If you are to help me win this war, you must be better prepared. To do otherwise will not only harm others besides your intended quarry but fail to protect you."

"I'm not sure I get your drift."

"By hitting out at Ware today, he learns of your weaknesses and will exploit them at the first opportunity. He knows that you are impulsive and quick to anger. The moment he emerges from that meeting, he will hunt you down. I can feel him probing your location now, can you?"

Could she? Gazing around, she was distracted by her first glimpse of Westminster Palace, by the Abbey's external scaffolding, by the busy road filled wagons burdened with goods being hauled by men and women, by people on horseback.

The sharp thudding headache hit her forehead out of nowhere. "Yes," she whispered, slapping her brow. "He's found me."

"Quick, shield yourself," Petrus ordered. "Imagine a castle wall protecting you in a cloud of light pushing back against his probing. Do it now and keep it in place while I take you someplace safe. It must be inside the Abbey for I cannot leave the premises."

Geri tried running after Petrus while attempting to hold her mental picture in place but it was bloody difficult.

"I am bound to this place until the floor is complete," he explained. "Why did you leave my rooms when I asked you not to?"

"I was looking for you and Lin."

"I told you to stay until I did my work."

"I'm not the waiting kind. Have I ever been the waiting kind?" she asked.

"Never and it has caused endless grief."

"Wait, where are we going?" Geri scrambled after him.

"Back the way we came. I must secure you in my apartments inside the Abbey and stave off Ware."

Only as Petrus entered the huge oak doors, Geri banged against an invisible barrier. "He's locked me out!" she cried.

Petrus turned. "I will protect you. He comes. Run! I will find you once I keep him from you!"

"Where should I go?" she called.

"As far away from the Abbey as you can manage! And know that you will not remain invisible to all. Guard yourself!"

Geri turned and scrambled away, unsure of which direction to head or how to get there. Granted, she was invisible, but this was still a strange new old world and she felt as lost as if she had had just fallen back into time all over again. And now on top of everything, she was terrified because she could feel Ware bearing down, feel Petrus blocking his movement, sense the struggle in progress with her at the center of it all.

Protect yourself, Petrus had cautioned but how? Yes, she could imagine a shield but holding that picture in place while bolting down a medieval street was the real challenge.

Maybe she could teach herself some kind of magic coating like a veneer that would offer protection while she went about her business ? (Not that she knew her business). Was there a spell for that? Why hadn't she studied magic when she had the chance? Her mother had been more than willing to help but, no, Geri had resolved to be an academic and saw no way for those twains to meet—fool! Why did she think that she could keep such a huge part of herself at bay for all her natural life? Maybe because she didn't realize how unnatural her life really was to become.

But now she needed to conjure something that Ware could not penetrate. That surely would take time, as would learning how to be more precise in her magic weaponry and to be more measured overall. If she were to survive long enough to rescue Lin, help Petrus repair the Pavement, and jump back into her own century, Geri had to get her magic act together. Only now she felt like a child just when she foolishly thought she was a fully mature adult.

Meanwhile, here she was, this invisible person trudging down a medieval road, assaulted by the sights, sounds and scents while being overwhelmed, terrified, and completely disorientated. Petrus said he would protect her but how could he do that if he couldn't leave the Abbey? How would she survive in the meantime?

Had she been her corporal self, she would have been mown down by a wagon twice, trampled by several horses, and probably pulverized by the assault on her senses alone. Being invisible and unsubstantial did nothing to alleviate the reek of human feces, mud, dung, bodies along with a whiff of an unsavory river to her right. All were enough to impel her to empty her well-fed stomach into the ditch.

But she was an archaeologist and this was living history. How fantastic was that? But she was too focused on getting as far away from the Abbey as possible to study the surroundings. Westminster was the ground zero that she had to escape. To that end, she kept stomping along the muddy road running next to the Thames, dodging horses and people where possible or just letting them ride right through her when her energy sagged.

And her energy was sagging quickly. Her memory of all things Medieval brought up an ancient map drawn in the days when Westminster was the royal seat down river from the center of medieval London. Though it shocked her how clearly the image appeared in her brain and how she could mentally zoom in on features as if her head contained some version of a smart screen, all that was irrelevant to her now. Really, everything was becoming a bit too much.

She knew that she must follow that road along the Thames to the old City. There must be a million places to hide in Old London, a million places where she could tuck herself away until either Petrus found her or she mastered her art enough to protect herself. She much preferred the latter. Playing the damsel in distress was getting old, even if she was dressed for the occasion.

But trudging in the muck and the cold was damned difficult and her pretty little slippers were hardly up to the challenge. She envied the peasant woman riding with her husband in their shabby little cart beside her. Though the poor mule groaned with exertion, at least the farmer and his missus were high and dry. Both husband and wife wore serviceable woolen cowled cloaks while she had to rely on her ermine-lined velvets to keep her warm, minus the cloak. Warm, yes, but weatherproof, no. It had begun to drizzle.

She was trudging between their wagon and the road's edge because the cart offered some protection from the mud flinging hoofs that galloped along the track. People were in a hurry on this road. They were either rushing to market or off to their manor houses and castles and who knew where.

It would take hours to reach London at the rate she was going. She was exhausted with bloodied blistered feet. She eyed the couple's cart and willed herself up into the back of the their wagon to squeeze herself down between a trussed pig, a bag of potatoes, and a basket of fresh buns.

Sitting up front with the woman and her husband would have been too annoying, since they kept bellowing out to anybody with a beating heart about their buns for sale. When they weren't calling, they were either singing obscene little ditties or squabbling with one another.

Besides, the buns smelled so much better than the pair up front and she rather liked the company of the pig better.

She lay back against the bag of potatoes until she was eye to eye with the pig, a big black and white spotted sow, probably too old to bear anymore piglets so ready for the bacon barrel.

The creature was terrified but seemed to have exhausted itself thrashing around. In a flash, Geri saw an image of the pig enjoying a morning snuffle in the trough with her fellows, happy, though happiness didn't extend farther than a barnyard. Suddenly, the creature had been ripped off her trotters and flipped on her side, legs brutally bound while she squealed in fear and pain. Geri felt the whole thing with every inch of her being.

"Poor little buddy. Don't much like becoming part of somebody's food group, right?" Geri murmured, stroking the pig's ears. "They think you're too old so it's off to market for you. Some members of the society in which I used to reside thought similarly of females of a certain age—minus the market part, except maybe the marriage market. In fact, to my century's way of thinking, being an older female puts you straight out of the picture in more ways than one." She laughed at the thought. What her colleagues would think if they could see her now.

The pig thrashed harder, shooting a vivid bolt of terror straight into her heart. It could hear her, it could see her, *it understood her* and she understood it in return! It was a startling sensation.

"Dost thou hear that, Morris?" The woman up front turned around to stare in Geri direction. "D'ye hear a voice?"

Geri looked around. No horses or other wagons were near them now, the others on this busy road being either ahead or behind. She'd best keep her comments to herself.

"I hear nothing, Madge. Now shut yer gob and hold the reins while I take a piss."

The wagon rolled to a stop by the side of the road as Morris jumped out to spray some dusty roadside weeds. A troop of men on horseback—maybe barons returning home after the Chamber meeting—galloped past, shouting a mix of greetings and rude remarks about Morris's working parts. Everybody laughed, including Morris. Geri stared at the pig and the pig stared back.

Help! it squealed in her head.

Geri fixed on the animal's eyes. Here was a brutal period of human history. There was little hesitation to kill man or beast and to do so without care for pain and suffering. All that consideration would come later in time, much later. For now, the people butchered animals and one another with little care and Geri couldn't stand the thought.

"This little piggy is not going to market," she whispered. All she had to do was insert one finger under the ropes that trussed the creature's legs and think *cut* and the ropes sliced apart like a fork through boiled linguini. In seconds, the pig was on his trotters, had hurled itself off the back end of the wagon, and was squealing across a field.

Geri briefly considered what she had just done: chosen the life of an animal over these poor serfs who had to scrounge for everything just to survive. It was all about survival in the 13th century. Nobody thrived but the very rich, and even they were prone to die from some terrible affliction or to lose their head at the drop of a gauntlet.

But still, she thought, here she was able to communicate with animals—amazing! It was at that moment that Geri realized that she stood on the side of not suffering over suffering any day and preferred to throw her hand in with the underdog—or underpig, as the case may be.

Meanwhile, Marge and Morris were screaming. Their fellow travelers paused on to listen to their distress while Morris took off into a field after the pig.

A few travelers, including a man wearing the king's own insignia, dismounted to assist with the hog retrieval efforts. Others had drawn up their wagons to commiserate with Marge who was wailing with gusto while another man leading a donkey burdened with a tinkling rack of knives and spoons peered into the back of the wagon. "Yer cut the ropes yerself, did ye, goodwife?" he asked suspiciously.

Marg was by his side in a second, leaning over the cart's open back to study the severed ropes. "Why would I do a daft thing like that, tinker?" she demanded. "I did no such thing."

"Somebody doeth such, woman. Be witchcraft, methinks."

"I be no witch!" Marg cried, her round face inflamed.

"Not ye." The man paused and sniffed the air, "but a witch be near at hand. I can smell it."

What? That had to be pig he was smelling or maybe magic was detectable to some based on other senses—something else her age had lost? Crud—trouble, either way.

Geri shimmied out of the wagon and stepped away from the tinker to stand by the side of the road with the other wayfarers to study the retrieval efforts. They were not going well. Clearly, the pig knew how to dart this way and that while the men crashed about the undergrowth calling out as if piggy would return to the noose of its own free will. Geri knew the pig would escape eventually. Again, she had no idea why she knew that but had stopped second-guessing herself.

Among the observers sat a man on horseback calmly surveying the scene. Accompanied by two men bearing swords and with crossbows strapped to their saddles, all three men wore a gold wolf insignia and sat mounted on fine steeds. Geri figured that the two companions must be guards or servants to the main man. Garbed in a thick red woolen cloak trimmed with fur, his legs encased in fine leather boots and the purse at his waist fat with gold coin, the boss man was clearly wealthy. Probably a merchant or maybe a lord.

One of his men asked if they could join the pig retrieval efforts but his master issued a curt dismissal while demanding a swig of ale as he had finished his own. One of his men dismounted his sleek-looking white horse to pass the master a flask while his fellow guard called out to the others: "Heave ho! Move thy wagons so that Lord Boniface may pass!"

But no one paid him any mind. Geri compared the lord's fat purse with Marge's which dangled at her waist like a wizened scrotum. She imagined the coins transferring from the wealthy man's to Marge's, giving the woman what would amount to a year's wages as a serf or peasant, certainly more than enough to compensate for the lost pig.

Within seconds, her heart fluttered in pleasure as the transfer of wealth occurred right before her very eyes like, well, like magic. One minute Marge's purse was empty and the next it was full. So she was now Robin Hood, was she? The wealthy toff probably wouldn't miss so much as a coin and had plenty left, in any case.

But now her headache was intensifying, bearing down on her forehead like a brewing storm. She had let down her guard and Ware had located her—bloody hell! Did that mean that Petrus had lost the battle?

Eyeing the horse, she knew that she must escape but how? Roiling with anxiety, she levitated herself up into the servant's vacant saddle and settled into the perch. It was like squeezing onto a bicycle seat, only worse, and the steed whinnied and stomped its hoofs.

The man tending his master shouted back to the horse. "What be thy problem, Wilder? Ye be still!"

Geri leaned over and whispered into the horses's ear: "Wilder, I don't know what that guy gives you in feed but I'll double it. Bolt, baby, bolt!"

Only Geri had not anticipated what bolt meant to a horse. She had no experience with the fine English art of horseback riding and discovered that it was not like in the movies—not her thing, either way. The bouncing, molar-dislodging bottom bumping was a total shock to her system as well as all her other parts, and Wilder the Horse seemed keen to buck her at the first opportunity. There was no way she could hold on at this speed as they hurtled down the road at full gallop.

"Slow down!" she cried.

Wilder did not slow down and considering that Ware was after her, that was probably a good thing. Obviously, she did not have a good connection with this beast and sensed that the steed's loyalty to his master was powerful.

Geri needed an alternate plan. Scrunching her eyes closed, she imagined herself as weightless, perched loosely on a foam-like cushion that absorbed the shock as well as keeping her butt firmly in the saddle. That took a lot of brain power which drained away whatever flimsy protective shield she'd managed to put in place. She feared she'd be open to Ware's prodding more than ever but suspected that it was already too late. An evil cloud was bearing down on her heels.

Shooting a glance behind her, she saw that a party of riders was barreling along the road attempting to capture this runaway horse. Geri was sure that she had glimpsed mounted monks at the back of the group. Did monks ride galloping steeds? If they were on Ware's team, probably.

Well, damn! Her mount was fast but the posse at her heels were speedy, too, and now a fancy wagon with a troop of mounted guards blocked the way ahead.

"Heave ho!" cried one of her pursuers. "Pray catch yon steed!'

Four riders left the group ahead and fanned out to oblige. Now she was tearing towards mounted men who appeared to know exactly how to catch a runaway horse.

"Head for the field, Wilder!" she called, and for good measure, sent a mental picture of him leaping through the meadow.

The horse veered off the road and began bounding across the field, the cries of her pursuers shrill in Geri's ears. She risked another backward glance long enough to see four monks jetting ahead of the others on coal-black steeds. What was worse, these monks had horns sprouting from their tonsured heads and eyes that seemed to burn like little pilot lights. And they were gaining on her. Shit and damn!

Magic steeds could outrun her mount any day and her fledgling magic skills were no match for Ware's agents of evil—yet.

She tried to swivel in her seat long enough to hurl a fire ball at her pursuers only to discover that there was no oomph left in her arsenal.

Now Wilder was stumbling as if suddenly hobbled by a stone or worse. Geri watched in horror as the ground rose and the horse fell to its knees, screaming in pain. Bastards had hamstrung him! She tumbled over the beast's neck to land sprawled in the grass, the sky spattering rain on her face, her heart rolling thunder.

As she struggled to rise, a monk suddenly appeared overhead. Peering down at her, his horns seeming to fade in and out as if her magic sight couldn't fix them in her vision for long. She was weakening. "Morning mistress," he said with a smirk.

Wilder whinnied piteously.

"For God's sake, help the horse, you demon spawn!" she cried.

The monk only beamed his fanged grin broader as his two comrades arrived at his side to enjoy the spectacle. The horse was of no concern to these bastards.

"I'm sorry," she whispered to Wilder, now foaming at the mouth in the grass beside her. "I broke my promise to you and I'm sorry." She felt his pain, the raging fear, as the other riders caught up with the brethren of hell. To ordinary people, they'd look like normal monks.

"What hath we here?" one man asked as he gazed down at Geri. Oh, shit! She was visible now, too?

"It be a witch, my goodly man," said a demon monk. "The pig, the horse, are but toys to such wicked creatures. My brethren and I shall taketh her away to trial where God will punish her most evil ways."

She tried to yell that these camouflaged spawn of the devil were the true evil ones but her lips had gummed shut.

"She be dressed in fine raiments for a witch," said one of the knights who had galloped up.

"Stolen, no doubt," said another. "Look at the how the cow lies there. She be a witch, I say."

Behind him, Wilder's owner arrived, riding double with his comrade. Jumping from the saddle, he fell to his knees beside his steed. "What be this?' the man cried as he stroked Wilder's neck. "My most noble mount looks fair done for!"

"Aye, the witch hath maimed thy steed, my goodly man," said one of the hell brethren. "She hath ridden him into the ground and severed the hamstrings from spite. Pray put the beast out of its misery now while we do likewise for this foul creature."

Wilder's master drew his sword, his face stricken with grief.

Geri lay mustering her strength. She could feel remnants of her power swirling away inside her like wisps of dissipating mist. Maybe she could gather enough force to become invisible again, or maybe find the strength to throw a fire puff—or smoke puff, more like it—anything that might save herself or delay the inevitable? It was either that or try to put Wilder back on his feet before his master was forced to draw his blade to put his beloved steed out of his misery.

That was Geri's choice: either save herself or save the horse.

She chose the horse.

Chapter Twelve

J ust before the hell brethren trussed her up and threw a bag over her head, Geri had the satisfaction of seeing Wilder lurch to his feet. The stallion shook his noble head and whinnied while the others stood by in stunned amazement.

"How could that be?" asked one of the spectators. "That beast be hamstrung but a breeze ago. I did see it with mine own eyes."

"Makes no difference," the horse's owner declared as he took the reins and mounted Wilder. "My horse be fit and hearty now and 'tis all that matters."

One monk looked ready to smite the horse again but another cast him a warning look.

That was just before the bag was yanked over Geri's head. She felt something hard hit her on the stomach, followed by another and another. The bystanders were hurling stones at her.

"Brethren, pray name the place of the witch's trial," a voice called out, "so that we may bear witness."

"Take the witch to Tyburn!" one cried.

"Torture her! Let us watch!" yelled another.

"Burn the bitch!"

The sick feeling in the pit of her stomach seemed to burrow into her very soul. So heartless. Was that Ware tipping the scales? Either way, she was done for. Had she stayed inside Petrus's protection, none of this would have happened.

Would there even be a trial? It would be a sham, if so. Courts of this age were steeped in prejudices and pre-determined outcomes, fixed with the fury of God minus compassion. Everything she said would be twisted, if she'd even be allowed to speak at all. And to make it worse, she always told the truth. There's the irony: she couldn't tell a lie to save her life. No real witch she knew could.

She could imagine a possible cross-examination: *Art thou a witch?*
Yes, actually, but not practicing until recently. Does that count?
Did thou stealest a horse and releaseth a pig?
Damn right!
Guilty!
People had been drawn and quartered for less.

She was tossed over the back of one of the demon steeds like a (large) sack of potatoes. She could see nothing through the hopsacking and could hardly breathe. The material was foul as if just seconds before it had held a load of excrement.

Even when the horse began to move, the crowd kept throwing stones, hitting her back and butt until tears burned her eyes. Seconds later, the sound of the jeering faded as her mount took off. Where the demon monks were taking her, she had no idea. She just knew that with the pressure on her gut and the inability to breathe, she'd never make it to London or back to the Abbey, for that matter. One way or the other, she was going to die and before she'd even been born without even saying goodbye to Randall or told him how much he meant to her. Of course, he knew but she had never said the words often enough. Too damn busy with her work, her all-important career as Geraldine Woodworth the archaeologist. And Petrus, her dream lover, and Lin, the person she vowed to protect. Such a failure!

She'd hoped to catch an inkling of where there were taking her by eaves-dropping on Ware's monks but their communication seemed nonverbal.

Thus, she had no idea why the horse beneath her suddenly stopped minutes or hours later or why she was tossed onto someplace hard, face-up. Her arms and hands were numb and every inch of her body seared with pain.

The sacking was suddenly whipped from her head, leaving her coughing and choking in some dark chill place. It felt like she was suspended in a black hole of nothingness. Not a crack of light anywhere. She could sense the pres-ence of entities all around but nothing communicated. Her lips were still gummed shut. When she attempted to cry out with her mind, even that was impossible. She had been shackled and gagged.

How long she remained in that state was a mystery since she kept fading in and out of consciousness but eventually she sensed a quickening of movement in the surrounding dark. A prick of red began intensifying overhead until something like a human-sized figure hovered above.

A chill seized her gut as she stared into the fire-pit eyes of Abbot Ware. The rest of his form was dark—darker than the surrounding nothingness—with just the faint outline of a skeleton or maybe that was a corpse? Gone were the rich vestments, the velvet robes, and fur linings, leaving nothing behind but that *thing*.

"So we meet at last, ye pitiful excuse for a witch." His voice grated like the lid of a coffin, iron upon stone. "I thank ye for thy bumbling for now ye have delivered forth my greatest foe and I shall hold him tight until it is time to drop the great touchstone in place. Then the world will tip into chaos and will become ours!"

Petrus, he had Petrus, too? She tried to ask what he had done to Lin and Petrus, but no words escaped her.

"Ah, thou shalt listen, witch. Thy hast not the right to speak or to move ever again from this day forth, but to stay in this hole until it is time for thy execution." He laughed, the sound affecting her like nails gouging into flesh. "I shall burn ye at the stake and make Petrus and your daughter watch from afar! And, yes, Geraldine, though ye will die in this age, I shall ensure that so, too, ye will burn in thy own. There, ye shall suddenly run afoul, be struck mute and uncommunicative as if by a terrible affliction, made dead though thou livest still. That shall be thy fate and I shall revel in thy despair!" More horrid laughter followed.

Geri bucked in her restraints, a thousand cries and insults flew to her tongue and died. He had her, he had Petrus and Lin! The world would tip into evil and fall apart and it was all her fault! But, wait—why did he refer to Lin as her daughter?

And then just as quickly as he arrived, he disappeared. Probably way too busy to watch her thrash in mute despair. He had things to do, people to harm. What was she in the face of all that? Nothing but a shroud of pain caught in the middle of an abyss with her heart throbbing in agony.

And then deep in her despair, it occurred to her that Eddy had been gone for hours. She hadn't seen him since escaping Petrus's apartments. Where was he? All these days and months when the glowing orb had followed her around like a puppy and now he chooses to disappear? Why hadn't he showed up back in the Abbey when she was in the Chapter House or beyond the Abbey walls when she was thrashing about for a place to hide? And now that she was to die a horrible death, he still doesn't reappear?

That was the last straw. A wrecking ball of despair and loneliness smashed into her. She couldn't even cry. It was as if everything that smacked of a juicy life well lived or even half-lived had escaped her, leaving her as dry and lifeless as Ware himself.

She felt dead inside.

Hours later, she was wrenched from the hole in which she had been bound and shoved into the daylight where the blaze of sun assaulted her eyes. She squinted against the unbearable light and winced at the cry of the crowds. Hands bound, she was shoved into a cart and rolled down the streets while people ran behind the wagon throwing stones and hurling insults. Had there been a trial and she missed it?

She saw what lay ahead of her—a platform on which a mass of sticks and wood had been piled. They were going to burn her alive. There would be no trial. The people had believed that they had witnessed witchcraft and the monks had deemed it to be true. What other proof did they need? Witchcraft or anybody of free thought brought raging fear in this age when justice was a fierce and feeble play enacted by brute force. The crowd wanted blood—or toast, in this case.

The cart rumbled up to the pyre. A scan of her surroundings revealed ramshackle timbered houses crowded together around a market square. More roofs huddled in the distance and the Thames curved it's grey-blue back mere streets away.

London, then. How she'd love to walk these lanes and experience the city she'd studied and excavated for decades, have it reveal its secrets to her eye and senses rather than just having to cobble together a picture through deductive reasoning and imagination. But that would never be.

As rough hands dragged her from the wagon and hauled her up a plank towards a hewn tree where she was bound hands, feet and body to the stake, all she could think of was failure. She had failed without ever really grappling with the enormity of the task ahead of her. Who was she to try to save the world when she could not even save herself?

She focused on the four monks standing before her looking pious though even with her magic vision stripped from her, she could see straight through them. Why couldn't the crowd? Maybe it was cruelty and hate that blinded them after being force-fed dogma all their lives. People act out what they experience. If it's hate, they hate.

The demon monks gazed at her with false compassion, one of them stepping forward to light the fire. All she could do was find a safe place in her mind where she could go while waiting for the flames to scorch her body. *Eddy, where are you? Lin, fight the bastard! Randall, forgive me. Petrus...Petrus!*

Petrus. Just thinking of him suddenly released the floodgates of her mind, dredging up memory after memory— intense, fevered, filled with joy. Across the centuries, they had been mates, husband and wife, partners, allies, and powerful counterbalances to one another all at once. There were days when she had lived for his touch alone and moments when she had been so angry with him that she stormed the skies and churned the seas, but always they had remained together. Such a powerful force, love, that it kept the world in check.

She loved him but now she'd never see him again with her eyes this wide with knowing. If Ware had his way, she'd never awaken whole again in this life or any other. She blinked back searing tears—she did not want these demon bastards to see her cry.

The pyre was smoking now but the hell brothers could not get the fire properly started. The crowd was yelling and both men and women stepped forward to toss torches and burning twigs upon the pile. Still it wouldn't burn, though the smoke billowed thick and black.

Coughing, eyes streaming, she peered through the breaks in the smoke searching for even one compassionate face. They were there, she knew it, and it only took one to bring comfort. And she found two—*two*—a man and a woman standing side by side watching with pain in their faces, empathy almost as searing as that which throbbed in her heart. And there was a cat—a cat?

Geri blinked away the tears. Yes, a cat. The cat was trying to tell her something but she was too weak to read the message.

The flame had caught and was crackling now. The crowd began to cheer but all she saw was the little black cat calmly sitting at the base of the pyre, green eyes fixed on her, oblivious to both flame and crowd.

One of the demon monks caught sight of it and tried to kick her away but to no avail. The cat remained right where she wanted, green gaze fixed on Geri.

Geri wondered how she knew it was a she...

Chapter Thirteen

G eri didn't believe in the traditional concept of heaven and hell but figured that whatever state of mind in which one existed while alive followed you into the next dimension. Therefore, it didn't follow that she would end up in gorgeously decorated room.

If the afterlife was a cushy boudoir draped in velvets and silks with paintings by Monet and Raphael, and a few bits of ancient monuments used as coffee tables, then it appeared that she had arrived. Maybe she had died and come back as a curator or maybe a gallerist?

Pitching herself to a sitting position, she fixed on the woman who sat on the couch across from her, writing in an enormous book. Pillows in jeweled shades of satin everywhere, bookcases on every wall and on what seemed to be shelves receding into the distance, though the room couldn't be that large. Teacups and cookies on the coffee table.

"Am I dead?" she whispered.

The woman looked up—intense emerald eyes, long red hair, skin as smooth as creamy silk. "Not yet." She tossed aside the book which flipped closed and settled gently on a nearby table by itself. "And you won't be any time soon, if I have anything to do with it, but you make it damn challenging, sister. Geri, how I've missed you!"

In seconds Geri was enveloped in a jasmine-scented embrace. She pushed the woman away. "Wait—what do you mean by 'missed me'?"

The woman tossed a glossy red strand from her eyes, and stared down at her. Impossibly beautiful, Geri thought. "Missed every persnickety, pugnacious, funny, and gloriously prickly inch of you, though I keep forgetting what a pain in the ass you are. You have a way of reminding me."

Something tugged at the back of Geri's mind. "I know you don't I?"

Yes, she did. She almost remembered, though her memories were as fleeting as fish glimpsed in a lake. Maybe there were long conversations and walks on the beach? Hell, yes, walks on the beach along with girly stuff and plenty of laughter. Geri didn't do girly stuff—or walks on the beach, for that matter. Even as a young girl she had refused to live her life like the subject of some smarmy greeting card, so this was yet another shock. It felt as if she was being assaulted by memories that weren't her own and yet she almost remembered them.

"We're sisters," the woman said with a smile. "I am Morgana, whom you sometimes called 'Ganny', though I didn't like the nickname then and I still don't, so spare me the moniker this time around, all right?"

"No 'Ganny'. Yes, all right then. So, does that mean that we are biological sisters?" Geri asked.

"Of course not. How can that be when I wasn't born in your century and we are certainly not from the same parentage? There are many ways to be sisters, Geri, which I'm sure you know. I, for one, prefer to move back and forth among the centuries where I can do the most good."

"Is that why you speak in the modern vernacular?"

"I adapt my language to the person to whom I speak, naturally."

Naturally? There was nothing natural about any of this. Geri stated at the woman. "You are so beautiful."

"An illusion. I can change my appearance to look like anyone I choose to be any time I want but I do prefer to look gorgeous for aesthetic reasons. Mostly that's just to please myself as I move among the centuries. Someday, maybe you will do the same but at the moment you're stuck, though getting looser, I'm happy to say. I just hope it's not too late."

"Dare I ask: too late for what? I think I just died so it's already too late for me by my estimation." Here we go again. Just when she thought the game was up, she discovers that existence is not finite, that it just changes again and again punctuated with more half-remembered relationships.

"Wrong."

"Look, if you don't mind, I'm a bit lost at the moment: dropping headfirst into another century; meeting the man I supposedly love and who loves me back but whom I can't recall with any assurance; losing my student down a hole —I could go on and on. So, if I don't recall my long-lost sister exactly or know why I'm not dead when I should be, I trust all will be forgiven."

She didn't want to anger Morgana. The woman looked as though she could become thunderous when roused.

But Morgana hooted with laughter. "I have more important things to forgive you for than that. Mostly, I'm furious with you for putting us in this horrible position. Do you see how your memory issues are inconsequential next to that?"

Laughing or not, little sparks were flying off the edge of the woman's aura. It wouldn't do to anger this one. "Oh, well, I'm sure everything will all come rushing back to me at some point but it's not happening at the moment—my apologies. So what exactly have I done or failed to do?"

Morgana crossed her arms. "You don't know?"

"Actually, I'm currently feeling a little fried, or should I say singed? Didn't I just die or something like it?"

"You almost died, yes."

There's the rub. "Almost? I have a clear memory of being burned at the stake and that does something to one's mind." Glancing down at her body, she found herself still wearing the red velvet gown she started with that morning with zero signs of scorching.

"Ware attempted to burn you as a witch and not for the first time."

"There were others? How did I escape?" Those dreams that had plagued her all her life—this had to be the source.

"You have me to thank for that," Morgana told her.

Green eyes, so incredibly green, like emeralds. Geri gasped. "You're the cat!"

"I am. And a witch—a damn good one, too, which is more than I can say for you." She stepped closer. "You've got to hone your skills and clean up your act before you get us all killed, including yourself."

Geri dug around in her memory banks. "Are Petrus and Lin all right?"

"Ha!" Morgana snorted. "Do you mean are they still alive? Yes, they are still alive but in captivity for the moment. You will rescue them and save the world."

Geri stared, every glib remark dying on her tongue. It was time to drop the defenses. She had to save the world, period. "I'll do whatever is necessary. Thanks for rescuing me, by the way. How did you and can you teach me to save them?"

Arms still crossed, Morgan stared down at her. "I shall try, believe me. As for how I saved you, Ware's not the only one who can conjure something from thin air. I shrouded the pyre in a curtain of thick smoke while projecting an image of you thrashing about being burnt to a crisp. It wasn't pretty, let me tell you, but it wasn't real, either. I've seen the real variety enough times to make it look authentic. I am an artist, after all."

She snapped her fingers which delivered what could have been a movie playing in the air between them. Tied to a stake a woman burned, crying for mercy with heart-wrenching despair, a woman that looked a lot like Geri. Geri barely recognized herself though the unfolding horror. "Did you have to burn my clothes off?"

"Verisimilitude, Geri, verisimilitude. What do you think happens to fabric when it burns? It goes up in flames first. Those bastards care nothing for your modesty. In truth, some come for the show. Watching you die gave the creeps thrills while allowing others to revel in their good fortune." She sniffed. "And they call witches the evil ones."

"They came to watch?" Of course, they did! She knew that but there was something more gut-wrenching about being the one on show. Geri caught sight of her pseudo suffering on the moving scene rolling before her eyes. "Oh, stop that thing! That's a horror movie!"

She covered her face with her hands, remembering all her nightmares of burning, falling, drowning. She dropped her hands. "That's where my dreams come from, isn't it, from all my prior witch deaths?"

Morgana snapped her fingers again and the picture disappeared. "Now you're getting it. That's exactly where all your nightmares come from and, deep-down, is probably why you've turned into such a lily-livered coward in your current life."

"I'm not a coward," she protested. "I'm merely careful and prone to utilizing a bit of self-preservation, which makes sense, under the circumstances. And by circumstances I'm referring to all the chaotic occurrences that manifest when I am not exercising self-preservation and the fact that I'm almost a senior citizen."

"Had you faced that chaos long ago instead of running away from it, you'd be much further ahead now. As for the other, you are timeless, as are most people if they only recognize it to be so."

"That's kind of hard to swallow when you live in my century. Anyway, I made mistakes because I'm only human—granted, in a witchy way. Surely, you've made mistakes, too?"

Morgana pointed to the walls of books receding into the distance. "A few. You may read about some of them when you have a spare decade or two, which won't be any time soon. I'm a careful diary-keeper. Let us consider *your* mistakes for a moment, the ones that have led to *your* traumatic moments. Consider the time that you were removed from the choir as a child," Morgana said.

"Oh, you know about that? Of course, you do, you being a witch, but that's the chaos I was referring to. I was in the Abbey during choir practice and all the ghosts started yodeling off-key making the choirmaster assume that it was me."

Morgan snickered. "That was hilarious, but all the spirits wanted was a little attention, Geri, and you kept shoving them away. That's all they ever want, usually: the living to recognize that they exist or existed. Had you taken the time to hone your skills and interact with them, you may have learned something. They were trying to communicate."

"I was a kid, okay?" Geri protested, her face reddening. She only liked to argue when she had a chance of winning the debate. She sensed that there would be no winning against Morgana.

"What was your excuse when you were Head Archaeologist? There you thought you could use the ghosts without ever hearing what they wanted in return. Because of that, they did whatever they could to trip you up. And then the Dean caught you having a hissy fit and decided that you were not of the proper temperament to work at the Abbey—too blasphemous, I believe he called you."

"He caught me at a bad moment," Geri huffed, remembering that humiliating period.

"You were cursing with so much fervor that apparently Queen Mary rolled over in her grave."

"Queen Mary is always rolling over for one thing or another—such a prude! Anyway, I banged my knee against a tomb chest that had magically appeared where it hadn't been seconds before and I let rip a few prized curses."

"In three languages."

"I thought the Latin version was impressively inventive, especially the fortification with parts technically unreachable by one's self. Unfortunately, the Dean could translate and wasn't amused. That man had no sense of humor. He has since vacated his post and I like the new one far better."

She stared fiercely at Morgana who stared back with equal intensity. They tried to stare each other down. The seconds burned into minutes and, finally, the two of them burst into laughter simultaneously. They laughed and howled until tears streamed down their faces.

"He was fuming!" Morgan cried, holding her stomach. "How dare you curse in Westminster Abbey!"

Geri could hardly catch her breath. "And in Latin, too!"

That cracked them up all over again and it took several minutes before they could regain their composure. Morgana, now sprawled across the velvet couch apparently exhausted from a bout of mirth, suddenly sobered. "Here we are laughing on the eve of the world's destruction—as if we had time for such levity."

"I can't think of a better time for a good belly laugh than during pending doom," Geri said, sitting on the floor with her legs spread wide. "It felt so good. My stomach has been in knots for days."

"More like centuries. In any case," Morgana sprung to her feet with a grace Geri couldn't manage under any circumstance. "What I was about to say before I lost it, was to point out that self-preservation is cowardice in another form. It is sometimes necessary to take a risk in order to truly live, Geri, and you have refused to live for far too long. Now look where we are?"

"Which is?" Geri asked, looking around. "I mean, I know you meant that metaphorically but is this another magic room tucked away in an alternate dimension?"

Morgan spread her hands. "This my home. Whenever you get your act together, you'll create your own sanctuary to protect yourself and your guests, providing we live that long. You will not survive another burning. I've witnessed your death for real countless times in the past and it's wrenched my heart each and every time. Let Ware think that he's killed you permanently in this round but this has got to be the last time that you end up tied to a stake. There are no more chances left."

Geri stared. "How many times have I been burned before?"

"At least three, that I was witnessed to, and once you were thrown into a river and didn't have the sense to stay down. You really lack common sense for one so brilliant. I kept you company during at least one death and was forced to watch the others through to the end though I, myself, remained alive. I could not let you die alone."

"Well thanks for that. One does not want to descend into the long good-night by oneself. My apologies for not remembering all of the details. I was literally fried," Geri murmured sadly.

"Don't jest, sister. Be serious. Every time we burn, we come back stronger, yes, but had Ware been able to light you up for real this time, it would have been your last. Even witches can't go on forever as our enemies gain in strength."

Geri's gaze reached Morgan's fathomless green eyes. "I have to get better at this, I know that much."

"And soon. You are immensely powerful—much more so than I. I've just had more practice—but as we grow in power, so do our enemies. If Ware weren't so busy putting out his own fires this time around, he would have been more successful setting light to yours. He left the task to his underlings and that cost him."

Geri thought back on all the mistakes she'd made. "And Petrus?"

"Imprisoned. The moment he let his guard down to give you an opportunity to escape, Ware located him. The snare had already been laid. Petrus knew it and still he protected you because, as powerful a wizard as he is, loving you makes him weaker. Pray that you learn to make him stronger because this is the last chance you'll have to do what he needs you to do, what *we* need you to do."

Geri jumped to her feet. "But I don't know what to do!"

"You'd better learn quickly. We're running out of time here. You have to be ready to lay that stone with Petrus at daybreak tomorrow and prevent Ware from contaminating the mortar."

"Can't you teach me?" she asked.

"I am going to teach you everything I can in the next few hours but that part is beyond me. The Cosmati Pavement is Petrus's design and only he can tell you how to help him put it back together, which he is in no position to do at the moment. He would have been had you not left his rooms prematurely. Now, you'll have to figure it out as you go."

"As I go where?" Geri wailed.

"To the Abbey with me tomorrow and as you leap into the flames to assist Petrus in saving the world. You can do it. You're that powerful."

"Wait—back up: could you change your language somewhat and eliminate all this daunting 'save the world' verbiage and maybe the 'jump into the flames' bit, too? It's rather daunting for a senior citizen approaching retirement."

"Will you stop with the senior thing? Being a senior, as you say, is irrelevant to who and what you are. Stop using it as a crutch."

"It's how the world treats people over fifty that prompts me to react this way. Besides, I'm afraid—afraid of all that swirling energy that fights to burst out. That's why I stifled my true spirit for all these years as an archaeologist in my current birth life because of fear," Geri whispered, stricken by the knowledge that now infused her being. She'd definitely label herself lily-livered now that she gave it thought.

"Yes, you went to your new birth century terrified of your very self. I watched from afar but could never reach you, though I knew that as the Cosmati cracks grew in strength, you and Silas would be forced to face your true selves eventually."

"Silas is Randall," Geri whispered. The realizations were hitting her one by one.

"Yes, but I know him as Silas, our brother. He must remain anchored in your birth century in order to help you return home, when and if the stars align, that is. There is much I must teach you first and none of it will be easy.

Now that both Petrus and Lin are imprisoned, your task has just become that much more enormous."

Geri straightened. "I need to see them."

"Well, go ahead and check them out."

Geri stared. "Me?"

"Have you seen them in Ware's detention before?"

"Not Petrus, no, but I saw Lin through the door of the Pyx Chamber."

"Using magic?"

"Of course, but Eddy helped. Where is he, by the way?"

"First things first. Back to checking on Petrus and Lin: if you've already seen Lin, then you know how to do it again so go ahead."

"As I've said, Eddy helped. Actually, I am quite certain that he was the one who allowed me to see the inner workings of the door. He's been immensely handy of late."

Morgana's face had settled into a cool resoluteness which Geri could read instantly. "I have to do it by myself, apparently."

"You already have at least once. Do it again."

Geri squeezed her eyes shut, imagining Lin in the Pyx Chamber surrounded by snarling dogs but in her imagination is where the image remained. When she opened her eyes seconds later, nothing had changed. Next, she fixed on Petrus, trying to conjure his smiling face, those flashing eyes, but again, nothing. "It appears that I'm stymied," she said after a minute.

"Emotion is fuel to the imagination, Geri. Put your heart into it."

She knew that. She knew everything that Morgana told her yet it rankled that she needed to be reminded. So, it was with anger that she imagined Lin next and, in return, she saw through swirling mist the girl still in the Pyx Chamber, head in her arms, apparently asleep. Relieved, she next thought of Petrus, exploring these feelings she'd recently been experiencing about the man until, at last, his image came into view. He was walking down the nave, sleeves rolled up, face grim, and Geri could clearly see the faint lines of prison bars around his form. He paused and looked right into her eyes. "I'll be there tomorrow, my love. Don't despair!" she cried.

When the image evaporated, she met Morgana's eyes. Her sister was studying her. "You have big emotions hidden away, Geri. It is time to give them a little air."

"Yes, ma'am. When do we leave?"

"Tomorrow before dawn. The center roundel is destined to be set into the Pavement according to the astrological and astronomical patterns that have been decreed by all the powers that flow through and around us. The King will be present as will be Ware and the Archbishop of Canterbury—no friend of Ware's, believe me. With Petrus shackled, he will not be able to keep the portal steady as he lowers it into place, something which Ware is counting on."

"Ware's locked Petrus inside a mobile prison," Geri was so angry, she wanted to throttle the abbot.

"Precisely so. His chains are invisible yet he is shackled. No one but the magical will see his true condition. To the mortals, he'll look like any artisan performing his craft but in all other ways, he is unable to function as his true self. He cannot even return to his real apartments but must live in a cell. You have no idea how that pains him. As an Italian, he loves beautiful things."

"And I presume that none of the real work of the Cosmati floor will be visible to the spectators."

"You presume correctly. You won't be visible, either, because you will shield yourself from Ware until the deed is done, at which time you will return to your home century with Lin. If Ware knows that you are present, all will be lost."

"Please stop saying that."

"Not until I hear you say that you will save the world and sound like you mean it."

"Oh, come now. That's a sizable request. What if I were to say that 'I will help Petrus begin to put the world to rights."

"Too limp. You will literally leap into the fire. Say it."

Geri glowered at her. "I, Geraldine Woodworth, will leap into the fire—is that as in literally burning?—to save the world with Petrus."

"The man you love. Say it."

"Oh, please. Why is that important?"

"If you have to ask that, I truly fear that you are not ready for this challenge."

Geri did sense a swelling in the area of what was theoretically her heart. If that was romantic love, she had pitifully few examples by which to compare it to in her birth lifetime. When she said his name, something physical definitely occurred but she thought that would more likely caused by lust, which had to mean something, too. She had to admit that she was beginning to understand the hype that surrounded romance—all those over-heated songs, the movies, the books—since the feeling was intense enough to create physical manifestations. Still she couldn't say the words because she wasn't convinced that she believed them. "Then I am not ready for the challenge."

Morgana stared at her. "You either manage conviction or our world ends." Turning away, she swept across the room, her long gown catching the light as she moved. Swinging back to Geri, she spread her hands. "You are going to school now. You must learn how to control your powers before we reach the Abbey tomorrow morning. At least you've grasped a few more key concepts and moved a little more forward by embracing your true spirit."

It was becoming increasingly tedious to find herself staring blankly yet again. Geri was used to being the one who knew everything, or thought she did. "Do you mean by attempting to work magic the way I did when I blew Ware off his feet or I burst out of Petrus's rooms?"

"Fool!" Morgan's eyes actually flashed. "Not that. You didn't know what you were doing then and it showed." Taking a deep breath, she appeared to gather her composure. "But, it's only fair to add that, at the very least, you managed to absorb your true self."

"Would you mind explaining that more fully? Absorb my 'true self' how?" she added air quotes. "Is that like a New Age proclamation or some weird yoga position?"

Morgan threw her hands up in exasperation. "By absorbing Eddy!"

"I beg your pardon?"

"Eddy is you. Haven't you figured that out yet?"

Chapter Fourteen

Of course, it made total sense now that she thought about it. Eddy had appeared when she felt the loneliest, the most isolated, and when she knew that despite her protestations, retirement with all its uncertainty was looming on the horizon. She had desperately needed a close confidant, somebody who would always be there for her rather than be tied up with their own problems the way Randall often was. She needed someone who would put her interests first—somebody like herself, actually. Let's face it—everybody else was busy with their own issues most of the time. And now she realized that such a friend existed inside her all along. The invisible friend that she had as a child was her inner self. It amazed her how in some ways she knew more when younger than she did as an adult.

No other shock affected her like this one. Not only was Eddy funny and strangely kind, but he/it/she was a magical being. If Eddy was her, or part of her true self, then she should get along just fine because she actually liked him/herself.

"Eddy became fully a part of me when I broke from Petrus's apartments, only I didn't recognize what was happening. Suddenly I had magical abilities—well, I always have had them but had refused to explore the potential. Eddy's the part of me I've refused to acknowledge."

Morgana nodded. "You have always been you."

And all she need do was reach deep inside herself to find that true center. Age and circumstances may dislodge one's sense of self, but it was always there should one choose to reach deeply enough.

She stared straight ahead, her eyes fixed somewhere in the distance, looking inside herself now. It baffled her how blind she'd been—she, the professor emeritus, the woman so confident in herself and her role in the world, slapped back down to the beginning like a child seeing the world for the first time.

"Where do we begin with my education?" Geri said after a moment.

"First, you will learn how to protect yourself, which means imagining a shield that remains in place regardless of what you are doing."

"I have attempted to do just that but as soon as I become involved in something else, wham—the shield drops."

"It must become as habitual as breathing," Morgana said, taking a step forward. "Stand up, Geri."

Geri stood. "Where are we going?"

"Beyond these walls lies London town where every person had best protect themselves against robbers or other unsavory types. Nobody fares well on these streets without wit, wile, or a good knife. We will go forth now and you will protect yourself using your magical self. We haven't much time—a few hours at the most. Let's make the best of it. Make certain you remain protected while fully in touch with your true abilities."

Geri sighed. It irked to be the learner—the child in this case—where she had no choice but to learn and learn quickly. It's not that the didn't enjoy learning new things—she always had—but to be plunged into a do-or-die situation so dramatically and without preparation or even consent? "My Eddy self, in other words. Very well. Let's get at it." She stared around at the walls. "Show me the door, please."

Morgana crossed her arms. "Find it yourself. As my guest, I've built no barriers against you through wards. Seek and you shall find."

"Mind giving me a hint?"

Morgana's face suddenly appeared overcast. The woman seemed practically able to conjure the weather over her eyes.

Geri turned away. "All right, I'll find it myself."

It was easier than she expected. Locating the door required her to plunge into her Eddy self, feeling her way with her senses the way one might reach into a murky pond to feel for something on the bottom. As it happened, the door was right in front of her the whole time. All she had to do was think *door*.

"A bit obvious, isn't it?" Geri asked.

Her sister's lips curled into a beatific smile. "You didn't find it at first, did you? The best hiding places are often in plain sight. Surely you know that?"

Geri stared at the outline of the door that had superimposed itself (in her mind, at least) right over the patterned curtains that covered what she had assumed to be a nonexistent window. "So, if I were not a guest and had broken into your apartments, what would I have seen?"

"Monsters and nasty things straight from your worst nightmares."

"Yes, that would certainly be a deterrent. Why was I able to walk around Ware's apartments unchallenged?"

"Because he has so many servants going to and fro, including various innocent women and children upon which he preys, that he leaves his rooms unguarded. However, every person who entered has left an imprint visible only to him. He knew that somebody magical had entered yet has remained so involved with other matters that he has given little thought to the details."

"Busy with the brewing mutiny, perhaps?"

"That and the ceremony for setting the center roundel tomorrow, which involves the presence of esteemed guests and requires Ware to put on his best performance. I say performance because all those who know him well will see him as the vicious tyrant he is rather than the religious leader he purports to be. He cannot risk his monks stealing a word with the Archbishop. Also, of course, he has been busy keeping a virtual eye on Petrus."

"The three monks who tended Petrus the night I came through were grumbling about the Abbot. They, I assume, were the good guys?"

"Some actually have halos—glowing auras—which tell you that their spirits are clear and that they are lights in the world. You have seen these halos in your birth century, yes?"

"Occasionally, in an unguarded moment, I will see them hovering around certain heads just as I will see the darkening around others. Mostly I found those kinds of revelations distracting. So Ware has his hands full at the moment, does he? That can only work in our favor."

"Yes, and that preoccupation will only grow more intense. There's the matter of the King's shrinking funds. Without more money, Henry will be unable to complete the Abbey renovations and will blame Ware, thinking that his abbot does not pray hard enough to God—which he doesn't, even if God were a bank. Oh, and then there's the fact that imprisoning Petrus has strained Ware's magical resources, in fact, more than he can afford to squander under the circumstances. That, too, is a good thing. These matters should keep him distracted as we go forth on the morrow. Still, it is best that you not think of him too often in case he senses the attention and realizes that you live still."

Geri nodded. "Very well, let's get on it. I'll practice my shielding skills. Any tips to share?"

Morgana gazed at her. "Keep the shield in place—however you choose to imagine it—while going about multiple tasks. It is the only way."

"I understand. Let's go." Geri turned to the door and thought *open*. Suddenly, intriguing glimpses of London town appeared beyond the portal, including cobbled streets and narrow wooden buildings huddling together like a clutch of gossiping men.

"Wait," Morgana ordered.

Geri turned. "What now?"

"Are you going dressed like that?"

Geri thought she'd never hear those words again once she left her parents' house decades ago. Her mother always objected to her short skirts but, gazing down now, all she saw was the red velvet dress she had donned at Petrus's. "What's wrong with this?"

"To begin with, no woman ventures into the streets of London in velvet garb unless accompanied by her husband or guardian, servants, and either mounted on a horse or in a litter. Secondly, look at what's left of that dress, Geri. Really, you must begin to truly see."

Geri cleared her vision with a mental blink, shocked to find her dress so fire-singed, so muddy and torn, that most of her lower half was exposed and part of the bodice hung in tatters from her waist. She swore. "Something more in keeping with what an ancient London working woman would wear, then," she muttered, "and not that kind of working woman." Though that could be interesting.

"Get on with it," Morgana snapped.

Geri met her sister's gaze. "Bossy," she muttered, but here was her chance to walk in the shoes of the very people whose remains she'd studied for decades. So many times she'd hold an object in her hand and strain to imagine these people living their lives centuries before. Now, here she was about to do just that. Perhaps she'd step out that door dressed like Madge—a serf seeking a living from the land her lord had provided, after the tithe was paid, that is., which wasn't much. Or she could go as a peddler, selling something to every passerby. What could a poor woman sell besides herself? Flowers, of course!

"Work up a disguise," Morgana advised.

"As in become a 'shifter'?"

"What is a 'shifter'?" Morgana demanded.

"It's a term in my century for fantasy creatures that change shape—man into werewolf, for instance."

"They have a name for that? Changing shapes is what all magic beings do." Morgana threw up her hands. "I keep forgetting how obvious the twenty-first century is—and so boring. There is a good reason why I never sally forth there."

"Magic isn't common in my century, remember?"

"It might be if people with abilities such as you and Randall were to fully use your gifts."

"And cause chaos wherever we go?"

Morgana's eyes did that flashing thing again—sparks, lightning? Could be handy during an argument, either way. "Is there not chaos in your century already? Besides, you wouldn't cause chaos it you had learned the necessary discipline in your youth. Now get busy and create your disguise and shield. Look what I have done." She spread her hands.

Her sister was now garbed in a long cowled robe made of rough wool the color of old mustard with her lovely face time-ravaged as if from a life hard-lived.

"I'd rather look younger, myself. I've been doing the senior thing for awhile now, quite naturally, I might add."

"Do what you want, just hurry up about it. Time is running out," Morgan snapped.

Geri was inspired. What woman wouldn't want to look younger? True, she hadn't invested many resources in the youth creams she saw marketed everywhere. Still, imagine the possibilities? And so she became a more nubile version of herself, remembering the way she had been back in the day when her body was a bountiful feast for living, had she but known it—no lines, no wrinkles, everything perky. As for her clothing, she saw the wisdom of dressing down for the occasion and chose a threadbare robe.

"You're taking a risk," Morgana whispered as she surveyed her efforts.

"A risk of what?" Geri asked.

"That every male eye will now be drawn to you and you will need to stay extra vigilant. Perhaps that is the best practice, after all. Now pull your shield in place."

"I can't recall the last time I had a bit of male attention so I'll make the best of it. Once you're my age, another kind of invisibility takes over." Geri imagined herself safely tucked behind a clear wall of light. "Okay, let's go."

"When I'm your age? I'm far older than you, Geri, but let's set that point aside for a moment. Are you sure you are ready?"

Geri paused. "If I weren't, would you tell me?"

"No," Morgana said with a smile, drawing her cape closer. "I would allow you to fall flat on your face. You'll learn faster that way."

"Excuse me, but as one who has been teaching for decades, it is not the best practice to allow a student to fall on his, her or their face. Teachers must guide and lead by example."

To which Morgana howled with laughter and stepped out the door, Geri following on her heels. She was about to protest further but the sight before her caused every word to die on her lips.

To an archaeologist, everything she saw was superimposed over the remains of what had last been seen as dust and crumbling bits during an excavation—a vibrant if ramshackle city reduced by time and the ravages of the Great Fire of London to nothing but layers of stone and soil. Of course, there were people on foot and on horseback about, but she couldn't quite tear her gaze away from the buildings themselves.

From where she stood, the city's Norman foundations rose strong and solid, the wooden buildings running proud and sturdy on either side of the cobbled street amid the squeeze of more ramshackle houses. The spires of the great churches were visible in a way that was no longer possible in modern London. By her estimation, they were in the old city center near the Temple Church, the round shape of which she could just see over the rooflines.

"Oh, look—I excavated that building over a decade ago. They were putting in a new sewer main and called us in to do our archaeological due diligence before proceeding. I can't believe I'm seeing it in one of its earliest manifestations."

The half-timbered building she referred to dominated that end of the street and the two wings were joined by an arch, which presumably lead into the courtyard and stables beyond.

"You can clearly see how they built the timbered structure onto of the remains of a Roman foundation, which is an amazing feat of non-engineering, when you think about it," Geri continued. "That timbered construction looks as though it belongs to a noble or maybe a wealthy merchant and must be only a few years old on this day. Oh my, how I wish I could show my students and colleagues this sight! Had I my phone, I'd take a picture right here. I dated it to 1263, by the way, and it looks like I wasn't too far off. We found a medieval shoe near what may have been a well in the courtyard. I—" She turned to point out approximately where she found the artifact and realized that she had been talking to herself. Morgana had disappeared.

"Witch!" she muttered under her breath.

"Good day, fair maiden! Why doth such a comely wench be about this day and wherefore art thou gazing at my abode with such interest?"

She looked up. The same wealthy man who had paused to watch the pig retrieval efforts earlier had arrived with his entourage. His two men, one of whom had dismounted Wilder to take his master's reins, were standing by watching with interest.

The lord was looking her up and down. She read his thoughts in a flash: his wife was off visiting relatives so it was a prime time for him to enjoy this tasty little thing while he was about his day. He longed to squeeze her breasts, damn him.

"Ranoulf," he called to one of his men. "Take this girl into the kitchen and feed her bread and honey."

"Yes, milord."

Come off your high horse, bastard. What if she hated bread and honey? She could be on a gluten-free diet for all he knew. Though seriously tempted to knock him off his mount, she decided to play the game. That would give her an inside view of this medieval mansion that she had previously known by its foundations alone. It was also an excellent time to test her disguise and protection skills since this bastard had plenty of bad intentions.

Flipping through her Middle English lexicon, she made like a poor flower girl and beamed at him with what she hoped were yellowed teeth. "Might ye wife like one of me posies, fine sir?" spoken in a Middle English manner. Holding up a bouquet of roadside flowers for the man to inspect, she waited to see how much courtesy he would afford this poor child.

The man dismounted and tossed Ranouf his horses' reins while Wilder stood by snorting and pawing the ground. At least the steed recognized her.

She shot a warning glance at the horse. *Shut your horsey gob.* The steed tossed its head as if to challenge her.

I saved your hide, remember? She had also put his hide at risk but hopefully these animals didn't have advanced reasoning skills.

Luckily, Wilder quieted while the other man lead both horses away, leaving Ranouf standing by with his master.

The lord whipped the flowers from Geri's hand, tossed them into the road and ground them into the dust with his boot heel. "My wife has a magnificent garden and has no need for such weeds. Go forth with my man to the kitchen and I will seek ye later. Ranouf, pray get the maid to give her a good scrub."

Obviously, a poor girl had no say in the matter.

"Aye, milord." Ranouf stood by waiting for Geri to follow him. Not a bad sort, Geri decided, sizing him up, but he'd do what he was told since his livelihood depended on it. He didn't agree with his master's dalliances and had aspirations to be a real knight some day.

It was at that moment that an image of four mounted monks popped into Geri's head like a sharp pain across her temple—on black steeds foaming at the mouth, faces deeply hidden behind dark cowls. Why the image came the way it did, she had no idea but possibly, just possibly, she had allowed her shield to waver for an instant. Damn! She strengthened her vision of the ring of light sealing her away from negative probings but simultaneously, she sensed that the monks still came.

A shock zipped through her spine. Could they find her? She looked in every direction as she followed Ranouf into the house but could see nothing behind her but a courtyard busy with women washing, somebody drawing well water, and others running errands.

Why were the monks still around if they believed she was already toast? Maybe they weren't the demons after all but every sense in her being told her that her initial instincts were accurate.

If Ware even suspected that she was still alive, everything was in danger of collapsing, including the plan to repair the Cosmati Pavement. And she could not risk putting out feelers to determine Ware's location without alerting him to her presence. Whatever the demon spawn were after, she could only hope it wasn't her.

"Pay, hurry, maiden," said her escort. "I shall taketh thee to the kitchens where ye will be treated well."

And on what experiences would he judge treating a poor girl well? No doubt he had mostly witnessed abuse of one kind or another inflicted about her class and station. The servants would probably treat her as they had been treated, which was not likely good by her standards. Besides, the master was only sweetening his afternoon dalliance. She knew he intended to take her in the hayloft with the horses standing by and perhaps allow the groom to have a go, too, since the lad had been working extra hard of late and the lord thought to reward him.

Geri briefly considered turning the lord's assets into a cocktail wienie but thought that too unkind even for her. Wasn't he behaving in socially acceptable ways for the time? The "Me, Too" movement was centuries away and women held little status here. But she wouldn't allow this nonsense to get that far. She'd just look around the mansion and leave.

"What be the lord's name?" Geri asked as she followed the servant. Tall and broad-shouldered, Ranouf was good knight material, if a little bandy-legged. At least his heart was in the right place.

"My master's name is Ricard Boniface, a most important man in the wool trade. Please him and ye shall be well rewarded. Perhaps he will giveth thou a place in his household."

Wouldn't that be a grand life for a young woman—a life of indentured servitude until pregnancy put her out into the street? "And how shall I please him, pray tell? I am but a poor flower girl promised to a good man to be married afore the winter comes."

Laying it on a bit thick, perhaps, but it was a kind of test. She witnessed how the man clenched his jaw as he ushered her into a dark room furnished with large tables and two monster-sized fireplaces suitable for roasting a boar in its entirety. The space was hot, smokey, and bound to lower the life expectancy of anyone who worked there, not that most people were assured of a long life in this century. She needed to get into the main house and soon. Could she pull off invisibility and still keep her protective layer in place?

"Wilda," Ranouf called, "This girl be the guest of our Lord Boniface. Pray, feed her milk and honey and bathe her."

Wilda, a dark-eyed girl with long lank hair tied in a knot under her scarf, looked up from the carrots she had been chopping. Her glower appeared permanently etched deep into the grooves around her mouth yet she couldn't be older than twenty-five. "Another, Ran? The last one did leave the house in tears. Said the master did fair beat her."

Ranouf shot her a warning look. "Our will is but to serve. Now do as thy are bid." With that he exited, leaving Geri in the company of Wilda and another, older, woman busy at the fireplace stirring something in a large pot.

"Sit ye down," ordered Wilda, pointing to a stool near the fire. "I will need to boil water now and with lunch nearing the ready, ye will be but an added chore."

The older woman turned from her stirring and pointed to Geri. "Make her do the work, Wilda. Put the kettle on, you."

Geri didn't have time for this. If the demon monks were near at hand, then she'd best focus on keeping her shield in good order, which might be a challenge when Boniface attempted to rape her. Best that she exit the stage now.

"I must use the chamber pot," Geri said, still standing.

Both women turned to stare at her, at which point she remembered that the term "chamber pot" was a thing of the future. "I need to pee," she clarified. Surely that term was suitable but, just in case, she added several others, including the good old Anglo-Saxon version.

What felt like sharp nails began stabbing her temples. Something evil this way comes.

"Well go on, then. Go behind the stable and be quick about it," said Wilda.

That was Geri's cue to bolt and bolt she did, straight out of the kitchen into the courtyard and headlong into Ricard Boniface and the toxic vapors of the demon monks.

Chapter Fifteen

Coughing and choking, Geri fell to her knees while imagining a strong, impenetrable cone of light surrounding her person. "Oh, I pray thee good monks, protect me against this wicked lord who doth desirest to ravish me!"

"What nonsense is this!" cried Boniface. "As if I would but touch a creature so foul. Pay her no heed, brethren, for she speaketh lies."

"Fear not, good sir. We seeketh a woman who may pray for refuge under thy roof," said one demon brother.

"And what woman would that be? Surely not this. I found her wandering around upon the street beyond my door selling wayside weeds," said Boniface.

"You spied whom we seek with thine own eyes not long ago when she stole thy horse. That hag is much older and corporal in bearing—a witch, she be."

"That witch, say you? Brethren, I hath heard that thou didst burn the thief just days past. Be that true?"

"T'is true but such creatures be most devious in nature so we continue the search to be assured she be dead. Rise ye, girl."

Every nerve in Geri's body tingled at the edge of her protective field. She dreaded looking at the demons directly in case that alone would be enough to reveal her true identity. For now, groveling put her at eye level with their clawed feet, which were overlaid with an image of leather shoes, masking what they wanted no one to see.

"He said rise, wench." When Boniface jerked up by her hood, she kept her eyes lowered as would any modest maid of the day. "Would I touch this?" said

Boniface, "an unwashed creature of low birth?' He gave her a little shake and tossed her back to her knees in the dust.

She felt a chill on her arm as one of the demons lifted her back to standing and said in a silky voice: "Doth thou fear this man, sister? Hath thou need of our protection? Lift thine eyes to mine."

It was all she could do not to cringe, yet to refuse the demon's request could give her away. She sent an urgent image to her shield, feigning fear of retribution, making herself quake as if nothing but the wrath of God and man made her tremble while behind that layer she imagined only blankness.

Slowly, she looked up through stinging tears while suppressing the shivering that threatened to wrack her body. That much was real. Gazing deep into those recesses this creature masqueraded as eyes almost undid her. The thing knew nothing of love and kindness, nothing of humanity, in fact, but fed on pain and despair. The smoldering red pits hidden inside the face of an ordinary man promised endless grief and it took all her concentration to push back innocence and visions of sunny fields, hope, and laughter.

The demon prodded along the premier of her defenses like an icy tong probing soft tissue, before backing suddenly away. "Come, brethren, there is nothing for us here. She be of no interest."

Geri sagged in relief but still called out: "Pray, doth bide awhile and protect me from this man," hoping her ruse would garner her more credence.

One non-monk nearly smirked at that. "Hold thy tongue, woman, and obey thy good master. We have work to attend."

No sooner had they strode from the courtyard (actually, they lumbered out under the arch like a bunch of orangutans but the ordinary eye saw otherwise), when Boniface swung on Geri and slapped her hard. Her vision briefly blackened as she fell to the dust.

"Thou dare insult me to those men of Christ? Did I not bid my man to care for thee yet thee cry that I would ravish thou?"

Geri was seeing stars. Never before had she been hit by anyone and to have such inflicted on her centuries before she was born was just too much. She flew to her feet, so angry that the air crackled around her, and in one burst of fury, she changed Boniface's appendage into a cocktail weenie and added a side of mustard for good measure.

He cried out, clutching his groin in dismay as yellow goo oozed from under his tunic and ran down his hose. All around, the servants stood by in stunned amazement.

"What hath thou done to me?" Boniface cried.

"What, you want Dijon now, maybe a side of relish?" she yelled back, one hand pressed to her throbbing cheek.

"T'is her, t'is the witch!" someone cried out.

"It be she! Grab her!" cried another.

Geri started to run, realizing that she was on foot and probably back inside her own body, too. And what would be the result of that fit of temper? Probably demon monks thundering down on her heels. She may have exposed herself to Ware, and every other demon spawn, besides. Damn, damn, damn! Temper had aways been an issue.

By the time she had stumbled out into the street and looked down at herself, she realized that, no, she still appeared as the nubile maid which she had been when she began this walkabout. That hardly made any difference since everyone had witnessed her doing something to Boniface. And then there was the little matter of springing to her feet in a totally creepy way. Yes, they'd cry witch, all right.

She needed an escape hatch. Standing in the middle of the street, by-passers and wayfarers began to circle her as Boniface and his servants came thundering out from the courtyard.

"Grab the witch!" cried Boniface still clutching his crotch. "She did maim my person, grab her, I say!"

But the crowd had no stomach for witch-grabbing, especially if she might work a spell on one of them.

"Stop your bleating," Geri called to Boniface. "Your appendage will return to normal in a few days but you'll continue to lure young maidens into your lair, won't you? You should be the one punished for I was not the first woman you tried to snare, is it not so?" She spoke in the language of the time and gained some satisfaction as all eyes turned to Boniface. Her words rang true to many, she knew. The neighbors had seen plenty and not all of them approved of the man's treatment of wives and daughters.

"Ranouf, bring her to heel!" The master was so red-faced and incensed by now that he could barely spit out the words. "Bring her back under my roof!"

Geri glanced at the young man as he broke from the clutch of gaping servants and strode forward. A hush descended the crowd. Ranouf would attempt to do as he was told and there was no way that she wanted to hurt him.

When he was just steps away, she addressed him in a low voice. "Ranoulf, change masters while you can because soon your lord will ask you to kill an innocent man. You will refuse, and he will not grant you a reference as a result. But a lord will visit Boniface within the week. Ask him if he will take you on as squire. That will be a good career move for you, though you think yourself too old to apply. In truth, you are not. Now, if you'll excuse me, I have the world to save. I'm one of the good guys, by the way."

Ranouf stood dumbstruck as something like an electrical storm whipped around Geri's feet. It took a great draw on her resources to suck herself upwards in a sparkly cloud—and maybe she used more special effects than what was strictly necessary, but she figured that those poor sods needed a bit of entertainment.

Seconds later, she landed on a faraway hill. She had no idea where she'd landed and at the moment, didn't care. Though exhausted, look what she had accomplished! She'd held her disguise against the evil brethren and rescued herself unassisted while working a little side spell while at it. Her Eddy self had been on demand and that left her tingling with jubilation. She was getting better at the magic thing.

"Finished congratulating yourself?"

She swung around. There stood Morgana on the hilltop, the wind blowing the long red hair about her face and sending her cloak into a purple sail behind her body. She was back to being beautiful.

"Where were you when I needed you?" Geri demanded but then just as quickly she answered her own question. "You were there the whole time."

"I was," Morgana sat down beside her, "and you sensed it but decided to go forth in your own headstrong manner, as usual."

"Nevertheless, I kept my shield in place while the demon spawn looked directly at me and managed to extract myself without losing a limb. Did you like the cocktail weeny spell? I'm rather proud of that."

"The mustard was a bit overdone," Morgana said with a laugh. "Now stop congratulating yourself and consider that any time magic is used in the realm, Ware will sense its presence, send forth feelers, to track magic to the the magician. He may not yet know your exact location, but will see that your signature is active. He will find you now as may others."

"There was a man back there, a tinker, who claimed that he could smell a witch."

Morgana looked away. "Yes, there are those with that ability in this age. Magic has a scent if one's senses can but detect it. A good shield should guard you against all sensory perceptions. It seems that you allowed yours to waver."

They sat for a few minutes admiring the view while Geri wondered where exactly she had landed. The surrounding mountainous terrain looked nothing like England, let alone London, but it was wildly beautiful. Maybe she should have been more precise in her imaginings?

"Yes, I agree, Geri, you should have thought clearly where you wanted to land."

"Will you stop reading my mind?"

"As long as you fail to guard your thoughts, I will read them, and what is the issue? I know more about you than you do about yourself, at least where your past existences are concerned."

Geri sighed. "Yes, well, all right, so I come from an age of spyware so i really should be used to that kind of intrusion. We think we have a bad situation with electronic trackings and online bots in the 21st century but we don't know anything."

Morgana stared at her. "I do not even know what that means."

"If you never visit my century, you'll never find out. Why don't you visit, by the way?"

"Too much foul air, dirt, and disease. I landed once very briefly seeking you and could not bear the sights and sounds that assaulted me—metal flying machines, hard-sided mechanisms that flew down the roads spewing toxic fumes, buildings as tall as mountains with none of the beauty. A horrid place. I no sooner had I landed in my cat form than I was flattened by a huge metal beast carrying multiple people. I vowed then never to return."

"So you were killed by a bus when manifested as a cat but instantly returned to life as yourself in another century?"

"My cat form wasn't real and neither was I, by your definition, so yes, I returned here. Existence is multidimensional as is time itself, as you have been informed many times. Now, let us stop the chatter and consider next steps. Ware knows that you live still but not that your powers have increased. No doubt he believes that it was I who rescued you yet again. I believe that together we have left a confusing mess of tracks in the magic realm that he will have great difficulty in deciphering. This gives us time to build our shields in preparation for tomorrow's ride."

"Won't he sense us when we approach the Abbey since he has it so well warded?"

"Perhaps, but our task will to design a shield strong enough to deflect his probing, at least long enough for you to enter the Abbey undetected, rescue your daughter, and jump into the Cosmati Pavement with Petrus."

"Why do you refer to Lin as my daughter? She's not my daughter." But she stopped and stared. "Oh, no, don't tell me that she *is* my daughter the way you are my sister."

Morgana smiled. "For one so intelligent, it does take you awhile to reach the correct conclusions."

Geri gazed off into the distance, all misty blue hills edged with white-capped blue ocean. "Damn. Why didn't I realize this sooner? And I suppose that Petrus is Lin's father?"

"I am relieved that you finally understand."

But it was almost too much for her to get her mind around at the moment. Of course, theoretically she believed in the six degrees of separation theory but across multiple centuries and in the midst of a time-travel event? No, she needed to shelve this along with everything else she'd had yet to get her mind around. At the moment, she had more pressing matters to deal with.

"In order to rescue Lin, I must stage a distraction, something that will keep Ware occupied while I make my way to the Pyx Chamber. Pardon me for a moment while I see how both of them are getting along."

She paused long enough to delve into her mind, seeking Lin, finding the girl attempting to kick out at a hell dog snarling at her feet. The girl was growing weak, the beast remaining too strong. Ware kept her bound and gagged by magic while feeding her just enough to keep her alive long enough to enjoy her when he had time. The girl didn't need to be her daughter for the sight of such abuse to cause her to seethe with rage.

"What does that beast plan to do with her?" Geri whispered.

"You know the answer. Let me just say that the girl will be altered to the core when he finishes with her, her spirit broken, her soul deeply wounded. Some souls become so marred by the pain inflicted upon them that they can never recover and sink to the depths of the very evil they once fought."

"That won't happen, if I can help it, and help it I will." Geri said fiercely. Her inner vision switched next to Petrus who now worked with two other men to set the outer mosaic pieces into hexagons. The Pavement was nearing completion. The final piece—the center roundel—was to be laid on the morrow and the hole where it would be placed still gaped like a blind eye gazing into space. Her heart did some ridiculous flutter thing at the sight of him but she remained firmly fixed on the issue.

Though Petrus had designed the schemata long before the laying of the tiles, she knew how critical it was that each slice of stone be placed exactly as required. To that end, he stood by to guide his masons to lay each accordingly. Tingling hit Geri's spine at the sight of him and as she gazed, she saw him pause and turn his head slightly as if to acknowledge her observation. She felt a chill in the air around him and pulled quickly back.

"Ware has Petrus under his thumb," she gasped. "I still can't believe that a wizard of his strength can be so bound by Ware's will."

"Petrus walks a delicate balance when laying a floor of this power," Morgana replied. "The balance of good and evil is always at war. Every bit of Petrus's strength must be vested into the Cosmati Pavement at the critical moment of its placement, which is now and tomorrow. Your presence both intensifies his capacity yet simultaneously distracts him. He let his protective aura slip so you could escape Ware and that gave the bastard the opportunity to enslave him. The Evil One plans to kill Petrus when the floor explodes tomorrow morning and that could be the ultimate blow."

"Explodes?" Geri gasped, turning to the woman. "Explode as in kaboom?"

"Shatter, then, completely destabilizing the portal so that evil can tip the balance and rule the cosmos. The effects are already apparent in your century. All that is good clings to the precipice by its fingernails. This you know for you have seen it with your own eyes. You must help Petrus shore up the Pavement and restore some measure of the balance. That is your task."

"Yet you can't tell me how I am to go about this massive feat?"

"That's not my role, but yours."

"Well, thank you very much."

"You will figure it out, Geri. Some things cannot be gleaned until we are deep into the thick of it."

Geri gazed at her dimly-remembered sister. "Always the encouraging one, aren't you?"

"Always the truth-speaker, remember?"

Geri searched her memory for the wisps of recall and was rewarded by glimpses of a woman wearing different faces over many centuries telling her things she didn't want to hear. "All my life I have studied time from the back end as what I call an 'underground operative'. Now I must shore up the past to preserve the future. The irony isn't lost on me." Turning away, she stared into the distance. "All righty, then, let's get started."

"First, we prepare for the ride."

Chapter Sixteen

"Why ride? Why not simply appear at the Abbey at the appointed time?" Geri asked, thinking, that if one could work magic, why not level up?

"Because of the amount of energy it would require to do so would drain us both."

"Yes, of course. I am quite exhausted already." Geri fell back on the grass to stare up at the clouds. "And I must conserve my batteries for the big event tomorrow."

"Exactly and so must I. I will use whatever is needed to deliver you to the Abbey safely."

"Perfect, thank you." Geri stared up at the sky. One cloud formation just above her head appeared as a herd of galloping horses. For a moment, she considered that it might actually be a herd of galloping horses until she assured herself that even in this world, some things were exactly as they seemed. "However, riding for miles on a lumpy horse will no doubt exhaust me in a different manner."

"We will not take lumpy horses but will travel by coach, a conjuring of my making while you recharge your batteries, as you say."

"Excellent." But the whole thing was hardly excellent, to her way of thinking. After all, she had no blueprint as to how she was to do any of the cosmos-saving events the next day. The risks were huge and the chance of failing huger still. And what experience did she have to draw on except her instincts? Never had she felt simultaneously so old and so young. Always, she had been the sage on the stage.

"There is a great deal for you to learn very quickly, Geri. and it is not possible for me to teach you everything in so short a time."

"So I gathered. Surely you can read the future and know whether I'm going to succeed or fail tomorrow? Each time I attempt to gain a sense of things to come, all I see is blackness."

Morgana stared at her. "As do I."

"You, too? That is not how I believe a prophecy works most of the time but, admittedly, this is a big one. Most predictions speak of an event that will occur in the future but in the case of the end of time, the outcome can't be foretold in exact dates like an appointment. The end of the world is not yet booked, in other words. I take that as a hopeful sign."

Morgana's forehead briefly creased before smoothing like satin in an instant. "How can the end of the world ever be a hopeful sign?"

"Because there's wiggle-room embedded right in Petrus's baffling verse: *each that follows triples the years before.* What does that mean when one speaks of tripling the lifespan of a species that rarely remains fixed across the ages? Look at humans, for instance. Our lifetimes have nearly doubled since this century alone. That's why Petrus used all those befuddling references to adding up the ages of sea monsters and the like. The Cosmati Prophecy is more of a warning than a proclamation."

"It is designed to be approached like a maze that requires all parts of one's being to find the way free. That is all I know." Morgana fell silent for a moment.

Geri sat quietly beside her, studying the strange feelings that suddenly assaulted her at the sound of Petrus's name. It took a moment before she could pick through them and realize that she was reading Morgana. Finally, she said: "How well do you know him, sis?"

"You know the answer to that."

And she did. "I want to hear you admit it."

"Geri, you cannot expect a man who has lived for hundreds of years not to have had a paramour or two along the way. Especially when his true love is busy in another century. You were not the only one but you are still the one and only; do you understand?"

Geri turned away. "Of course, I understand. And, I hardly know the man, or at least, I am only now remembering how well I know him. But still, to have him fool around with my own sister?" She waved her hand. "Never mind, Morgana. Having the weight of the world on my shoulders is a bigger issue right now."

"You will succeed because you must."

"It's that simple, is it? Let's fix on practicalities for the moment. Tell me this: how will we safely arrive at Westminster Abbey in a coach, which is still a slow and laborious method of travel even for those supposedly comfy sitting inside? Ware will be watching every road heading for the Abbey." She paused. "I know that we will be disguised."

"Obviously. Ware will have the roads watched by his demons, whom you've already deceived once so we'll assume that you can do so again. There will be hundreds of travelers to London as the King has announced a feast day to celebrate the completion of the Sacred Pavement tomorrow. Anything that smacks of the holy gives these poor souls an opportunity to take a break from their laborious lives and have a bit of fun. Some will take it as a kind of pilgrimage and if they are able, pour into London to enjoy the treats King Henry will provide."

"King Henry will provide treats?" Geri asked.

"He will have his men toss alms into the crowd, which will cause the poor to go scrabbling in the dust to fight over a handful of coin—hardly worth the effort but when one is desperate, one grasps at every opportunity. The King will feel beneficent because he has given something to his people even if it be but a token and then only to the fortunate few. To him, it will be this great Abbey which he sees as his true legacy and his gift to the people."

"Providing one is Catholic. Everyone else will be persecuted in this age, especially the Jews who have already been forced to empty their coffers or else— and don't even get me started on the Muslims." Geri pushed herself up to sitting. The sun was setting over the headland and she felt chilled to the bone.

"True enough but what Petrus has created in the Cosmati Pavement involves all beings, regardless of religion."

"The universal principles of sacred geometry." Geri stared off into the distance, considering. What she could tell Randall about this experience, if she ever saw him again, that is. And Lin, she had her whole life ahead of her, or so she desperately hoped. Geri sat back down on the grass imagining a comfy pillow under her bottom until she finally felt moderate comfort. "Tell me more about you and Petrus. Spare me the details since I'm getting enough of that going on in my head. Sometimes I think I've inadvertently dialed into a porn channel."

"Enough talk. We must sleep deeply in preparation for tomorrow."

"Do you mean as in take a power nap?" But before Geri could hear the answer, presuming Morgana even gave one, she fell deeply asleep, awaking what seemed like seconds later.

"What's with these magic sleeps?" she demanded, bolting upright on the grass. "One minute I'm in the midst of a thought and the next I've tumbled over the velvet cliff. I didn't even have time to yawn!"

"I put you under a sleeping spell," Morgana explained beside her, "cocooning us both in a safety net until the daybreak."

Geri blinked. What she had seen as a sunset seconds before was actually the break of day? "I hate that! Never do it again without my express permission. At least give me the dignity of controlling my own brain."

"I apologize," Morgana said. "I am perhaps too aware of the need for haste and did not give enough consideration to your feelings."

"Apology accepted." Geri turned back to stare at the hills. "I do feel considerably refreshed, though. Where are we, anyway?"

"I believe that you call this place Scotland."

"Scotland?" Geri stiffened. "I sent myself to Scotland?"

"What were you thinking of when you willed yourself away?"

"*Outlander*, one of my favorite books when I was younger. I was thinking, *what would Claire do at a time like this*? Not that I had a standing stone's hope in hell of touching a magical Scottish rock in the midst of a London street but it was all done in such a hurry. Surely we don't have to travel by horse all the way to London? We'd never make it in time."

"Of course not." Morgana got to her feet. "I will magic us to the Roman road just north of London where we will join the traffic making their way to the Abbey. Come, take my hand."

Geri reached out, a shock coursing through her system at the moment of contact. Seconds later, she found herself dressed in a black robe sitting beside a much younger lady swathed in velvets and furs.

"You made me into a nun?" she cried, touching the wimple that rode her head

"Hush!" Morgana warned. "There are ears everywhere and, yes, I have made you a nun," she whispered fiercely. "What better way to gain entrance to the Abbey as one of the elite guests? Anyone not on the King's list at the door will be forced to wait until the guests take all the seats and then will be made to stand in the nave, if they are granted entry at all. Besides, at least you're a Gilbertine Canoness."

Geri leaned back in the seat. "That's some consolation, admittedly, since the Order is just obscure enough that not every sundry personage in Britain will know of it. Established by the Countess of Essex, if I recall correctly."

"Yes, and my identity as your companion puts me from the house of de Vere, the family who founded the Chicksands."

"All right, good for you, so this was—is—one of the wealthiest Gilbertine orders in Britain at the time—I mean, now, as in this time here, the thirteenth century. Will I ever get used to this?—And wealthy despite their vows of poverty. Anyway, Archbishop Thomas Beckett hid out there during the King Henry II debacle a few decades ago, did you know that?"

"Hush!" Morgana warned.

Geri glowered, running her hands down her woolen gown. "Being a canoness doesn't make this gear any less itchy."

Whatever they were sitting in began to move. She realized that they were seated in what appeared to be a velvet-lined box with two leather chairs each positioned beside a curtained window. The front was open and ahead she could see the rear ends of two horses. "We're in a two horse-powered cart. Top of the line, I see."

"As best as existed in the thirteenth century. I modeled this one on The Luttrell Psalter, which is a bit of a later model and much smaller, but I knew you'd complain if I provided anything less."

"Indeed I would. Who's driving this thing?"

"The driver sits just above the opening ahead but not in our line of sight. He is not real."

Geri closed her eyes to see the illusion using her inner vision: sunshine illuminating the coach's exterior with her inner vision: wooden, richly painted in vining swirls with a border of blue along the bottom edge. Two fine horses drew the cart driven by a man who looked to be made of vapor. Before she could study the details more carefully, she was briefly distracted by the sheer number of other vehicles on the road. Besides horses and foot traffic, there were many coaches, litters, and carts, including those more ornate than theirs.

"Isn't ours a bit luxurious for a canoness?" she asked.

"It is the litter of my husband, Lord de Hewitt, and as the youngest daughter of a count—that's my late father and your husband, by the way—I will travel in nothing less. You as my noble mother, doth travel in style also."

"How can I be your mother and a nun, too? Oh, wait: I entered the convent upon my husband's death and quickly rose to this exalted state no doubt because of the generous contributions to the convent made on behalf of my husband's estate, but what about my children?"

"You have two, both daughters, both married off at twelve years of age. I am your eldest, mother. May I call you 'mommy'?" she asked with a smirk.

"Don't even try." Geri drew back the curtain beside her and peered out, squinting into the sunlight. Beside them on eye level was a lovely male leg encased in chain links. Her gaze traveled upwards to their owner, a mounted knight with a long grey beard who upon seeing the curtain open, called down in French:

"Good day to you, good Mother. Be you away to the Abbey this fine morning?"

Geri squinted up and smiled, taking in the long-faced man at whom she couldn't help but stare. The knight was dressed in a white wool tunic emblazoned with a red cross that clearly denoted him as a member of the Order of the Knights Templar. All the mystery that surrounded these incredibly powerful and wealthy knights, all the study she had invested into their movements in Britain in her younger years, and here she was face-to-face with the genuine article. And, to make the sight even more awesome, this one appeared to be shimmering. She was so star-struck, she could hardly speak.

"I be John de Ferres from Temple Church. And from which convent be thee from, my good Mother?" the man continued.

She mustered her best French accent. "From the Chicksands Priory, my goodly knight," she stammered.

"A noble holy house, indeed," said the Templar with a gracious nod.

Morgana leaned over and beamed the man a beatific smile. "Do pardon the Canoness, my mother, most noble knight, for as a member of the Gilbertine order, she hath taken an oath of reduced discourse with strangers." *Not that anything could keep this one quiet for long* came the voice inside Geri's head. She swore that the knight's lips twitched as if he had heard the silent remark.

"Pardon me," the knight said, nodding. "I shall not disturb thee further," and he proceeded to trot off, Geri leaning out far enough to see that he was accompanied by at least twelve other knights of his Order before Morgana pulled her back.

"What?" she asked Morgana crossly.

"Do not stare. No canoness would behave so."

"But they're Templars! Don't you get that? The Templars are like the rock stars of history!"

"Rock stars?" Morgana asked, "What are rock stars?"

Geri turned back in her seat and stared straight ahead. "Do drop by my century someday when I can explain it better over a cup of tea or a swill of ale, your choice. Here's the short story: the Templars have an almost mythical air to them in my century—possible keepers of the Holy Grail, hoarders of vast treasures, one of the original elite fighting forces—on it goes. In my century, rock stars are like enormously famous bards who people idolize as if they were the religious figures in this century. They inspire icon-like objects, relics, great festivals, the whole show."

"But bards are mere entertainers. We enjoy them well enough but why would they be so exalted?"

Geri sighed. "As I said, you need to visit my century—I mean really visit my century. I'll put you up in a spare bedroom—to understand how our need for heroes has manifested in peculiar ways. Trying to explain that is challenging. And by the way, John de Ferrers is a wizard. Did you see his aura?"

"You will see many of magical powers here. A Templar so enhanced is not surprising as they have been amazingly successful in their endeavors. Currently they hold favor of both pope and king."

"Well, they will rather run out of luck in the next century."

They carried on without speaking for what seemed like hours while the coach's jostling made Geri's stomach queasy. It had to be nerves, among other things, she thought. Was she really up to the challenge that lay ahead, especially since she had no idea what exactly lay ahead? "Are we there yet? That's a joke, by the way."

Morgana sighed. "I know it's a joke, Geri, but I don't understand why it is funny, nor do I ever when you make jests and, yes, we will soon reach our destination. Do you see how the traffic slows?"

"Definitely slower." Geri pulled back the curtains again and saw with some relief that the foot traffic had thickened. She watched in amazement as a juggler strode past tossing balls in the air while a bard strummed on his lute nearby. Others dressed in their best clothes and smocks traveled on, chatting and laughing while still others whistled or sang. It was like Chaucer's *Canterbury Tales* manifested.

Geri pulled back. "So, tell me, what happens after we arrive?"

"We will leave the coach and proceed towards the Abbey. Our names are so listed on the roll as honored guests so we will be seated close to the altar. One of our servants that I have yet to manifest will announce our arrival to the herald when we reach the door. We cannot approach the Abbey directly without our servants present though they must wait outside."

"Protocol, protocol," Geri murmured.

"It's important that we not draw attention to ourselves. Once inside, we will enter the Abbey and take our places. After that, I have no idea." Morgana touched Geri's hand. "Are you ready for this?"

"Certainly not," Geri told her, "but I'll just dig in and figure it out as I go, won't I?"

Their wagon was making slow progress, moving along bit by bit. "Yes, you will," Morgana said with a nod. "You must. I will remain close and if there is anything I can do to help, I shall." The couch lurched to a halt. "We have arrived. The Abbey door lies ahead but no doubt the demon monks are watching the entrance."

"The first thing I must do is release Lin," Geri declared, more to herself than Morgana. That would mean gathering all her power to break down the Pyx door, wrestle the hell dogs, and release the prisoner, and, really, if she couldn't manage that much, she was hardly up for the rest of the challenge, was she?

"However, if you break down the Pyx door, Ware will surely detect your presence and know that you are inside the Abbey."

Geri swung to Morgana. "Would you please stop reading my mind?"

"Quickly, look ahead."

Geri turned to look beyond the horses. Westminster Abbey rose above the heads of the crowd, much closer than she had expected. Focusing her inner sight more acutely, she peered ahead. Shock hit her spine at the sight of the hell monks barricading the Abbey, looking to the casual eye like a brethren of greeters. There were thousands of them teeming about the foundations like a churning storm, invisible to all but the gifted.

"Damn! How do I get through that lot?" Swinging to Morgana, she asked: "Can you create a distraction?"

A slow smile crossed her sister's lips. "Distraction is one of my many skills."

"Wonderful. I'll leave that to you, then" and with that, Geri lifted the latch and jumped from the coach.

* * *

There were people—and demons—everywhere amid the festivities. A trio dressed in yellow tunics and multicolored hose strolled by playing lutes and flutes, laughing and playing jokes on every passerby. One man tooted a crumhorn in her face and then swiftly apologized accompanied by much bowing and clapping.

"Many pardons, Holy Mother, for I did not mean to frighten thee."

"Yes, you did, you scallawag. Be off with thee!" Did they even use that term in this century? She lifted up the hem of her robe and steered through the crowd, head down and hidden beneath her wimple while keeping one eye fixed on the rising spire of Westminster Abbey ahead.

Then her feet sank up to her ankles in goo and she nearly toppled over. A force of some kind was swirling around her feet as if she had just been caught up in a riptide of sludge. Eddys and undercurrents snaked around, tugging at her focus, attempting to knock her off-balance.

She knew at once what was happening: entities were probing her field. These were like random feelers—paranormal bots scouring the crowd for magic creatures. Crowds were a seething maelstrom of energies, both positive and negative, through which Geri must navigate. After a moment, she intensified her wards, sending zaps in all directions before plowing on.

Behind her somebody screamed. A quick glimpse over her shoulder revealed what looked to be Morgana—or at least Morgana in disguise—screaming as her gown leapt into flames. Morgana was using herself as a decoy? No, no, no. Geri's first impulse was to rush to her aid but that would be foolish. She needed to get on with the job and let her sister complete her performance.

Resolve fortified, she focused on the path ahead and waded through the crowd, part of which was now pouring back to watch the spectacle. Most people kept her canoness persona at a respectful distance, all but a small black creature that looked like a miniature gargoyle, that is. Geri noticed the thing dogging her heels when she glanced behind her and now all her super senses told her that it was a demon that had somehow latched onto her witchy scent.

That wasn't good. How could she penetrate the Abbey without that thing calling the alarm or, worse still, maybe it already had? There was nothing to do but soldier on. Maybe seconds before she entered the Abbey, she could turn and zap the thing but for now, there were more worrisome things to keep her occupied.

That evil fog encircling the Abbey, for instance. She was shocked at the sheer number of creatures that roamed inside that toxic mist. Besides the demon monks, creatures like the gargoyle she'd spied that first night in the Abbey and the one that followed her now, there were wicked twisted things that defied description—alien beasts? All prowled inside the sludge waiting for something to tear apart. It would be at Ware's command, though some of the creatures could be programed to detect any enemy whose defenses wavered. Geri suspected that the creature at her heels was sniffing down a whiff of magic so faint, that it was merely stalking her for more information.

Meanwhile, Westminster's great wooden doors yawned open, flanked on either side by greeting monks, some with halos, some with horns. Several brethren not on Team Ware appeared to be rubbing their temples while mustering fleeting smiles at the visiting dignitaries—bishops, wealthy landowners and nobles alike—as if it was all they could do to hold up their heads. King Henry was already inside, comfortably seated on his throne while the Abbey readied for the big event but Geri knew that everyone would be feeling the effects of Ware's poison including the king himself. Every citizen inside and near to the Abbey was beginning to sicken.

Behind her, Morgana's distraction was going up in flames—literally. Geri sensed that her sister would continue to power up the display proportionally to Geri's need for a diversion yet nothing seemed to be luring the demons away. They eyed the ruckus suspiciously but made no move to investigate further. With all that festering goo sticking so close to the Abbey and at her heels, Geri worried whether her shield could hold up.

As soon as she stepped into that murk without an escort, Team Ware might detect her magic but that was a chance she would have to take. Would the gate-keepers let her in?

And then a scream hit Geri between the eyes. She swung around, searching for the source while simultaneously realizing that the cry came from inside her head. In an instant, she saw Lin caught in a mammoth struggle with one of her demon keepers. The girl was thrashing with the beasts while trying to escape her prison.

Geri spun on her heels and began to dash up the walkway, pushing past the guests lining up for entry. She knew that going to the entrance without an escort was a bad idea. She knew that Ware must be looking out for her. She knew all that and yet still she ran headlong into the devil's jaws.

Chapter Seventeen

S uddenly, she spied a potential ally. John de Ferrers was standing with twelve other Templars close to the Abbey doors. Geri hastened towards him, nodding to everyone with her hands in prayer mode. Surely the waiting dignitaries would not stop a poor canoness from pushing ahead of the line? They didn't.

"My good knight, I beseech thee to offer me your assistance," she cried, once reaching the Templar.

Taking him by the arm, she stared straight into his blue eyes. *I am a witch and you are a wizard and I need your help—the world needs our help.* And in a flash of fleeting visions, she filled him in on what was unfolding inside the Abbey and beyond. She posted images of a horned Ware, portrayed the Cosmati floor crumbling even in the process of its creation, and revealed Lin being attacked by the hell dogs. De Ferres grasped it all in an instant. Geri had no doubt that the knight already suspected that something evil was afoot.

"Hail thee ahead," he called out to the gate-keeping monks. "The Canoness doth feel faint. Pray, clear the path!"

With that, he took Geri's arm and steered her through the doors while Geri kept her eyes cast down and a hand pressed to her forehead.

One of the horned gatekeepers made to block their entrance but John de Ferrers gave the creature such a withering look that it visibly cringed. It didn't hurt that de Ferrers was a member of one of the most feared and respected fighting orders of his time, one that had the backing of both king and pope, or that he was in the company of fellow knights, all looking equally armed and dangerous—a Medieval S.W.A.T. team if there ever was one. Even a demon couldn't challenge him in full view of the citizens without causing a scene.

De Ferrers led Geri deeper into the shadowy Abbey unchallenged as if seeking somewhere for the Canoness to lay her head. Immediately, a posse of brothers scrambled up to assist, some but not all of the normal variety. While they swarmed around, Geri swiftly probed the surrounding darkness, alarmed at the thick toxic vapors attacking those waiting for the ceremony to begin.

So many people were seated or standing facing the altar, candles burning everywhere, the scent of evil so thick that she nearly choked on the phlegm. The life was slowly leaching out from many of those gathered. Geri could feel it though they remained unaware. Maybe they thought their sudden exhaustion was due to stale air, the incense—anything but the truth.

But then she felt Petrus as a glowing source of light and beside him, a hole of impenetrable darkness. Petrus and Ware standing together at the altar? It was as if they were caught in an invisible stand-off, each unable to move from the other's orbit, struggling to remain in sync. No, Geri realized—only Petrus was attempting to keep the balance while Ware was weighing down his side to the tipping point. Geri felt the struggle like a constriction around her windpipe.

Ware must have believed that he had conquered his adversary only to discover that Petrus held power still. To the average observer, they were only the Abbot and the chief mason standing side by side before the beginning of the great ceremony. To beings with the sight, they were readying for a great battle. At least that struggle might hold Ware's focus long enough for her to rescue Lin.

But where was Lin? Geri tried to glimpse her through the thickening fog but could see nothing. Her anxiety spiked, prompting her to mentally scream into the Templar's head: *Quickly, John! The ceremony will soon begin and we must free Lin! Get me to the Infirmary!* The Infirmary was on the way to the Pyx Chamber and the best chance she had to get to Lin's prison unseen. She hoped that Ware was so busy struggling with Petrus that her safe passage might be possible. Meanwhile, de Ferres was leading the charge.

"Pray, brethren, thy assistance is needed," the Templar told the posse of monks. "We must take the Canoness to the infirmary to recover for she doth feel faint!"

Geri studied the four approaching brethren. Some she recognized but where they had been ordinary Benedictine brethren only hours before, now those same men sprouted horns. They had been possessed! Only one brother in the group remained uncorrupted—Brother Stephan from the infirmary.

Immediately, two of the brethren including Brother Stephan and one horned monk, rushed to assist Geri, intending, she realized, to carry her by the feet and shoulders down the hall to the infirmary. At least that got her away from the crowd and, being horizontal, out of sight of Ware.

The demon monk took her by the ankles and Brother Stephan lifted her by the shoulders while the other monks returned to their posts. She allowed them to carry her down the corridor accompanied on either side by four Templars while she fought off the numbing sensation resulting from the demon's touch. She desperately hoped that the creature could not detect her powers. Its intention might be to ultimately poison her once she was safely in the infirmary since most of the human guests were already falling ill.

They were halfway down the north transept and away from the altar when Geri heard a growl somewhere near her now-frozen feet—the demon scout had followed her in and now trotted beside the devil monk. An instant of communication passed between the two demons that Geri felt rather than saw.

Before she could respond, de Ferres had drawn his sword and hacked at the gargoyle while the demon monk let out a high-pitched squeal inaudible to human ears. It was an alarm. Geri kicked out at the demon that gripped her ankles while demanding that Brother Stephan put her down immediately. The moment her shoulders touched the tiles, she zapped the demon monk between the eyes, vaporizing him on the spot.

"Brother George!" cried Brother Stephan, aghast as he witnessed the man he believed to be his brother turn to ash. "What hath thou done, Canoness?"

"He's not Brother George but a demon infiltrator," Geri told him but had no time to explain further, "and I'm not a canoness. Quick, hide! The Abbot Ware is not what he seems and evil consumes the Abbey!"

With that she tried to scramble down the hall towards the Pyx Chamber, found her feet too numb to move, and nearly toppled onto her face. In seconds, John de Fares had hoisted her back to standing.

"Who be this girl that we shall now rescue?" he asked.

"My daughter who came through with me from the twenty-first century," she told him, struggling to find her balance.

"Twenty-first century?" he asked, surprise lifting his otherwise severe features.

So the Templar was not a time-traveller, then? Interesting, but she didn't have time to press him for details. "Thank you for your assistance, John de Ferres. Much appreciated. Must be off." He'd done enough already. The rest was her battle.

And with that, she made herself invisible and floated towards the Pyx Chamber, sensing a dark army gathering at her back. A jolt of fear hit. The scout had sounded the alarm, meaning that Ware now knew that she was near. Though he could not leave his post to tackle Geri, he had enough toxic minions to do the job in his stead.

Her head was spinning with no time to consider how to protect herself while simultaneously breaking down the Pyx door and battling the demons inside. As a newly-minted witch, learning battle strategy had yet to make it to her to-do list but she knew enough to protect her back.

As the Pyx Chamber grew closer—shrouded in dark mist like everything else in the Abbey—she spun around to face her pursuers. It was as if an army of evil was snarling and hissing at her heels. She stared into the churning, seething, mass tumbling down the hall towards her like some pyroclastic flow and wondered what it would take to stop that, or even what technique she should deploy.

She needed to preserve her strength for releasing Lin and for the even bigger battle to follow yet nothing would be possible without first dealing with this lot. A big fire ball? Somehow she doubted that fire would work against something made from poisonous gas. A blast of water, maybe?

And then her eyes picked out beads of light in the oncoming storm. Barely visible through the roiling murk, she began detecting the shapes of men and horses, caught sparks flying off swords being weilded in the darkness, saw creatures being obliterated one by one.

Moments later she was able to distinguish shapes—the Knights Templar were hacking away at the evil swarm. She was temporarily blown over with wonder before turning on her heels and zooming towards the Pyx Chamber.

She was ready to catapult a crushing force at the door when the murk cleared long enough for her to realize that nothing remained of the door but a mass of charred timbers. She stared: the Pyx Chamber was already open and gaped like a blackened craw.

Chapter Eighteen

D e Ferres and the Templar warriors arrived at Geri's side moments later. "What hath happened?" de Ferres asked, gazing at the charred remains of the door, the chamber's empty cavity exhaling foul smokey tendrils.

Geri was close to crying. "I don't know!" she wailed. "Lin is gone! What if the gargoyles tore her apart? The last time I saw her, she was on her back struggling to fend off one of Ware's guard demons, kicking and screaming. She was already weak! What if they tore her to bits?"

De Ferres laid a land on her shoulder and even through his chainmail glove, she felt a calming warmth. "Fear not, Geraldine, and do not make so hasty a conclusion. Perhaps the girl hath vanquished her enemies."

Okay for him to say since he wasn't the one who had just let down the daughter she never knew she had and how did he know her name, anyway? Geri wiped her eyes. None of that mattered—the hourglass was ticking. "We have no time to look for her since, if I fail to arrive in time for the ceremony, all and everyone will be lost, regardless. I can only hope that she's okay." She glanced at the sheer number of Templars that now stood ready to serve. "I'm very glad that you lads hung around, by the way. Did you bring an entire army or what?"

"Just the London Order. Our fellow knights are spread about the world but now that we have no holy wars to fight in Jerusalem, we hath focused our attentions on magic."

So the Templars had transformed into a magic force post-crusade? She'd like to give them a good dressing down about the Muslim-whacking thing but knew it was pointless in this century. Religion was a complex matter at the best of times, which this wasn't. No time to think about any of that now. Lin could be dead, for all she knew. Her heart felt like a lead weight strapped to her chest but still she must put one foot after the other.

"Good, good—glad to hear it," she said absently. "All right then, lads, let's get to work." She began floating back the way she'd come, noting how the murk had dissipated from the corridor in the wake of the knightly defense though isolated goo patches quivered here and there. One of the Templars strode ahead hacking at shadows and stabbing at puddles. Geri wondered how she'd have managed without them. Their arrival had to be fate.

Meanwhile, she tried probing the dark-consumed Abbey for Lin but felt nothing after seconds of exploring with her senses. Next, she attempted to connect with Petrus but knew before she began that the struggle with his adversary required every scrap of his concentration. Should he let his focus waver for an instant, Ware might gain ground before they even began the ceremony. Though he desperately needed her assistance, he was not available to provide instructions as to how she should proceed. She deepened her resolve to work things out on the fly.

Doubling down on her invisibility, she approached the transept. The crowd had thickened, each guest standing or sitting quietly, all sense of joviality gone. The ladies in their finery, the gentlemen equally garbed in their best tunics, sat gazing straight ahead as if locked in some alternate state while bishops, priests, and nuns stood in the front row looking equally stunned. Behind them stood the masses of peasants and serfs that had managed to gain admittance, all of them wearing blank stares. Fear clutched Geri's throat. All color had leached from the space. No more vivid reds and golds. Everyone now wore black.

Their expressions reminded Geri of one of those Zombie movies she'd fast-forwarded through but refused to watch—the same dead stare, the same expressionless features. Ware's evil influence appeared to be affecting everyone like poison, sucking away their will to live while devouring life of all color.

Turning, she tried to catch de Ferres' eye, finding that only he and the original twelve knights accompanied her now. However, de Ferres had assumed the same stunned stare as the audience and was gazing straight ahead. Right—he was a visible Templar guest and must appear as the others but she didn't believe for a moment that he had succumbed.

Meanwhile, the Archbishop of Canterbury was intoning in Latin while Petrus and Abbot Ware stood side by side on the near-finished Pavement as if unable or unwilling to move. Before them and just to the right of the Archbishop, stood a pedestal on which a black velvet pillow held the great polished onyx roundel waiting to be positioned.

The floor was complete but for that central stone. Geri knew that the crowning part of the ceremony was the moment when Petrus and Ware would together lift the stone and lower it into the Pavement. Upon that one act the fate of the world hinged.

Meanwhile, Geri floated unseen amid the Zombie-like guests to hover beside the altar. Ware's cold gaze never wavered and yet she knew that he was aware of her presence as was Petrus. Neither could lift their concentration long enough to either help or hinder her. But that would soon change.

The swirling gaseous fumes began to intensify around the Cosmati Pavement, thickening and darkening as in a gathering storm. A foul wind whipped at everyone's clothes as if the Abbey itself had been suddenly dropped into a hurricane and soon Geri could barely see more than a few feet ahead.

She tried to focus on the Archbishop's words but they were making no sense. Where he had been previously been speaking Latin, now he babbled in tongues, muttering incantations that she grasped the essence of without comprehending the words: everyone was being assigned to hell and eternal damnation. So, the Archbishop, too, had been corrupted.

And then Geri realized that the vortex was emanating from the great hole itself and in a flash saw how the surrounding murk consisted of deadened souls soon to be sucked down the cosmic chute which was the very place where the center stone would soon rest. All that blackness that clogged the Abbey consisted of once-human spirits drained of light to become nothing but charred remains reeking of evil and despair destined to be sucked down a kind of cosmic drain. The murk was once human. Was this the shape of the world should Ware succeed?

Panic gripped as she peered through the gloom and saw the Abbot and Petrus lift the roundel from its pillow, one on each side, and approach the Pavement. The Archbishop's voice was growing louder and louder and soon the wail of a thousand spirits joined the lament. Still Geri hesitated, unsure of what to do next.

The dark maelstrom churning around her thickened with agonized spirits and now she could pick out faces, the open mouths crying for help, the eyes stark with despair. Her heart would surely shatter into a thousand pieces if she stood by doing nothing for much longer but what could she do? What was her role in this? She stared into the gathering of souls, suppressing a scream.

But then a single face paused for a second before her in the midst of the soul soup. One elfin face stood out from the others, eyes wide, mouthing something that Geri couldn't grasp. She held out her hand, the other apparently gripped John de Ferres. Come? Surely she didn't expect her to jump into *that*?

In seconds they were gone and Geri could see Petrus and Ware lowering the roundel towards the floor. As the vortex continued to yank Geri towards its maw, she felt her inertia release, her energy returning proportional to the surge of the vortex's power.

Seconds later, she dove head-first into the soul storm.

Chapter Nineteen

I t was like swimming upstream in a river of sludge with one's head submerged, unable to breathe. Geri could see nothing but the occasional spark and everything below and around was a blur of gummy darkness. Yet she was gripped by a fierce resolve. She knew nothing for certain but that she must follow the light at all costs. Whether it be spark or blaze, those small flashes were all she cared about and in that direction she must head.

But she was dealing in mere seconds and couldn't squander a single one.

She tried to locate the strongest spark upon which to fix but even those were fading fast. Then she saw a shimmering glow ahead. Positioned as it was next to a hole of impenetrable darkness, that could only be Petrus. She kicked herself forward, noting how the dark hole beside him seemed to be hauling everything into its depths, expanding inexorably as a result. Around these dual orbs of light and dark, a shimmering wall seemed to be revolving.

In a flash of insight, she knew that she needed to seek inside rather than out for help, and to call on her Eddy self once again. She was shocked and relieved to find it burning intensely, vividly multicolored, and growing stronger by the moment. With a tremendous force of will, she turned herself inside out so that her inner self shone brightest on the outside, bright enough to illuminate the surrounding darkness, bright enough to lead the way. If she couldn't find the light, then she'd better become the light.

Now she was like a lighthouse in the churning sea of darkness with all the sparks near and far swimming in her direction. More merged into her field by the moment until it was if altogether they became a powerful thundering force. So fueled, she steered them right for Petrus.

I'm coming, darling!

The moment of impact hit like a magnificent explosion of brilliant, saturated color. Suddenly, everything illuminated around them and all the souls that had been languishing in the darkness burst into life, powered by the will to survive, to thrive in a world worth saving. It was at that moment, that Geri saw Ware waver, shrinking like a tumor against the assault.

But it didn't last. As soon as the light spirits revolved around her, she witnessed a dark stream of evil pouring out of the chute to bolster Ware. Geri fixed on Petrus's light and reached out towards him. Though his hands still physically held the Cosmati roundel, his spirit reached her in a tingling blast. Suddenly, it was as if she were being filled with everything warm and loving. Together, they now held the shockingly heavy Cosmati roundel.

Geri didn't know how that happened—how any of it happened—but she felt the weight of the round stone tip towards the dark mass that was Ware. Ware—that churning hole of nothingness—strove to slam the stone and the cosmos into oblivion. Geri took a deep breath (at least there was air as well as light surrounding her) and held fast.

She was no longer swimming in a spirit sludge but seemed to have been suddenly elevated into air in a kind of skydiving position—on her stomach, legs and arms outstretched for balance as if riding celestial currents. Gaseous clouds sparkling with filaments spiraled around and around. Petrus flew directly opposite while to her right, Ware blasted darkness in their direction, leaching the light at every attack.

At the center of this power circle, the Cosmati stone whirled with twisting streams of fiery gold and red, darkening to the color of dried blood after every Ware offense only to restore its brilliance when Geri and Petrus had regained the balance. But after each attack, the colors appeared to wane as if unable to grasp back the original force, the fiery core weakening at every attack.

How long could they continue like this? Petrus's strength was waning as was hers, both exhausted before they had even begun. He had been battling evil for much longer than she so, of course, he'd already been severely taxed. It pained her to know that she had got this far and still couldn't help him right the wrong to win back the future.

Other spirits that surrounded them offered up their charges but even all those souls together were not enough to stem the endless march of darkness swarming into Ware's craw.

Dismay gnawed at Geri's confidence. How could there be so many on

Ware's side and so comparatively few on theirs? How could evil have been permitted to gain such dominance? She knew that this pestilence hadn't begun in this century any more than it had in those before or after but had been mounting over time as more and more people populated the globe with their greedy wants, their fixation on the individual instead of the whole. It was shattering to see where and how it would all end.

Petrus was attempting to communicate something. Gazing at her across the swirling Cosmic stone, he was telling her not to succumb to negativity, not to capitulate to despair but to hold tight. She gazed into his eyes and fortified herself, calling out for help as she did.

Taking her eyes from Petrus for an instant, she glanced behind her, deep into the tempest of light that kept them buoyed. One spark dominated the others, one young being desperate to join them. Holding onto the stone with only one hand, Geri stretched out the other and pulled Lin into ring. The current from the girl's being instantaneously fortified both Petrus and herself. A beam of light ran from one of them to the next and on to the next until they formed a glowing triangle. They had formed a triad, a foundation of three equal points, one of the most powerful units in sacred geometry, and together they ignited the Cosmati Pavement.

A cosmic explosion followed akin to a supersonic boom with fireworks and microbursts. Geri, Lin, and Petrus were now linked in a fierce band of white light as if they were holding hands—though they technically weren't—while flying around and around in churning colors like a rainbow mixing hues on the move.

Together, the three of them lowered the roundel into the hole, oblivious to the screeching wail of the negative forces now being shoved back down the chute. Ware was nothing but an open mouth of screeching protest and his followers foul wisps dissipating in all directions when the stone settled into place with a thunderous thump.

Petrus, Geri and Lin barely heard Ware's cries over the music that had suddenly erupted. Choruses of hymns and prayers in multiple languages and denominations were now chanting over musical instruments in the symphony of the spheres. And when the singing began, so did the laughter.

A massive party was breaking out around the widening circle, a chorus of music and song as other souls joined in the celebration.

Geri caught flashes of thousands of faces, some she recognized, most she did not. Queens and kings, poets and musicians, artists and writers along with countless strangers all whizzing past in a fast-forward of joy and relief. Geri swore she spied John Lennon in the crowd. "All you need is love!" she called out, waving.

It was intoxicating. She was intoxicated—the singing, the music, the laughter, all of it. Petrus was beaming, enjoying the festivities. Lin flew by. "I'm looking for my mom," she cried.

Geri figured that she really should find her parents, too. Wouldn't that be something to tell Randall when she got home? *I saw Mom and Dad while helping to save the world. They send their love...* But then she sobered: what if she and Lin couldn't get home? What if she ended flying around in this phantasmagorical swirl forever? She swore that she heard Randall calling her home or maybe tats his voice praying somewhere.

She searched for Petrus and found him at once. He had been hovering nearby the whole time and now, still in skydiving position, revolving around her as if only the two of them existed in space and time.

"Petrus, we need to go home," she gasped.

"I, know, Geri, my love. I have always known that should we succeed in our quest, it would only be to part again."

"But I remember everything now," she said, tears rolling down her cheeks. "I remember you, all of what we meant to one another, what we mean to one another still. I understand, I mean truly understand. Now that I have found you again, I can't bear to say goodbye and yet I must. Will you come back with me?"

"I cannot do that, Geri. My work is in the past, which is where I must stay as long as I have work to do."

"But what about me? Isn't my work here with you?"

"Sadly, no, but I will help you both to return."

"But will we meet again?"

"We must, for our greatest tasks will always be done together." And he spread his arms wide and she sailed right into them.

Chapter Twenty

Geri landed on her stomach, wincing as chin, bare breasts and belly skidded against the cold tiles. She heard cries and gasps all around when she finally stopped a few seconds later but her head was spinning so badly that she couldn't tell up from down. Every time she moved, the vertigo struck more violently.

"Call an ambulance!" she heard a man cry.

Someone threw a coat over her. "Geraldine!" Randall's voice in her ear. She was back?

"No ambulance!" she whispered. "Get me home. Where's Lin?"

"She's here, too. What happened?"

"Get us home!" she whispered.

Everything that followed came in a blur of whirling images, the sense of a moving vehicle, and Randall and Soo's voices ordering everyone away.

Somehow, she ended up in her own bed where she slept for what may as well have been a thousand years. When she awoke many hours later (she had no idea how many), objects no longer spun in her vision, and she could see the dark sky through her half-opened window. Her nightlight glowed on the table nearby and voices were speaking softly in the lounge.

According to the alarm clock, it was only 7:12 PM.

Slowly, she dragged herself up to sitting and dangled her feet over the edge of the bed, soaking her senses in the twenty-first century. Cars honked in the street below along with the faint thumping bass emanating from some live band playing in the corner pub, everything accompanied by the whiff of diesel fumes riding the autumn air.

Home.

But what struck her most intensely was what she couldn't detect—no animal smells or the musky warmth of human and animal bodies pressed together in close quarters. No tingling inside her, either, as if all magic had dissipated. Surprisingly, that felt like a powerful loss. Everything felt lonelier and emptier somehow.

Yet, her sense of bereavement went much deeper. For the first time in her current life, she had fully touched another soul, experiencing the deep connection that surpassed anything she had understood could exist between individuals. And, she thought as she stared into space, that person or individual or partner or mate—what could she call him?—was no longer sharing this same lifetime with her. They didn't breathe the same air and could not share the same room. He was gone and she was alone again.

The minutes ticked away in the manner that minutes do in her century yet she was still shocked when the numbers on her little digital clock turned into 8:23. Her stomach emitted an almost leonine growl. Time for its regular feeding, then. Could it really be a few centuries ago since she had last eaten?

Sighing, she got to her feet, went to the bathroom, and glared in the mirror at her haggard face with the scratches and scrapes, most of which covered the entire front of her body, too. Damn. There was no easy way to travel between the centuries, apparently.

She got busy cleaning herself up, though by the look of the bandaids plastered here and there, somebody (probably Soo) had tended to the worst abrasions. After she had tossed her nightgown back on and added the red Liberty paisley print robe from the back of the door, she took a deep fortifying breath and went to join the others.

Soo and Randall launched themselves from the lounge chairs and ran towards her in a flurry of hugs and exclamations, relief pouring off them in waves. They had been waiting for her to rouse, they said, drinking copious amounts of tea and nibbling on ginger biscuits and sandwiches all day long. Nobody asked her a single question accept how she was feeling. Fine, fine, she assured them.

Geri sniffed. Something delicious was simmering in the kitchen. Her brother and friend appeared to be holding back questions like they were stifling a pending volcanic eruption but somehow they ushered her into the kitchen without asking a single one.

Randall passed her a cup of tea. "I trust that you are hungry?"

The table was set for four.

"Very and that smells delicious. Where's Lin?" Geri asked, taking the cup gratefully.

"I was letting her sleep but I shall rouse her now," Soo explained, dashing away. "Sit down."

That left brother and sister seated opposite one another, the little pseudo Tiffany lamp glowing in the center of the table between them. Geri realized with a pang that she missed Eddy, which was beyond ridiculous, considering.

Her dear's brother's face—oh, how she missed him—was looking worn out with strain but simultaneously elated with relief. She could only imagine what it must have been like for him for all these days.

"You haven't slept, have you?" she asked.

"Soo and I dozed while we were waiting for you to arouse but were reluctant to leave you unattended. Geraldine, I have so many things to ask you, so many questions. I—"

"I know and I promise to answer everything as fully as I am able as soon as I've been suitably restored," Geri said, thinking how glad she was to be in his company again. No matter what our losses, there is usually something or someone left for whom to be grateful.

"Of course, Geraldine, and I do not wish to push you, truly I do not, but please answer me this: has the world been saved? I did sense the retreat of the darkest energies in the Abbey moments prior to your arrival so I have cause to hope." For the first time, she realized that he wore the blue crewneck sweater that matched his eyes, the one that she had given him for Christmas years ago. She hardly ever saw him in civvies these days.

"Keep hoping Randall. Always keep hoping."

A sleep-tousled Lin entered at that moment dressed in a pair of black leggings and a grey hoodie, her hair wrestled into submission with one of her aunt's red scarves. She flashed a shy smile at Geri and sat down next to Randall. "Morning, Rev."

"Evening, actually. Good evening to you, Lin. I trust that you are recovering from your ordeal?"

"Was it an ordeal?" the girl asked softly, holding Geri's gaze. "I suppose it was."

"Your aunt and I have agreed not to assail you both with questions until after our repast," Randall continued. "Shall I lead us in saying grace?" He did anyway with everyone around the table silent until his prayers of thankfulness were complete.

"Eat, everyone!" Soo cried afterwards, clapping her hands. "Fresh buns are on the table and I'll just dish up the chicken stew now, shall I?"

"Yes, please," Geraldine and Lin said more or less in unison as they gazed at one another.

No one said another word until well into the meal except to exclaim over the deliciousness of the food.

"Do you recall when and what you last ate?" Soo asked as casually as if this were an ordinary meal shared among homecoming travelers.

"I had gruel—yuk. Horrible stuff. Oh, and copious amounts of mead, which I detest, by the way."

"I believe it was pasta and wine in my case," Geri mused, surprised that it had been that long since she'd eaten properly. "I was served that shortly upon my arrival."

"Pasta?" Soo inquired, looking up. "They served pasta wherever you were? I know that I mustn't ask exactly where you were as yet, so pardon me, please, but pasta?"

"Not common in the thirteenth century, I agree, but these were extraordinary circumstances and the chef was Italian, after all," Geri explained. "He was a wizard in the kitchen," she added with a sad smile.

A spoon clattered to a bowl. "Thirteenth century, you were in the thirteenth century?" That was Randall. Maybe she shouldn't have landed that on him quite so soon.

"Where did you think we had gone, Randall? Oh, never mind. Yes, we were sucked back to Westminster Abbey days prior to the ceremony that was to mark the completion of the Cosmati Pavement. How long have we been gone from this end, may I ask?" She scooped up another spoonful of Soo's incredible peanut strew.

"Approximately ten hours and forty-five minutes," Randall said, staring at her with a gaping expression.

"That's all?" she gasped.

"We were both rather afraid that we'd never see you again," Soo explained. "It was dreadful. One minute you were in Westminster Abbey and the next you weren't. May I ask if you were, indeed, caught in a wormhole?"

"We almost didn't come back and it didn't look like I'd expect a wormhole to look like from all the sci-fi shows," Lin remarked after a hasty swallow. "It definitely had a gravitational pull, which we know is intense enough to absorb even light and maybe time itself, so maybe. Anyway, we got held up trying to wrestle the stone away from Ware."

"The stone?" Randall enquired.

"She's referring to the Pavement's central onyx rondel," Geri remarked, "which turned out to be key in stopping the evil and negativity from seeping into our world. Think of it as a giant bathtub stopper."

"Ware was the agent of evil, by the way, and Petrus the dude determined to stem the cracks. He's a super powerful wizard and calls himself the Mason to the Stars," Lin said with a grin.

"Mason to the Stars?" Soo gasped. "Is that a joke?"

Lin nodded. "Petrus is pretty cool and has a good sense of humor."

But Geri was fixed on Lin. "You met Petrus then? Did he rescue you from the Pyx Chamber?" *And did he mention that he was your father?*

"I rescued me," Lin said, one finger tapping her chest. "I'm a much more powerful witch than I knew and, honestly, those monster mutts were just air and teeth in the end. I imagined a giant pork chop and made them choke on it. Okay, so Petrus did send me a few hints telepathically and was a great comfort when I thought I was a goner but once Ware imprisoned him, I had to figure out the rest on my own." *Wait—what do you mean by 'mention that he was my father?*

Not now, Geri thought. She needed to mind her thoughts.

"Monster mutts?" Soo asked with a squeak.

Geri turned back to her two other companions. "This will be a very long story. Perhaps we'd better head for the lounge where we can tell it to you from the beginning over tea."

"I believe that should I drink any more tea, I would begin to slosh," Randall said.

"Something stronger, then. In your case, sherry, perhaps?" Geri suggested. "I have that and more besides."

An hour or so later, the story was still unfolding after Geri had requested that all questions be held until she had finished her side of the tale, though Lin interjected with her own embellishments, here and there. Neither Randall nor Soo breached the flow with so much as a single query though both seemed to be taking advantage of Geri's offer of alcoholic refreshments. In all fairness, they appeared to be in desperate need of fortification.

"So Petrus was trying to protect the stone against Ware and Doc here jumped in to help but together they still couldn't keep it steady until, in a burst of brilliant insight—I mean, I was attempting to catch her attention all along but maybe she couldn't see me—Doc called me in to help and—wham! Together we got the stone in place."

"It wasn't quite that simple," Geri remarked.

Randall cleared his throat. "So, you formed a kind of...trinity, then, despite the fact that none of you are holy?" Poor man was definitely having trouble with this, as Geri expected.

"We don't need to be saints to do good, Randall. I am a witch, after all, which is rather like a license to be a little bad. And, yes, we formed a triad, a triangle of power where the three points forged an immovable foundation that the instigator could not overcome," Geri explained. "And not a second too soon, I might add. The light was evaporating before our very eyes."

"And the devil Ware shriveled before our very eyes, too!" Lin exclaimed.

Geri sipped her gin. "Actually, the Abbot began as an ordinary man who became corrupted and possessed by the forces of evil. I don't believe for a minute that he was born inherently bad any more than anyone else is who is born into this world. He, too, was a victim of a force greater than himself."

"So," Randall began, his voice trembling ever so slightly, "Ware is not Satan and therefore Petrus was not the Great Almighty."

"No, of course not, Randall. How could you think such a thing? Petrus is— was—" Geri took a moment to steady her own voice, "an agent of good just as Ware was the agent of evil in this particular battle. You don't have to be perfect to do good or purely evil to do wrong, and Petrus, as extraordinary as he was, could not be said to be perfect. However, his intent has been fixed on repairing what's broken so in that sense, he is very good, indeed. That was him you saw on the Cosmati Pavement, by the way. You were witnessing him right after I had landed on top of him and perhaps, had you studied the green mist more closely, you may have seen me, too. I hit him on my way through and lay stunned for a bit."

"On your way through what exactly?" Soo asked, trying to remain as calm as if discussing a scientific principle. "Is this the cosmic black hole of which we are speaking?"

Geri attempted to clarify. "Through the Cosmati aperture, the opening through which time and evil were leaking. If it helps to think of it in astronomical terms, then by all means use that analogy, but it's really much more complex and multilayered than that. Everything we understand about the world can be viewed in several different viewpoints which never quite capture the entire picture. Speaking in magic terms, Ware and his forces were taking advantage of the Cosmati fissure to tip the balance. When Lin and I were sucked into the hole, we ended back in Westminster Abbey during the time of the Cosmati floor's creation."

"I didn't end up there," Lin said quietly. "Something dark and mean snatched me from the vortex and dragged me off to prison—Ware, apparently. I didn't even see the Cosmati floor until the end."

165

Geri looked at her. "So that's what happened. Petrus wasn't expecting you, otherwise he would have fought off the demons for you the same way as he did me."

Lin nodded. "He found out about my existence later and tried to help me where he could—very apologetic. I didn't get any pasta, by the way. Nothing but stale oat biscuits, putrid mead, and gruel for me, complements of Chef Ware, but Petrus provided comfort as best he could."

"I'm sorry that I wasn't there for you," Geri said softly.

Lin shrugged. "That's okay. I was there for me in the end."

"You had your own Eddy," Geri said, smiling. "Did I mention that I swallowed him—no, that's not true: I *absorbed* him. Eddy is my special power enhancer."

"You swallowed him?" Randall asked.

"No swallowed, exactly. As I said, I absorbed him," Gerri stated.

"Hate to mention it, but it doesn't look that way to me," Lin said.

"I beg your pardon"" Geri asked.

"I'm just very relieved that you are all right," Soo interrupted. "May I ask how Eddy got along, by the way? Though, I admit that I may not be properly prepared for the answer. He looks rather subdued at the moment, much as do you.."

Geri took a deep breath and exhaled slowly. "Subdued? Well, I suppose I am. You see, I am Eddy, too. Yes, as odd as that sounds, it is the truth and, really, I should have understood that point far sooner. You might say that I became one with him the moment I came into full possession of my powers. Now we've been assimilated. One minute he was floating before my eyes being his annoying self and the next he was gone, though not very far gone, as it turned out."

"Did you just cough him back up or something?" Lin asked, "because I'm trying to tell you that he's over there on the floor."

All eyes turned towards the door where Eddy now sat dimly glowing beside Geri's battered bag.

Geri jumped to her feet. "Wot? How'd you get there?" she demanded.

"I forgot to mention that the bag did come through with you from the other side," Randall explained.

But Geri was still addressing the orb. "You're supposed to be inside me, not back to being some external annoyance!"

Of course, Eddy remained silent. Geri glowered at the orb and almost sensed it glowering back.

"Neither of us have powers in this century though, right?" Lin reminded her. "I mean, that must be why Eddy's back to his orb self , right? We're no longer back in the thirteenth century. Do you you remember recently coughing him back up?"

"Certainly not," Geri said, sitting back down, her gaze following Eddy as he rolled across the floor to stop at her feet. She felt suddenly a little disorientated, even lost. "Well, now what?" she asked. In response, the orb jumped into her lap.

"So, briefly you and Eddy were one?" Randall asked, gazing at the ball of softly luminous light.

"Well, figuratively speaking. I didn't gobble him down or anything. Yes, I absorbed him," Geri said, still fixed on Eddy. "But I have no memory of us becoming separated in the recent past. It must have happened during the return."

"So you are no longer super-powerful," Lin said sadly, "and neither am I. That explains why I couldn't just imagined myself dressed awhile ago."

"No, we will have lost our powers in this century, which will feel very much as though we're missing part of ourselves." Even though she half-expected that to happen, it was a stronger blow than she anticipated. To be separated from Eddy before she really grasped how to properly live as her complete while self. "Our powers will be diminished in this century as is everything else, so it's best that we don't go thinking we can jump off buildings and fly, for instance. It will take some time for us to realize exactly what we can and cannot do."

"How do you all know this?" Lin pressed. "I mean, I didn't come away knowing all of this."

"First of all, you are still younger than I am, even in terms of the number of prior lives we've lived and, secondly, I encountered my sister and your aunt from another life who informed me of that fact and much more during my training session."

Randall gasped. "Your sister?"

"I knew it—you're my mother!" Lin exclaimed.

Geri held up her hand. "I am not your mother now but was at some point. We have all lived prior lives and been connected before. Yes, Randall, we have a sister, Morgana, though she's not of this century and refuses to visit ours. We were all siblings in another century, possibly many other centuries."

"May I call you 'Mother'?" Lin asked with a grin.

Geri smiled. "You may not but if ever I were to have a child, I assure you that I'd be very happy for them to be just like you."

Lin seemed momentarily at a loss for words. "Well, thanks. Ditto," she said after a moment before wiping her eyes on her sleeve. "So, that means that Petrus was/is my father in another lifetime, too," she continued, "making Rev here my honorary uncle and Auntie Soo's sister, too. Wow, like this is all hard to get my mind around but it's like we're family."

"Indeed, we are, and that's rather wonderful, don't you think?" Geri glanced around the table. "I am certainly pleased to have you in my circle." Because she was missing so many others, including part of herself.

"I am happy for this, too" Soo exclaimed, "but I do rather think that we all need time to process. Personally, I am a bit overwhelmed."

"So," Randall began, "we are all in some way related? How extraordinary."

"In a manner of speaking," Geri attempted to clarify, "but Morgana and I didn't have an opportunity to untangle the centuries of our twisted family forest. Perhaps we are now a family by virtue of our shared experiences and mutual caring for one another. Personally, that's enough for me."

"Ah, calling you 'Doc' doesn't seem quite right now but neither does any other term. You and Petras were lovers, right?" Lin said, gazing at Geri with something like a twinkle in her eye . "I saw how he looked at you when we were rotating around and around that stone and then after the stone was dropped into place, he tugged you with him behind a cloud, wrapped you up in a rainbow-colored blanket, and sparks seriously flew. I can just guess what happened in there. I mean, that's seriously romantic."

Geri flushed redder than her robe.

Randall who had been holding his breath, let it out with a gust. "Is that why you were expelled from the floor stark naked?"

Geri rolled her eyes. "I knew we were going to get to that. Nobody comes out of the vortex fully clothed, Randall. Do give it a think. Were you born with clothes on?"

"Certainly not! But to hear that my own sister was cavorting in a cloud with some man—" He stopped himself. "That sounds utterly ridiculous."

"It does, doesn't it?" Geri remarked calmly, "but just to appease your prudish sensibilities, Petrus and I were cavorting in that cloud as mates, as in married, though I'm not sure where or when that particular ceremony took place. Regardless, Petrus is, as the saying goes, my soul mate."

Soo was wearing an expression of utter shock but managed to pull herself together. "How blessed you are to find your soul mate at last," she said, "let alone encounter him in the filaments and stars. Now, pardon me please but I would like to question you about the stars you saw—did you see stars?" she asked.

"Mostly gasses and clouds," Geri answered. "I have to admit to being a bit preoccupied, generally speaking."

"And would you say that it is possible to flow in and out of time?" Soo pressed. She was sitting beside Lin on the couch holding the girl's hand but Geri sensed that she was trying to divert the topic to less emotional ground.

"Time is not linear but a multi-dimensional free-flowing tide that we can slip in and out of, providing we can identify the entry point," Geri began. "It turns out that the Cosmati Pavement was a powerful portal that has now been closed. There are others."

"Others? But where?" Randall asked, leaning forward.

"That will be revealed at another time. It must be." Geri pulled her robe closer. "To use an old saying: we have won the battle but not the war. Ware has been defeated, yes, but there will be and still are other agents of evil who will attempt to tip the scales, other cracks in the world's great sacred places that will require fixing. We have pulled the world back from the precipice but our efforts won't hold forever. We have much work to do still and all of us will be part of the next battle."

"We will?" Lin was sitting up straight as if ready to get started.

"But not today," Soo said with a note of determination, patting her niece's knee. "Come Lin, let us leave our new family to recover while we go home to do likewise. We will see you both soon, I am sure," she said as she got to her feet. "I shall call a cab."

"Wait, you called me *Lin,*" the girl said.

"Yes, I did, didn't I? I believe that you have earned the right to define yourself in your own terms and I apologize for not acknowledging that sooner. Now, let us be away home and allow our friends to have some privacy."

Much hugging followed during the goodbyes while Eddy hovered about beaming a warm glow but it was close to eleven o'clock by the time Randall and Geri were alone and sitting across from one another in the lounge. Randall had the fire burning in the grate and had returned to tea as his brew of choice and Geri sat with Eddy in her lap. A kind of weighty silence had fallen in around them.

"I do not quite know how to process all of this," Randall said after a few minutes.

"No, of course not. Perfectly understandable," Geri said absently. "There is a great deal to take in."

"And firstly among the concepts I must grapple with is the idea that you are married in some confounded way and have far more experience in certain matters than I could ever have imagined."

And he didn't know the half of it. "Randall, of all the things that I've told you tonight—admittedly, some of which even I have yet to get my own mind around—are you truly fixed on my marital status?"

Randall rubbed his eyes. "You must admit that that changes things."

"Why, because you have an absent brother-in-law in another century?"

"That and the fact that I cannot quite remove the image of my big sister making out with this man behind a brightly-colored cloud."

Geri grinned. "Now, why are you fixed on that? We have more important matters to consider such as what is occurring globally, don't you agree? At some point, and I have no idea exactly when, we will be called to duty once again and we had better be ready because there will be even less time to prepare than what we have recently experienced. You will not be able to remain in the Abbey this time, Randall. The Abbey has been healed and you will be needed elsewhere."

"Where elsewhere?" he asked, blanching.

"I have no idea." She leaned over and patted his knee. "It's all right, Randall. This won't happen right away. I'm certain that we will have some time before it does."

"But what will we do in the meantime?" her brother inquired, his stricken expression still in place. "I feel as though everything has changed in some ground-breaking manner and that I shan't be able to find my footing."

Geri took the last gulp of her gin, rattling what was left of the ice cubes for good effect and laid a hand on Eddy. He felt comfortingly warm. "I suppose that you will go on as the Right Reverend of Westminster Abbey for awhile longer. In my case, I shall pass in my notice the first thing Monday morning and ensure that George Bolten assumes my duties. Then, I shall find a way to become my true self in this century so that I can locate another portal linking this world to another sacred place that requires healing. I must return to the past, Randall, as must you some day. Part of me still resides there, and we both have work to do."

Eddy floated from her lap and hovered in the air between them.

"But I'm not ready," Randall gasped, gazing at the orb.

"Neither was I," Geri said.

Ready for more Geri and family? Pre-order the Cosmati Connection.

About the Author

JANE THORNLEY is an author of historical mystery thrillers with a humorous twist, mysteries, tales of time travel and just a touch of the unexplained embedded into everything. She has been writing for as long as she can remember and when not traveling and writing, lives a very dull life—at least on the outside. Her inner world is something else.

With multiple novels published and more on the way, she keeps up a lively dialogue with her characters and invites you to eavesdrop by reading all of her works.

To follow Jane and share her books' interesting background details, special offers, and more, please join her newsletter using the link below. All newsletter signees will receive an option to download *Rogue Wave*, book 1 in the Crime by Design Series.

NEWSLETTER SIGN-UP

SERIES: NONE OF THE ABOVE MYSTERY

None of the Above Series Book 1: Downside Up

None of the Above Series Book 2: DownPlay

SERIES: TIME SHADOWS

Consider me Gone Book 1

The Spirit in the Fold 2 (companion to The Florentine's Secret)

SERIES: THE CSMATI CHRONICLES

The Cosmati Prophecy, Book 1

The Cosmati Connection, Book 2

Printed in Great Britain
by Amazon

33287659R00099